D0912510

Victorian Bookshop Mysteries by Kate Parker

THE VANISHING THIEF
THE COUNTERFEIT LADY
THE ROYAL ASSASSIN
THE CONSPIRING WOMAN

Deadly Scandal

Kate Parker

JDP PRESS

Deadly Scandal copyright © 2016 by Kate Parker

ISBN: 978-0-9964831-2-4 [print]
ISBN: 978-0-9964831-3-1 [e-book]

Published by JDPPress
Cover Design by Amber Shah
Book Beautiful

Dedication

To booklovers everywhere,
Particularly Nancy, Patti, Ruth, Merry, Anna, Louisa,
the Baden ladies, and a host of others. You know
who you are.

London, September 1937

CHAPTER ONE

WHAT I SAW was all wrong.

I gasped as I looked down at Reggie's face and reached for him. My hand jerked to a stop as reality hit me.

Reggie wasn't sleeping on that cold metal table. He looked too sunken and gray. A large round red spot marked the bullet's entrance above his right ear. The damage was to the other, the left, side of his head. Even at this angle, I could tell we'd need to keep the coffin closed. What I saw, despite everyone's attempts to keep me from seeing, would never go away.

My vision shattered like glass into shards. The room became disconnected visions and sounds. I took a deep breath and choked on the overwhelming smell of bleach. I felt Sir John grab my arm as if he feared I'd faint.

"The Foreign Office has already identified him, Mrs. Denis," a man's voice said as he attempted to take my other arm. "You don't need to be here."

I shook him off. "Yes, I do." They were wrong. Reggie hadn't committed suicide. He couldn't have shot himself on the right side of his head.

Reggie had been murdered.

I couldn't mourn him. Not yet.

The garishly lit room smelled of disinfectant, smoke, and rotting meat, incompletely masked by a strong scent of perfume. I became aware of other people, living people, moving about the large basement space and murmuring.

A lifetime of training at boarding school and living under my father's roof forced me to pull myself together.

When and where had Reggie been discovered? I realized I hadn't asked even that basic a question. And I needed answers. "What was he killed with? And where?"

"A Webley British Bull Dog." Another man joined us. He was large, solid, rumpled. He introduced himself as a police inspector. He and Sir John shook hands.

"Who killed him?"

"He killed himself, Mrs. Denis," the inspector said. His tone said, *I'm tired. Let's get this over with.*

"How did he shoot himself in the right side of his head if he shot left-handed?" I stared at the inspector.

"Our records say your husband was right-handed."

"He was. But he didn't shoot right-handed. He couldn't. His right trigger and middle fingers didn't bend." I looked at the men's faces staring blankly back at me. "Don't you understand? He couldn't have killed himself. Not this way."

The doctor shared a glance with his assistant, who draped the sheet over Reggie's head. "Mrs. Denis, I realize this is a shock—"

I grabbed Sir John's arm. "He didn't do this. He was murdered. Where was he found?"

The inspector reviewed some notes. "In the service alley behind St. Asaph's Hotel. A couple of waiters leaving for the night found his body with the gun lying next to him. A suicide note was found in his pocket. He hadn't been dead long, maybe a couple of minutes."

"May I see the note?"

The inspector nodded and handed me a paper. "There

were no fingerprints."

The note said, *This can't continue. I should have done something earlier. I accept responsibility*

"Do you recognize his handwriting?"

"Yes. But he accepts responsibility for what? And why had he gone to the St. Asaph's after the theater? He was never out past eleven or midnight on a weeknight. Ever." The more I learned, the less Reggie's death made sense.

"Apparently, your husband went to the theater with some work colleagues. They split up after the performance. No one saw him after that. Didn't you wonder when he didn't come home last night, Mrs. Denis?" the policeman asked. I heard criticism in his tone.

"I wasn't home. I was visiting friends in the country when the Foreign Office came to tell me of his death." There. I hadn't lied.

"Your husband owned a Webley British Bull Dog, didn't he?" the inspector said, taking back the note. "We'll have to go to your home and make sure it's still there."

I peered into the inspector's eyes. "Of course, but you don't think you'll find it, do you?"

"No."

"Reggie had no reason to take his life." This was turning into a nightmare. My temper made my head pound. How could anyone do this to Reggie?

The inspector avoided my gaze as he folded his arms across his chest. "The coroner will determine the reason."

"You're wrong, Inspector." He didn't know Reggie at all. The whole idea was preposterous.

I was about to continue arguing when Sir John pulled me aside. "Keep quiet, Livvy. They'll find out you didn't come down to our place until…" He glanced toward the detective.

"And usually, husbands are killed by their wives. They'll think you killed him."

"I couldn't kill him, John," I whispered back.

"I know that."

"But somebody did."

"Now is not the time to discuss it. Do you want to see any more?"

I shook my head. All I wanted was to get the sight of Reggie, gray and broken, out of my mind.

Sir John told the doctor to release the body to the mortuary when they were done and hustled me out of the room.

When we reached the sidewalk and I could no longer smell disinfectant and the metallic tang of blood, I took a deep breath. We traveled with the inspector and a constable to the flat and found the short-barreled gun missing from the drawer where Reggie kept it. I couldn't think of anywhere else it could be. After a cursory search, the policemen thanked me and left.

I wandered from room to room. The flat felt achingly empty. Yesterday morning, Reggie had gone into work, promising to meet me the next night at Sir John's estate, Summersby Lodge, taking an evening train to Sussex. He'd been his usual self, wishing me a safe journey, nearly forgetting his umbrella, kissing my cheek. I'd burnt the toast.

I gasped from the pain of the memory. The refrain of our mornings for the past three years would never happen again.

I needed the truth.

I faced Sir John and said, "I want to see where he died."

"Livvy—"

"Please. I really need to see the spot. He's dead, John, and it makes no sense. Help me, please."

"It's not a good idea, Livvy. None of this is."

"Someone murdering Reggie wasn't a good idea, either," I snapped. Then I put up my hands in a conciliatory gesture. "I'm sorry. I won't get hysterical on you, I promise. Please. I want to retrace his steps."

He glanced at me, sighed, and said, "Oh, all right."

We took a cab to Soho and, at my request, climbed out in front of the Windmill Theater. I don't know what I was expecting, but it was a dreary brick building with triple entrance doors chained shut at this time of the day. Posters for the revue flanked the entrance.

"If we leave for the station now—"

There was more for me to discover. I was sure of it. "Where is St. Asaph's Hotel from here?"

He glanced around. "I think down Haymarket and then Pall Mall and across St. James Park."

I began to walk in the direction he pointed.

"Livvy, we have a train to catch."

I glanced back at Sir John, who reminded me of a teddy bear as he trundled down the pavement in his brown suit. "There will be other trains."

I kept walking, checking the pavement and gutters for a clue. If he had asked me what I was looking for, I wouldn't have known. I was only sure Reggie had gone to the St. Asaph's for a reason.

A short distance down Pall Mall I came to an abrupt stop. "That's the German embassy over there."

Sir John gave me a dry look. The huge swastika flag flying from the roof was a giveaway.

"Would he have had some reason to come down here?" I turned toward the embassy entrance on Carlton House Terrace.

"I hope you're not planning on dropping in at the embassy and asking them," Sir John said, looking horrified.

"Not today." I'd been told the reason for his suicide was that Reggie was suspected of giving secrets to the Nazis. To have the route to his death go past their building made me uneasy.

I kept walking until I passed the Foreign Office where Reggie had worked. "Did he see something here, John? Something that meant he had to be killed?"

He didn't answer. There was no answer.

We'd reached the alley that ran next to St. Asaph's Hotel when I spotted a garishly colored booklet crumpled on the ground a few feet away. When I retrieved it, Sir John looked over my shoulder as I skimmed the pages. It was a theater program for the Windmill Revue, damp and wrinkled, with a few notations in Reggie's handwriting.

"It's his program. See? He always made notations about performances. He has every program for every show he's ever seen, going back to his school days." A moment later, I caught my mistake. Had, not has.

Sir John ignored my verbal slip. "So he dropped it and it blew over here."

"It's a clue."

"You're not Agatha Christie and it's not a clue. Keep the program by all means if it makes you feel better." His voice had an edge.

I walked to the spot where Reggie must have died and looked around, but I found no other sign that Reggie had ever been here. It felt as though he had vanished. Two men in white cook's aprons came out a back door and stared at me as they lit cigarettes.

I started back the way I came.

"Hold on, Livvy. We need to return…"

I slid the program into my purse and kept walking. It would have taken Reggie ten or fifteen minutes from the time he left the theater to reach the spot where I found the booklet. The street was well lit. People would have been out on this street at that time of the evening even in the rain we'd had last night. Plus, rooms of the hotel overlooked this spot.

"Why did no one hear the gunshot?"

Sir John shrugged his wide shoulders. "Perhaps they did. There was only one shot. People don't usually respond to one of something. It takes a few noises to make people sit up and take notice."

I nodded. He was probably right. "No witnesses have come forward?"

"Apparently not. Now, let's go." He took my arm and walked to the front of the hotel where he hailed a cab. It was only then that I realized how very tired I was. We rode to the train station in silence and didn't exchange a word until we settled into a first-class compartment by ourselves.

Sir John, who'd kept his mouth shut, now blasted out his words at me. "Olivia, suspecting your husband was murdered is one thing. Setting yourself up to be hanged is quite another."

"You went hunting with Reggie. You know he couldn't shoot right-handed." I stared at his face as he turned his gaze to the floor. "You think he was murdered, too."

"Yes, all right, what you say makes sense. But it's dangerous for you to say so. Whoever killed him did so for a reason. He might come after you next. And the police might decide you're the murderer. You have no alibi."

"I had dinner with my father last night."

"Well, that's something. How is Sir Ronald?"

"Unchanging and unchangeable."

"Ah." He knew my father well.

We arrived back at Sir John's country house to find my father, like bad news, had arrived there ahead of us. When the footman opened the door, Father pivoted around in Sir John and Lady Abigail's best parlor and marched into the hall. "Olivia, are you all right? What is the meaning of this, Summersby?"

Sir John's eyebrows rose to his thinning dome. "She was determined to see him. I couldn't let her go on her own."

"Of course not. Good thinking. But Olivia, why put yourself through something so distressing?"

"At least now I know he was murdered."

Lady Abigail, Sir John's wife, gasped as she came over and took my hand. "Are you sure?"

"Very," Sir John said. I caught the look that passed between them. He believed me, and now his wife did, too.

"Preposterous," my father said.

"Have you ever known Reggie to shoot right-handed? Have you ever known him to stay out late on a work night? Has he ever taken his pistol to a theater performance? None of this makes sense." I was very near tears and not doing a good job of hiding them.

Reggie and I were seldom apart for long. His job was one of minutiae, details of documents, ceremonies, diplomatic credentials. Sometimes he would work late at the office. He never came home smelling of brandy or sex. No lipstick smudges. Never a hair out of place.

He was my anchor, my rudder, while I dashed off in all directions. Writing, sketching, going out with girlfriends, always busy while he sat observing.

I'd married him against the advice of my father, which

was a major point in Reggie's favor. I'd never had an instant's thought that my father could be right.

My father's tone turned pedantic. "I always knew he was capable of deceiving you, Livvy, but I never thought he'd do anything like this. There's an investigation into papers stolen from the Foreign Office. From his section. Reggie must have done it. His note is a confession."

"I don't believe it."

"He said he took responsibility. What else could he mean?"

"I plan to find out. Reggie wasn't a traitor."

"Well, someone in his department is working with the Nazis."

"It's not in Reggie's character," Abby told my father, her lips thinned in anger. She was Reggie's cousin and the sister I never had.

"Don't be too sure. He could have hidden all sorts of secrets from you," my father told her.

"I've known him all my life. He might as well have been my brother." She took my hand. "Oh, Livvy, I don't believe any of this. He was too bookish for his own good, but he didn't have a criminal bone in his body. He'd never steal, he certainly wouldn't commit treason, and he didn't like the Nazis."

"I know. People don't suddenly change like this." Reggie certainly hadn't.

"He worked for the Foreign Office. You have no idea what those people are capable of," my father said.

"You work for the Foreign Office," I snapped at him. I'd spent my childhood furious over his deceits.

"And I'm a better judge of character than you."

That stung. "I'm going to find out what Reggie was

capable of."

"There's more." My father stood there in his black three-piece suit, his back soldier-straight, and stared at me with a grim face.

"You just insisted my husband died by his own hand, he's suspected of being a traitor, and now you're telling me there's more?" My voice rose in a wail.

"Reggie had been under investigation for the theft of those papers for some time. The Foreign Office won't admit it publicly, but they believe he was the one who committed treason. They were closing in on him. And he knew it. This would explain why he," he drew in a breath, "took this step."

I looked at their faces. Abby's concern was written on her features. John looked shocked.

"Never." Why would my father think my calm, brilliant, sweet husband had killed himself? "Reggie would never divulge secrets from the Foreign Office. He was an honorable man, not a traitor. He followed all the rules. And now that he can no longer defend himself..."

My breaths shook my body. I took the handkerchief Abby had been holding out to me and dried my eyes.

My father's expression softened a little. "I don't like telling my only child her husband was a traitor. Naturally, the Foreign Office will do what we can to avoid a scandal."

I looked him straight in the eye. "I'm going to investigate the circumstances of my husband's death."

"Livvy. No. It will only mean more pain for you. Leave the investigation to the professionals."

"He was my husband. I have to do this." I'd seen the professional detective. He had no interest in plunging in to find the truth. And that wasn't the only reason. Some compulsion was driving me on—anger, disbelief, a rejection of all I'd been told, but I couldn't admit this out loud. They'd have stopped me.

My father put on his best Victorian head-of-the-family tone. "You'll do nothing until after the funeral. Then we'll talk about it. Oh, why did I let you attend university?"

"Why did you *let* me...?" I allowed my anger to boil. It was the only thing that kept my brain functioning after the shock. I knew I'd need my nerve and my mind working at full steam if I was going to catch Reggie's killer.

CHAPTER TWO

THE FOLLOWING day, I rode back to London with my father on the train as he listed the tasks that needed to be done to bury Reggie properly. Measures had been passed by Parliament with less thought.

I wished he'd just stop talking. I was so tired. I wasn't up to any tasks, each seeming more monumental than the last.

Then I went home alone. The flat had never seemed so empty. I managed to make a trunk call to the vicar of Reggie's family's home parish in Wiltshire before the tears rolling down my cheeks turned into gasping sobs.

Oh, what a silly girl. Reggie was dead. Murdered. And I sat crying because of what I'd lost. Reggie was no longer there to buffer my dealings with my father. I no longer had a social life as a married woman. There was no one to anchor my days. To commend my efforts.

Now I was a widow. It sounded so ancient, and I was only twenty-five. It wasn't fair.

And then I shed fresh tears of guilt, ashamed of my childish feelings. Poor, dear Reggie. I so wanted to hug him one more time. And that was not to be.

I needed to pull myself together. Wallowing in pity would not tell me what happened to Reggie. I needed to know, for myself and for him. He'd encouraged me to keep trying to discover my talents, and I owed him.

After I dried my eyes, I found the strength to call Lester Babcock, Reggie's closest friend in the office, to find out who Reggie had left the theater with.

Lester answered the phone with a cheery "Hello."

"Lester, it's Olivia Denis. I wondered—"

"Livvy. Oh, dear. I'm so sorry. I should have walked with—I don't know what—who could have—?" His tone was immediately apologetic.

"Did Reggie leave the theater alone?"

"Yes. Of course. The Windmill really isn't as bad— nothing happened—I don't know how—"

I wondered if I was going to have to go over there and slap him to get any sense out of him at all. "Lester. Stop. I'm sorry to interrupt your Saturday afternoon, but Reggie was murdered and I want some answers."

"Livvy. You know I'd never—"

"I know. That's why I'm asking you. What time did you leave the Windmill?"

"When the show let out, at eleven."

"You walked outside as a group?"

"Yes. The weather was drizzly, but not too bad. We discussed the show for a minute, and then David Peters said he'd had enough and was off. He headed toward Piccadilly with Fielding."

"Fielding?"

"Blake Fielding. The new man in the Eastern European section. Nice chap. Just finished a rotation in our embassy in Prague. You must have met him. He was introduced at a party a month or so ago."

"I'm sure I have." Actually, today I wasn't feeling certain of anything. "You were saying?"

"I grabbed the first cab. Just as we were pulling out, I

saw Edward Hawthorn grab the next one. At the same time, Paul Chambers and Reggie waved to each other as Reggie headed down Windmill Avenue toward Haymarket and Paul headed along Shaftesbury toward Charing Cross. He lives in that area now."

"I knew he was thinking of moving." He'd told me the house was too depressing after his wife had died. I hoped I wouldn't feel that way about my home with Reggie.

"He got a modern flat off Charing Cross. It's very small, but he finds it convenient."

"So you actually saw Reggie leave by himself?"

"Yes. We weren't told much at work. What happened, Livvy?" Lester's voice sounded cautious for the first time.

"Reggie was murdered. He was shot in the right side of his head. And I found his theater program at a distance from where his body was found. There was no reason for him to be there. I want to know what happened to my husband." If I ended in a wail, I hoped Lester forgave me.

"Oh, Livvy. I'm so sorry. I should have seen him home safely."

"Had something happened at the office that would have made him wary? Had Reggie been threatened by anyone?"

"No." He paused and added, "I don't know. He was quieter than usual. I just wish I'd done something."

"Was there anything different about that night?"

"No. Well, not really."

I jumped on this. "What do you mean, 'Not really'?"

"Just sort of an atmosphere. That's what Mary would call it," he said. Mary was his wife, a nice woman, and a good friend. "Nothing I could explain."

No matter how hard I pressed him, Lester couldn't give me any more details. In the end, I told him the funeral would be in Wiltshire and I'd call Mary later.

I hung up and walked into the parlor, my gaze falling on our framed wedding portrait. Reggie, slender and studious, squinting nervously at the camera since the photographer had made him remove his glasses. Me, beaming, my curly hair in place for once, looking so young and excited.

It had been Reggie's thirty-seventh birthday.

People whispered at the time that I was looking for someone like my father. Just the opposite. My father drove me mad on a regular basis. I loved Reggie. He would patiently explain things to me. I had learned so much from him. About myself. About life. I didn't know how I'd do without him.

Reggie never told me anything about his work because he said I would find it tiresome. He knew I was quickly bored. Reggie helped me see I needed a purpose, a cause. Few jobs were open to married women, and nothing available had ever appealed to me. So I'd written a few short stories that were rejected by everyone. My efforts at sketching would never sell. I knew I didn't have the drive to try acting. But Reggie had continued to encourage me. He was the only one who had.

I stared at the portrait. He was such a private person that after three years of marriage, I still didn't know him. Not truly. And now I'd never get answers to those questions he'd deflected.

There was a knock on the door. I went into the hall and shouted, "Go away." I heard heavy footsteps do exactly that.

* * *

The inquest was held a few days later in a dreary courtroom full of heavy wooden furniture and peopled with the interested and the nosy, all dressed somberly.

Police evidence was given by the police inspector I'd

spoken to at the morgue. He still sounded tired and ready to be rid of this case. He made the note discovered in Reggie's pocket and finding the body in the shadowy alley behind St. Asaph's Hotel the main points suggesting suicide. The type of gun, the same as the one missing from our home, was explained as evidence of a thought-out plan.

Medical evidence told us only that his death had been quick and relatively painless. That was small comfort.

Reggie's supervisor, Sir George Rankin, wore an expression that made it obvious he could taste the anger and fear of previous defendants in this courtroom. He stated that Reggie's work was not dangerous, he was a conscientious employee, and he didn't seem worried about anything.

Sir George didn't mention the search for the Foreign Office traitor or his suspicions about Reggie.

Lester Babcock testified next that Reggie hadn't appeared worried about anything. That he seemed perfectly normal the day of his death both at work and at the theater. He didn't mention the odd mood within the group that night.

Then it was my turn. As I sat in the witness seat, I could feel hundreds of eyes boring into me, trying to guess my secrets, wanting to strip me bare of my thoughts and my dignity.

The coroner spoke in a mild voice, asking simple questions. When was the last time I'd seen Reggie? Were there any money problems? Were we happy?

The last was the one I replied to the most forcefully. I gripped the wide wooden railing in front of me and snapped, "Yes." Taking a deep breath, I added, "Well, we were content. After the first flush of marital bliss, I think most marriages fall into a routine both parties find satisfactory."

The coroner cleared his throat. I think I shocked him a

little. Then he asked me about the pistol, and I told him it was missing from our flat. I also told him about Reggie's inability to shoot right-handed, although he did everything else with his right hand.

He dismissed me then. I looked at him, surprised. "But I have more to tell you."

My father, sitting in the first row of spectators, came halfway out of his chair. I ignored him and looked expectantly at the coroner.

He blinked and said, "Please continue, Mrs. Denis."

I pulled the dirty, wrinkled theater program from my purse. "I found this at the entrance to the alley where Reggie's body was found. It's his. It has his notes in it. Reggie kept every theater program from every production he'd ever seen."

"You found this in the alley where your husband's body was found?" the coroner asked.

"No. I saw it near the entrance to the alley where he was found. This was after I went to the morgue. I—"

"You went to the morgue? My notes say Sir George Rankin identified the body." He peered at me with a no-nonsense look.

"He did. But I wanted to see for myself. Make sure there hadn't been a mistake."

"And had there been?"

"Not on the identification. But there had been in the police assumption that Reggie committed suicide. It was quite impossible. And then when I saw how far his program was from where his body was found, I knew someone else had been involved." I was rambling, but I didn't care. I couldn't mourn Reggie's passing properly until I could get him justice.

"Perhaps you'd better explain to the court your activities on the day your husband was found."

I did a little judicious editing on where I was the early part of that day. I wasn't going to explain anything to the ghouls in the gallery. "I was a guest at the home of Sir John and Lady Abigail Summersby when Sir George Rankin arrived. My husband was supposed to meet me there that evening. Sir George told me Reggie was dead and it was believed to be suicide. I insisted on seeing his body, so Sir John went into town with me."

Taking a deep breath, I continued. "After visiting the morgue and discovering with the police inspector that Reggie's pistol was missing, Sir John and I went to the alley where my husband's body was found. His going there after the theater on a work night was completely out of character. And he never went down alleys. It was a little obsession of his. He would never have gone in there of his own free will."

Aware of the stares of the coroner and the crowd, I took a deep breath while I tried to sort out my thoughts. I finished my explanation of our walk to the St. Asaph's in long-winded detail as the coroner glanced at the clock.

"And Sir John Summersby can verify all of this?"

"Yes, sir." I'd done my best. Now it was up to the coroner.

I think that was why he entered an open verdict. At least the court could reconvene at such time as the police had more information. I suspected it would be a very long time before they looked. And that wasn't fair to Reggie.

* * *

Two days later, we traveled by an early train for the funeral and burial in Reggie's family's home parish in Wiltshire. I wore the long-sleeved, black dress and large black hat I'd worn to the funeral of Sir John's sister.

Reggie hated me in black.

Sir George Rankin represented the Foreign Office. Reggie's few remaining local relatives, second cousins, attended. My father stood on one side of me, Abby and John on the other.

Dry grass lined the church wall and stood in tufts by the worn headstones. Trees were in glorious color beyond the low hedge. Reggie had liked autumn. Someone had cheated him out of it this year. That wasn't fair.

The vicar did an admirable job of ignoring the circumstances of Reggie's death after listening to my father and me argue over whether he was murdered or a suicide. Everything the vicar said was so bland that I could almost believe Reggie died in his bed of a lingering illness. Almost.

After the funeral and burial service was completed, Sir John pulled me aside and said, "What were you thinking of, saying all those things at the inquest?"

"They were all true."

"But if they start questioning me about that, what's to stop them asking me when you arrived at Summersby Lodge?" A scowling Sir John then set about the business of lighting his pipe as we skirted around the side of the ancient stone church.

So far everyone had assumed I'd been with them overnight. I hadn't killed Reggie, but I didn't want anyone looking at my alibi too closely. Anyone who read the newspapers would believe wives killed their husbands with boring regularity.

And the last thing I wanted was to be suspected by that lethargic, disinterested police inspector.

Abby came around the corner of the church after us. "Everything all right?"

"Perfectly, dear." John's words floated on a puff of smoke.

Abby raised her eyebrows as she looked at her husband and then turned to me. "Is there a problem?"

"Your husband isn't happy with what I said at the inquest."

"Neither is your father. I've had an entire lecture on the subject."

Poor Abby. I had suffered through enough of his lectures to know how tiresome they could be. "Sorry."

"Don't be. So far as I know, you arrived at Summersby Lodge late in the evening. It's not a problem."

That was wonderful of Abby, but I'd have to make sure she didn't perjure herself. I'd have to get justice for Reggie without hurting anyone I cared for.

After a short luncheon at a local inn and a stop at Reggie's now-covered grave, we returned to London by train to hear our family solicitor, Mr. Peabody, read the will. There were no surprises. I inherited Reggie's meager estate after a few bequests. He left the gun, the lethal short-barrel Webley British Bull Dog, to Sir John.

* * *

I spent the next few days wandering from room to room in the flat, feeling lost. I was unable to concentrate on reading or housework. I didn't want to talk to anyone. I lacked the energy to even fix a cup of tea or comb my hair.

Whenever I heard a knock on the door, I shouted, "Go away" in a tired voice. Whoever it was must have heard, because they always obeyed.

What was I going to do? My life had revolved around Reggie. Fix his breakfast and then take care of the chores. My day was mine. Then a peck on the cheek when Reggie came home, dinner together, and an evening spent listening to the wireless or reading.

Now my routine was gone. Cooking one chop, washing one tea cup, seemed silly. I had to lick my wounds while I figured out my next step. Figured out how I would spend my time. Figured out what had happened to Reggie.

A sharp rap on my front door made me jump. I shook my head at the fancies growing inside my mind. "Go away," I shouted, stronger this time.

"I will not."

I rose and opened the door.

My father brushed past me and strode in—all Westminster government official in his black three-piece suit, old school tie, silver hair, and sleek disapproval. He kissed my cheek and walked into my parlor. I shut the door and followed, wondering what had brought him here in the middle of a workday.

"Reggie didn't leave you well provided for, did he?" he asked without preamble.

"No, he didn't." I wondered where this was headed. So far I hadn't given my bank account any thought. Even though I knew better, in my heart I still expected Reggie to walk through our front door.

After all, this had been Reggie's flat long before it was ours. We'd done some redecorating, but every room held Reggie's imprint. In a way, I was just a tenant.

My father began to pace the room. After four or five steps, he had to turn around. "I'm sorry to admit this, but my investments have done poorly for years. I simply can't afford to support you. Not in your own flat."

I pressed my nails into the palms of my hands, trying not to snap at my father. "I don't expect you to."

"You'll have to give up the flat and move home."

It was a good thing I hadn't eaten lately, because the idea made me ill. This had originally been Reggie's flat. The idea of giving it up felt like another shovelful of dirt on his grave. "No."

"Olivia, be practical. This flat must be costing you a fortune. Sell up. Move home. The house will be yours someday. Why not take advantage of part of it now?"

I stared into bright blue eyes flecked with gray, so much like my own. "Because we didn't do well living under the same roof when I was a girl." I saw him wince and I dutifully backtracked. "Father, I appreciate the offer, but you'd be as miserable as I would."

"Are you looking for another husband already?" He looked shocked. "I didn't realize your marriage was in such pitiful shape."

All I could do was shake my head. "I'll have to get a job."

"No" came out of his mouth in a scandalized screech.

He was as stubborn as I was. Part of the reason we didn't get on. "I'll get a job and pay my own way."

"Where? Be practical. There must be ten people out of work for every job available."

An exaggeration, but not a large one for a female with few skills. "You have contacts. You could help me."

"Why would I do that when the idea of a daughter of mine working is abhorrent? You're not part of the working class."

"I'm going to look for work, and if you don't help, you won't like the jobs I'll apply for. You don't want to introduce me to your associates as my daughter, the shop assistant."

"Hardly worse than my daughter who sits around all day and writes fluff or sketches nudes or drinks coffee with her girlfriends."

"No. On the weekends, I play bridge or go to the theater." Saying those words made me realize how settled my life had been. And how protected Reggie had made me.

"Not while you're in mourning, I hope. And how can you work while you wear mourning?"

"That is so Victorian, Father. No one goes through all the mourning rituals these days. At least, no one in my generation."

"Another reason not to trust your generation." Picking up his bowler, gloves, and umbrella, he said, "Think about it. You won't be able to afford this flat for long without income. More income than a shop assistant makes. If you moved home, you could find a volunteer position to fill your time. Something more challenging than working in a shop. Something respectable."

I'd escaped the prison my father had built with his rules for proper, young, almost upper-crust ladies, but I'd landed in a jail called "married woman." Now I'd have to find the keys before I landed back in my original prison.

CHAPTER THREE

TALKING TO MY father propelled me out of my grief and into action. Now that he'd made me face my choices, I knew I had to find a job that paid well enough for me to stay in the flat. And a friend who would understand my predicament, and might be able to help, was Esther Benton Powell.

As soon as I convinced my father to leave and let me think about my situation, I called her and made a date to meet for luncheon in an hour. She immediately suggested someplace swanky.

Esther and I had gone to boarding school together, where she was largely ignored for being clumsy and nouveau riche. I hadn't been anyone either, my father only being a baronet, so we'd gotten along fine. Then we'd gone up to Cambridge together, where we were both serious students.

She'd married a powerful young man in the City right after university. Since then, she always wore furs and said it was at his suggestion.

The idea of seeing Esther and doing something about my situation gave me the kickstart I needed. I put on the soft black wool dress with a black hat, stockings, and heels I'd worn to the inquest, picked up my umbrella, and headed out.

When I reached her table at the restaurant, Esther was wearing a fashionable black-and-yellow dress with padded shoulders and a narrow skirt. Her hat, which had a hint of a veil, picked up the yellow in her dress. She rose and kissed both my cheeks. "Livvy, I am so sorry about Reggie."

"Thank you. And don't believe what you hear. He was murdered."

She jerked back and blinked her dark, deep-set eyes. Esther would never be a beauty, but current styles favored her. She had managed to look slender and wistful in school and she'd never changed. "What happened?"

I knew she asked as a friend and not as her father's daughter. Sir Henry Benton was one of the most powerful newspaper publishers in Britain, maybe *the* most powerful. I was sure the newspapers would just love my story. But that wasn't what I wanted.

The waiter took our orders and returned with our soup. As we ate, I gave her the short version. Really, there wasn't a long version yet. I had no idea why anyone would kill Reggie with his own pistol. Unless someone stole his Webley to make his death look like suicide.

Esther studied me for a full minute, the silence at our table lengthening while around us, china clinked, voices murmured, and heels clicked on the tile floor as diners passed by. "You're determined to find out who killed Reggie."

"Yes."

Esther tapped an expensively manicured nail on the table. "And the police?"

"The coroner gave an open verdict, but the police believe it was suicide and aren't looking any further."

"And you want to use my father's newspapers to find Reggie's killer."

"No. I want a job on his papers because I need the money. Reggie was not a rich man. We lived on his wages. With a salary of my own, I can be independent, which will allow me to hunt for his killer."

"You could move home. It's just you and your father, isn't it?"

"Yes, and that is exactly why I can't move home. We've never gotten along."

She smiled then and her face transformed to one of beauty. "He won't help in your job search?"

"No. And I don't think I'd like any job he'd find me. There are very few fields my father thinks women should enter."

"Your father is so calm and traditional. I've always liked that about him. How is he?"

"Still calm and traditional. And well."

She leaned back in her chair. "I can't imagine any job my father could give you that would help in your search for a killer."

"It will allow me the luxury of keeping my flat and therefore my sanity." I leaned forward. "I finished my studies at Cambridge. And you can tell your father I have experience as a typist. It was only for a few months before Reggie and I married, and it was a volunteer position, but I can type." I hoped that hadn't been a better use of my time than the years I spent at Cambridge.

"It might give you an advantage." Esther waited until the server brought our almond-crusted fish with spinach before she said, "Do you still have contacts in the Foreign Office?"

"Yes." I remembered that tone from school. "Esther, what do you have in mind?"

"There may be a way we can help each other. You're aware of the political climate in Europe."

"I'd have to be blind and deaf not to know Hitler hasn't reached the limits of his ambition."

She studied me for a moment. "And you're still as

ingenious as ever?"

"Hopefully smoothed over with a little maturity." I watched her, unable to guess where this conversation was leading.

"Have you done any amateur theatricals since our university days?"

"None, unless you want to count some of the tales I've told my father."

"Ah, well. It will all come back to you, I'm sure. My father needs to know when Hitler plans to move before the Nazis do anything irreversible."

"For the paper?"

"No. It's a private matter. Your husband had the German desk. Would you be willing to keep in touch with your husband's coworkers? Find out what you can about contacts between Germany and the Foreign Office and report back to my father?"

Spy for Sir Henry Benton. It was a distasteful thought. And I knew how closemouthed Reggie and his coworkers were. Still, if it would get me a job... "Yes. Although I can't promise that they'll tell me anything useful."

"There is one more thing. Father doesn't want anyone to wear mourning while working for him. He says it attracts attention, and the last thing he wants his reporters to do is attract attention to themselves. He wants everyone working for him to blend in."

That was fine with me. I didn't want to mourn Reggie. I wanted to see someone pay with their life.

* * *

I returned home in a good mood. The sun was shining. Esther would put a good word in for me with her father. I opened the door to my flat and skidded to a stop.

Everything I owned seemed to be scattered on the parquet floor along the entire length of the hall and trailed through every doorway. The place was a shambles, but nothing seemed to be broken. I stepped over my belongings to reach the phone and dialed the police.

They advised me to step out into the relative safety of the landing and they'd arrive shortly.

I hung up the phone and stood there, wondering how much damage had been done. Slowly, I picked my way down the hall, checking every room as I passed. My burglars had kindly left every door open so I could tell at a glance that they'd overturned drawers and cushions.

All of my jewelry appeared to be on the rug in my bedroom, along with my mattress. Reggie's large collection of books was flung about, clothes trampled, beds undone, the desk turned upside down, and pots and pans dumped on the floor under a fine covering of flour. They'd even upended his theater playbill collection.

When I heard the tap on the door, I jumped over books and pans in the hallway to find a tall blond man with hazel eyes on my landing, gray fedora in one hand that matched his well-tailored double-breasted suit. He gave me a quick smile and walked in before I could say anything.

"I can't say much for your housekeeping."

I glared at him. "Not funny. Are you with the police?" If so, this one showed a spark of dry wit and some fashion sense. I had the feeling the one who'd concluded Reggie had committed suicide never found anything amusing or looked other than rumpled.

"No, it's not funny. And no, I'm with a different branch of the government." He tossed his hat on the hall table and moved silently down the hall, peering around the first doorway before continuing.

"I just looked in. They made a mess of every room."

His look said he couldn't believe how foolish I was before he began to enter each room in turn. My husband was murdered, and now a strange man was walking through my flat. Where were the police?

"Excuse me. Who are you?"

He ignored me as he moved like a cat through the wreckage, every muscle ready to strike at the first hint of danger.

I followed him down the hall. "If you're not a policeman, why are you here?"

He came out of the guest bedroom last, slipping a wicked-looking knife out of sight up his sleeve but not before I saw the gleam of the blade. "Whoever did this has left."

"I know that." Who was this man? He didn't look frightening, but I'd seen his knife. My flat no longer felt like my sanctuary. "I've called the police. Did you find out from them? Why are you here? And who are you?"

I kept backing up as he walked toward me until we were at my front door. He gave me a quick smile. "Don't tell the police I was here. And don't tell them we've already checked for anyone lurking. That's their job, and they tend to take offense when we do it for them. Let them check out your place and make a report." He peered closely at my face. "Are you all right?"

I nodded and realized I was shivering. "Who are you and why are you here?"

He gave me a sympathetic glance. "Now that your burglars have looked, either they found what they wanted and you'll never see them again, or they didn't, in which case they know you don't have it and won't be back. Either way, you should be safe enough now."

He moved out into the landing and turned away as he put on his fedora.

"Have what?"

"If we knew that, things would be simpler."

He didn't look completely batty, but his answers were. At least he was out of my flat. "Why were you here?"

He swung around to face me. "Someone I've been watching came into this building. He stayed inside some time, so I left and looked up the address. I discovered your Foreign Office husband was recently killed. It didn't take a genius to put it together."

"Put what together? Who was this person you were watching? And who are you?"

"Better you don't know. Just think of me as someone who came back to make sure you were all right." He tipped his hat to me.

"Wait."

I watched him as he nearly ran down the stairs and probably passed the bobby in the lobby. My fear was rapidly turning to fury. He suspected someone had searched my flat and didn't call the police. And he had the nerve to say it was better that I didn't know who he was. Or who'd burgled my flat.

The bobby who came to check out my flat was young, polite, and nearly as confused as I was. "How long were you away, ma'am?"

"Nearly two hours. I went to get a bite to eat with an old school friend and came back to this." I hoped he didn't ask me the name of the friend. I didn't want Esther to find out. It might ruin my chances for a job on her father's newspaper.

For some reason, he didn't. There mustn't have been a

box for that question on the form he filled out.

He checked the door handle and showed me the scratches made when someone picked the lock. Then I went over the flat room by room with him. There was little damage, just incredible disarray, and nothing appeared to be missing.

Sutton, our doorman and porter, came up as the bobby was finishing. "I want you to know, Mrs. Denis, no burglars got past me. And I don't sleep at my post, not like some others I could name." He peered through the doorway. "Made a right mess of things, didn't he?"

"You didn't see anyone suspicious lurking about, did you?" the bobby asked.

"No, I didn't. Everyone who came past me was respectable. And had good reason for being here."

Liar. I knew of two people who'd passed him recently without a reason to be here other than to frighten me. Or one, if the blond man with the knife had lied and was also my burglar returning for a second look.

I'd never get rid of the bobby so I could clean up the debris if I didn't stop Sutton's denials. "The burglar must have found a way in through the cellars, maybe with a skeleton key. Don't they all carry skeleton keys?" I asked.

"Maybe we should take a look at the entrance to the cellars," the bobby suggested, putting away his pencil. "Let me get the forensic men in for fingerprinting first. Don't touch anything, ma'am, and stay in the hall, please."

Sutton led him away and I shut the door and took up a seat on the stairs.

It took a team of white-coated men a short time to spread fingerprint dust over my flat and leave me with a greater mess than I had before. After they left, I started by putting my bedroom to rights. Once it was back to normal and I had a whole sack of laundry to send to the cleaners in the morning, I began on the kitchen.

I had barely begun when my phone rang. Drying my hands on a towel, I hurried into the hall to answer. I was afraid it was my father and I didn't want him to see what had happened. Our war over whether I would move home would only intensify if he knew I'd been burglarized.

Instead, a frosty female voice came over the line telling me I had an appointment to see Sir Henry Benton the following morning.

Esther had worked fast. I returned to my cleaning with a smile, determined to put this behind me before I faced my interview.

My flat had never felt as large as it did that afternoon and evening. By the time I finished cleaning and putting everything in its place, it was the small hours of the morning.

* * *

I'd met Sir Henry Benton at parents' days at school and later during visits at university holidays. He was rich even then, and loud, and an embarrassment to his daughter. I thought he was wonderful, so different from my stodgy father. When I arrived at the top of his building on Fleet Street, I was shown straight in to his office.

"Olivia, it's a pleasure to see you," he said, rising from his desk and walking over to me with his hand extended. He was nearly a head shorter than I was and stocky, with what was left of his brown hair now turning gray. "My condolences on your loss. Reggie was a good man."

I pressed my lips together to fight an unexpected flash of tears. I was sure they wouldn't help my job prospects. "He was."

Sir Henry led me to a straight-backed wooden chair and then crossed behind his desk to sit facing me. He looked so tall behind his desk I would have bet his feet didn't touch the floor. "Esther tells me you need a job."

I was comforted to notice he hadn't lost his Newcastle accent. "Reggie left me a bit, uh, hard up." I was going to say "short."

"He was in the Foreign Office, wasn't he?"

"Yes." Here came the part Esther had mentioned the day before. The part that sounded confusing, difficult, and a little exciting.

"He dealt with credentials, official functions, and so on?"

"Yes."

"Do you know his coworkers well?"

"We socialized with them, so, yes, I know them."

"And you have contacts in high society from your school days and your father's connections?"

"Yes." I wondered how my contacts with the rich and powerful would help if Sir Henry was interested in Foreign Office gossip.

"No reason for them to shun you?"

"None."

"I remember your performances in your student plays. Clever. Are you still as resourceful as you were as a student?"

My cheeks heated. Esther must have told her father some of the stunts that high spirits and curiosity had led us to. "I'm sure if the opportunity arose—"

Sir Henry Benton nodded to himself. "Good. Esther also said you have some experience as a typist. That's a bonus."

"From before my marriage." I wanted to be honest. If he was expecting a good typist, he was in for a disappointment. Somehow, mentioning my unsuccessful efforts at writing fiction didn't seem wise.

"Excellent. You'll soon get up to speed. I want you to talk to Mr. Colinswood. He's our foreign desk editor. We have a special role in mind for you. Colinswood will spell it all out. It was his idea originally. Good man, Colinswood. Nice seeing you again, Olivia." He pushed a button on his telephone and glanced at a typewritten paper with numerous scratch-outs and corrections.

After a moment, a rumpled man of about fifty walked in. "You wanted to see me, sir?"

"Colinswood, this is Mrs. Denis. The woman I told you about."

"Excellent." He gave me a smile and his fatigue slipped away. I changed my estimate of his age to forty. "This way, Mrs. Denis."

I followed him down to another floor and through a field of heavy wooden furniture, ringing telephones, clanking ticker tape machines, and shouting men beating on typewriters. Somehow, it reminded me of the courtroom where the inquest had been held, but with noise and frantic activity added.

Colinswood's office, when we finally reached it, was as rumpled as he was. We sat facing each other over his paper-strewn desk with its overflowing ashtray. "Sir Henry asked me to give you the particulars of the job we have in mind for you."

Then he told me the salary—and I'd have agreed to anything. It was more than enough to keep me from having to move home, considerably more than I'd get as a shop assistant or a file clerk.

"You will officially be part of our society page staff. You will cover your assignments and type up your stories to pass on to Miss Westcott, our society page editor, and the rewrite staff. You'll be replacing a woman who's left us to get married."

Then he leaned forward. *Here comes the catch.*

"On occasion, we'll have special assignments for you. Assignments given to you by either Sir Henry or myself. Assignments we hope you can fulfill by using your contacts at the Foreign Office or in society. Assignments that will require tact and imagination. And a bit of acting talent. Do you have any problem with this?"

"No." Not with the salary he'd promised.

"You understand you're not to mention these extra assignments to anyone. Not the possibility of doing little odd jobs for us, and not once you do them. Am I clear?"

"Completely. I'm being hired as a society page reporter."

He looked relieved. "Good. Report to me at half-nine on Monday morning and we'll get you started in Miss Westcott's reporting pool. Oh, and no wearing mourning in the office or on assignment. Official policy. Any questions?"

"No." I couldn't mourn Reggie yet. Not until I found his killer. I left with a smile and a handshake. Outwardly, I kept calm, but inside I was a quivering mass of excitement and terror.

As I entered my flat, I reached down by habit to pick up the mail. On the floor under the mail slot were some black-edged envelopes containing sympathy messages and one large, official-looking envelope creased to fit through the slot.

Curious, I carried the stack into the parlor and looked at the large envelope. It was addressed to Reggie.

I smiled at the first positive thing to come out of Reggie's death. He'd received various letters I was curious about during our marriage. I never learned the contents of any of them.

For a while, I'd been nosy. But I'd never learned anything, not even the sender. When Reggie and I were newlyweds, Abby had told me he liked to keep his life compartmentalized. Since I told him every stray thought that ran through my mind, it seemed odd, but I learned to let him have his privacy.

With a little whoop of joy, I opened his mail.

Inside were a number of sheets of legal pages, all neatly stacked. I read the top page. It was a petition for a divorce. With my name and Reggie's. For adultery. Adultery? How could Reggie believe that?

I flipped through the pages frantically, making a mess of the neat pile. There was also a will that didn't mention me. He'd left everything to a woman named Claire deLong.

Who was Claire deLong? And why should she get anything? I was Reggie's wife.

CHAPTER FOUR

THE PAGES FROM the large envelope slid onto my lap and spilled across the floor. My heart squeezed in my chest. How could he? I picked up the last sheet of the will and noticed it was dated that day but unsigned. I scattered papers as I searched for the last page of the divorce petition. It was likewise unsigned.

Was he so miserable he had to kill himself to escape? Drops fell on the divorce petition before I realized there were tears running down my cheeks.

Who was this Claire deLong? And who was Hamish McDowell, Esquire, besides being the solicitor who had written this travesty?

I pulled out the phone book and looked for his listing. My hands shook as I dialed the number, listening to the clacks as the dial returned. After a short pause, I heard ringing.

The line rang and rang. And like the questions forming in my mind, there was no answer.

I wanted answers if I had to shake them out of Hamish McDowell, Esquire.

Fortunately, I reached him on a later try. To meet with Mr. McDowell, I traveled by Tube to a musty area just outside the limits of the City of London near the Inns of Court. His chambers were up two flights of grimy stairs to a dark landing. Light came out of the frosted pane in the door marked "McDowell Solicitor." I knocked and walked in.

No one was in reception at the desk with water marks and crumbs, so I walked to the door on the far side and put my ear against it. Not hearing any sound, I knocked.

"Come in," said a voice from within.

I opened the door to an even grubbier office.

"I thought I heard someone in the other room. You must be Mrs. Denis."

I walked in as stale tobacco smell hit my nose. "I am."

McDowell, a chubby, red-faced man with dark greasy hair, rose from behind a desk that appeared ready to shed an avalanche of papers. He cleared several large books off a chair so I could sit. The dust marks left on the seat told me no one had dusted or swept in this office in months. He glanced around and then decided to set the books next to another stack on the floor. Another wooden chair and the tops of the file cabinets already held piles of books and sheaves of papers.

I sat, knowing I'd have to dust off my skirt later, and McDowell hurried around his desk to sit in the swivel chair. It squeaked in protest before I could say, "I'm here because you did some legal work for my late husband."

"Mr. Denis?"

"Yes."

"Mr. Reginald Denis?"

"Yes."

"I began some work for him. He never returned with the signed papers."

"I know. He was murdered before they arrived."

Something flickered behind his eyes. "Really. I heard he died from a self-inflicted gunshot wound."

"A physical impossibility. When did you begin work for

him?"

He raised his eyebrows but said nothing at my claim of impossibility. "Let me see."

McDowell opened his calendar and flipped through. "He came to see me a week before he died."

"And how did Mr. Denis plan to prove in open court that I had committed adultery?" I was losing my natural deference to solicitors. This man was trying my patience.

"You've seen the papers?" Something reptilian flashed across his features.

"Yes."

"He didn't tell me. He only assured me of the fact, just as he assured me you'd been married three years so he could now divorce you. I would have learned the details in due course, once a trial date had been set."

"What would you have done if there were no evidence?"

"Excuse me?" His red face had turned crimson.

"I have, uh, had never been unfaithful to my husband. There could be no evidence. What would you have done then?" In my demand for an answer, I heard my father's combative voice.

He shrugged. "That would have been up to your husband. He never returned the signed papers, therefore they were never filed. I'd say you had a lucky escape, Mrs. Denis."

"Or you did, peddling this nonsense." I snapped out my words, close to losing my temper.

He smiled and shook his head. "Not me. But by saying your husband was murdered and by wanting to know what evidence he had of your adultery, you have raised my suspicions. The police might find this conversation interesting. Very interesting, indeed."

His words felt like insects walking over my skin. I leaned back in my chair in an effort to get away from him as I thought about my lack of an alibi. "Why is it interesting?"

"I should report what you've said to the authorities. But perhaps we could come to some arrangement."

My puzzlement must have been written on my face. "What are you talking about?"

"I could be persuaded to keep my silence. And in exchange, you could show your appreciation." His smile deepened and his eyes glittered with avarice.

I thought my breakfast of tea and toast would land on his filthy carpet. How could Reggie have stood to deal with this slimy creep? I jumped up and strode from his office, saying, "Do what you want. There'll be no arrangement between us."

I rushed out to the landing, leaving the door open behind me. I ran down the staircase and didn't stop until I was out on the busy pavement.

I began walking toward the Underground station when a man fell into step with me. I sped up; he matched me step for step. I slowed down; he did the same.

"Mrs. Denis?" He had a nice baritone voice.

"Yes." I glanced his way once. Well-tailored three-piece suit and a snap-brimmed fedora in gray. I didn't want to look at his face. I just wanted to get out of there.

"Mrs. Olivia Denis?"

"Yes?" After my experience with Mr. McDowell, I was wary of everyone.

"I'm a friend of Colonel Summersby."

"Sir John?" I stopped then and actually looked at the man. He was the first to arrive at my flat after the burglary. Why did he choose to mention Abby's husband now? And why was he back?

"Yes." He smiled quickly. I had an impression that all his movements were quick, precise. "Civilians call him that. What were you doing talking to Mr. McDowell?"

"That's none of your business. Who are you? And what were you doing at my flat before the police arrived?" I jerked back a step and then hurried toward the station.

He kept up easily. "Ah, the burglary. I wanted to make sure the burglars were gone so you weren't in any danger. And I'm afraid your presence here is my business. Mr. McDowell is suspected of unsavory legal practices and dealing with criminals. As a friend of Colonel Summersby, I felt you should be warned."

"You said before you aren't with the police. So what business is any of this of yours?"

"Your husband's death could be involved tangentially with my work."

"What does that mean?" Despite the pedestrians around us, I was growing increasingly uneasy. And more than a little annoyed with his riddles.

There was that lovely smile again. This time it lingered a moment longer. "It means I'm a government employee, but not with Scotland Yard. I'm an army officer. My name is Adam Redmond. I'm a captain, British Army." He stood a little straighter as he spoke.

"Well, Captain Redmond, have you been following me everywhere and watching me?"

"No. I've been following and watching some other people, unsavory people, and lately when I follow them, I find you."

"Are these unsavory people following me?"

"Either that or meeting with you."

I gave him a dirty look as I moved to walk around him.

He held up a hand. "Of course you're not involved, so they must want something from you."

I decided to take a chance at hearing the truth from this man. Stepping aside on the busy pavement, I asked, "Would Mr. McDowell manufacture evidence for a court proceeding?"

"I wouldn't be surprised."

"Oh, wonderful." He would have to if he brought divorce proceedings for Reggie against me. The only way Reggie could have divorced me was by using false testimony.

"What did he say?" Redmond sounded very interested in Mr. McDowell.

"Nothing." I started to continue on my way.

"You believe your husband was murdered, and you want to know what sort of evidence McDowell had that you committed adultery. An interesting combination."

My gasp gave me away. How did he know these things? "I didn't."

"The divorce papers your husband never signed said you had."

"How do you know what papers my husband had and whether he signed them or not?" I glanced around. Not a bobby in sight.

His quick smile flashed again but didn't reach his hazel eyes. "What was your husband up to, Mrs. Denis?"

"I wish I knew." Nothing I'd heard since Reggie died made any sense.

"Perhaps we could get a cup of tea, and we wouldn't have to carry on this conversation in the street." He gave me a disarming smile, which made me more distrustful.

I felt much safer in the street with this man, and even there I was nervous. "I don't know you."

"If Colonel Summersby were here, I could ask for an

introduction. Since he's not, you'll just have to trust me."

Trust had been in short supply in my life since Reggie's murder. Redmond was dressed like any middling office manager in the area. Gray, unremarkable, bland. The sort of man who would fade into the background and be hard to describe. The sort of man, I imagined, who would be hired by sinister people to commit sinister deeds.

There was no way I could trust him. Anyone who'd been following me would know that I was a friend of John and Abby. And I suspected this man was very good at watching from the shadows.

"I think I'll just wait until Sir John is here to introduce us." I turned to walk away, terrified he'd grab me before I could put some distance between us.

"I didn't murder your husband, if that's what concerns you," he said to my back.

I faced him once more. "You agree he was murdered." I was glad he admitted it. If he knew, then others did as well.

"Yes. It was either a murder by someone who didn't know your husband well, or a warning to someone who did."

I blinked. "Who would be warned by my husband's death?"

"You."

Despite the warmth of the day, I shivered. "Warn me about what? And who is warning me? And why? This makes no sense." Fear and desperation gripped my vocal cords.

"If you don't know, the answers wouldn't make any sense to you."

"None of this makes any sense to me," I said, my throat dry, and then realized he was looking past me. I turned to look over my shoulder, but all I saw were men and women walking along the opposite side of the street. Normal men and women who didn't appear to be involved in murder and burglary.

I swung back around to find Redmond pointing toward the Underground entrance.

"You'll find it that way, miss," he said and then turned away.

"What?" Now I was completely confused.

Captain Redmond walked away at a good clip as if he were headed to an appointment. Not running, not looking back, but blending into the heavy foot traffic as his cuffed trouser-covered legs marched with precision. Everyone around me appeared to be focused on their own affairs, not noticing a frightened-looking woman in somber colors standing on the sidewalk.

But if I guessed correctly, Captain Redmond had seen one of the unsavory people he'd been following among the pedestrians around me.

I hurried away, my heels rapidly clicking on the pavement. Was the person he'd seen now following me? I all but ran to the Underground.

* * *

When I reached Summersby Lodge that Friday afternoon, I was starting to feel much like my old self. As long as I kept busy, my sorrow and anger at losing Reggie only struck at odd moments.

As I looked at the men around me since his death—my father, Sir Henry Benton, Captain Redmond—I could clearly see what I'd lost. What the world had lost. Reggie was a good, kind, honest man. I admired him. There were too few of his type around.

Abby and John's sons were down for the weekend from their boarding school. I couldn't believe how fast they were growing up, and how much taller they were than when I'd seen them during their summer holidays. We played a raucous game of something resembling cricket before cleaning up for dinner. The meal was enlivened by stories involving lessons and schoolboy pranks.

It wasn't until after dinner when the boys went to listen to the wireless that the grownups could sit and talk. I immediately raised the question I most wanted answered. "Do you know a Captain Redmond?"

"Redmond? Can't say that I do. Why?" John said, fiddling with his pipe.

"I met him in London. He said he was your friend, and he'd ask you to introduce us when he next saw you. He called you Colonel Summersby."

"Then I know him through the army, but I don't recall the name. How did you meet him?"

"The first time was a few days ago just after I came home to find my flat had been ransacked."

"Good heavens." Abby seemed ready to spring from her chair before she sank back down. I was again struck with how much she resembled a female, animated version of Reggie. Slender, traditionally good-looking, fair-complexioned. "You poor thing. You must have been terrified. First this business with Reggie, and now the flat. Why didn't you come straight down here after the police left?"

"Because I had a job interview."

"Did you get the job?" Abby always focused on what she considered the important details.

"Yes. Society reporter for the *Daily Premier*."

Abby smiled, but before she could say a word, John asked, "And you think this Captain Redmond had some role in the burglary?"

"He told me he'd been following the man who broke in and then he checked to make sure the flat was empty of criminals." Said that way, the story sounded amusing. And untrue.

"I hope you avoid him in the future," John said.

"Actually, I saw him again two days later."

"Livvy!" Now Abby sounded as worried as John sounded concerned.

"He came up to me on the street and called me by name. Then he introduced himself and said he knew you. As Colonel Summersby."

"Blasted cheek," John said. "Using the slightest acquaintance to start up a conversation."

"I don't like it," Abby said. "Reggie is murdered, your flat is broken into, and then some man comes up to you on the street. He knows your name and claims to know John. Oh, I don't like it at all."

I was glad I was away from London and the likes of Hamish McDowell and Captain Redmond. Here, surrounded by friends, I felt safe. I caught Abby's gaze and held it. "Worse, he stopped me after I left Mr. McDowell's office. What I'd just learned and Captain Redmond already knew was that Reggie had requested divorce papers and a new will from this solicitor McDowell. Unsigned papers at least, so they carry no weight."

Thank goodness. The scandal of being divorced and disinherited by a dead man, a man believed to be a suicide, would force me to leave for the colonies.

Abby's eyes and mouth rounded. "What? Divorce?" Somehow she kept her voice down. "Reggie divorce you? That's preposterous. Unthinkable. He adored you."

John banged his pipe on the table next to him. "A new

will? This Redmond chap must be a confederate of this solicitor, but I'll be dashed if I can figure out what their game is. You need to be very careful, Livvy."

"I agree. But if he's working with McDowell, why did he say he was a friend of yours? And why did he warn me away from McDowell?" It made no sense, and I was getting nervous all over again. *Reggie, what were you mixed up in?*

"It wouldn't be hard to find out we're friends. Perhaps he was trying to catch you off guard by using my name."

"What did the unsigned will say?" Abby asked.

"Everything goes to a Claire deLong. Have you ever heard of her?" I wished I hadn't.

"I believe she's an American. I only know the woman by reputation. I don't think Reggie ever met her. They didn't run in the same crowd."

"Who is she friends with?" Reggie had never met her? This was becoming odder by the moment.

Abby moved next to where I was sitting and took my arm. "Mrs. deLong is a divorcee. She's rumored to belong to a fast crowd. Reggie certainly didn't."

Reggie running with a fast crowd. The thought was so ludicrous I nearly burst out laughing.

"You've received unsigned divorce papers and an unsigned will where Reggie gives everything to that shocking woman?" Abby asked. "It must be some kind of a hoax."

"What were the grounds for divorce?" John asked. "Obviously not desertion."

Wonderful. He wasn't saying "obviously not madness." But then, John probably thought me a little mad. "Adultery."

"Livvy?" Abby asked in a breathless voice.

"Oh, I don't believe this. How could you think it could be true? I'd never cheat on Reggie."

"Who would pull such an elaborate, nasty trick?" Abby asked.

"You think it's just a trick?"

"Oh, most assuredly. Maybe it's some ploy for money," Abby said.

"Has anyone tried to blackmail you about these papers?" John asked.

"No. Well, except for McDowell."

"That would be the only way I can see someone making money with them. Threaten to show them to your father or something." John relit his pipe.

"Tell me about your new job." Abby sounded eager to talk about something pleasant, so I told her what little I knew. Without mentioning spying on Reggie's coworkers for Sir Henry.

I normally told them everything, but this time, I'd been sworn not to tell anyone.

"Oh, how exciting," Abby said, giving me a big grin. "Reporting on fashions and parties and galas."

John frowned. "Does your father know?"

"Not yet, and I don't want you to tell him before I can. He'll be against it, but he doesn't want me to move home any more than I do. And please, never mention my burglary."

John held up a hand. "Wouldn't dream of it."

I didn't believe that, but I let it go. "Back to this Captain Redmond. He said he worked for the government, but not Scotland Yard. Then he said he was an army officer. What kind of an army do we have that watches people's flats being burglarized without calling the police?" I was still incensed by his actions.

"Of course!" John bellowed through a plume of tobacco smoke, making Abby and me jump. "Now I remember.

Redmond's in Army Intelligence. Specifically counterespionage. Of course, I don't see him around much. They're short-handed and their workload's jumped since the abdication. The Germans are trying to find sympathizers with the ear of the new king."

"Why did he approach me? And why was he hanging around my building when he watched this person that he wouldn't name break into my flat?"

"I'd suspect the burglar was a German."

"I don't know any Germans."

John shrugged and looked away. "Reggie was in the Foreign Office. He was the head of his department's Northern European desk. He dealt with the Germans."

"He dealt with ceremonial issues." Reggie always said you could paper the entire country with the forms and certificates that went through his office.

"Usually."

Alarm bells went off in my head. "What do you mean, usually?"

He looked away. "With all these foreigners in town pushing this treaty or that pact, credentials have become very important. Reggie, of course, didn't tell me anything, but I could read between the lines. His duties had expanded. He had to be more thorough in checking paperwork."

"Reggie never told me anything about his work. Is this why Captain Redmond keeps popping up? Is this why the flat was ransacked?" My skin itched all over with the slime of dread. Would I never feel safe again?

John still didn't look in my direction as he examined the rug with surprising interest.

Abby finally said, "Perhaps we could have Captain Redmond here next weekend so he and Livvy could talk.

After being properly introduced, of course."

"I'd like that." Anything to eliminate the creepy feeling along the back of my neck every time I thought of him following me.

"I'll try." John didn't sound hopeful. "I don't think any of those counterintelligence chaps get out of London much."

"John, I expect him down here. It's the least you can do."

Sir John looked at his wife with an expression that said he knew when he was beaten, but he wasn't happy.

I didn't care if he was happy, as long as I could get answers out of Captain Redmond.

CHAPTER FIVE

MY FIRST WEEK at the *Daily Premier* was a disaster. My typing was rusty. I interviewed debutantes and society matrons as I covered bridal showers and teas in aid of good deeds. Miss Westcott put me on the mail desk where all the announcements of births and engagements and marriages were dumped. The low point was when I made a typo and reported an earl's daughter had given birth, baby's father unknown.

I meant *I* didn't know and needed to find out. But we were rushed as always and I forgot to ask who the earl's daughter was married to. Then someone came along and picked up all the announcements for the composing room.

Miss Westcott was heard to sob after one of the rewrite girls went down to the composing room and discovered the men guffawing. She returned with the offending notice and a tale that followed me for days.

Some of my reports were covered with so many typos and cross-outs that the articles were nearly impossible to read. Miss Westcott spent far too much of her time looking over my shoulder either in an attempt to hurry a report out of me before deadline or rewriting in her head as I typed. She never raised her voice, but one of the rewrite girls looked at me as she said, "If things continue this way, Miss Westcott will be forced to take up drinking."

The harder I tried, the worse my work became.

And then came my big break. I was sent to a concert where my job was to describe the dress of a minor member of the House of Windsor and get a quote for a story in Friday's edition. I was told to dress like a guest to this affair so I wouldn't stand out as a reporter.

Apparently Miss Westcott saw the benefit of sending someone with a gloss of aristocratic bearing to cover the event. Or perhaps she'd rather I messed up somewhere other than in the office.

Whatever Sir Henry had in mind, Miss Westcott found a way to use my talents first.

I sidled up to the minor royal during intermission for the concert and complimented her on her gown while taking mental notes on its design.

She thanked me.

I asked if she were enjoying the concert and she said it was wonderful. Then I was shoved aside by a member of her party and I left to wonder how I could make a story out of that.

The next morning, Jane Seville, a photographer who worked on photo essays as well as the society pages, showed me how to write my piece with enough detail to give the public a view into that concert. Glancing at the sketch of the royal gown in my notebook, she nodded appreciatively and pointed out a better way to describe the dress. She also showed me how to give the royal a few quotes that wouldn't offend Buckingham Palace.

"But she didn't say that to me," I said.

"She probably said it at some point during the concert. We don't report the literal truth here, Olivia. We report what these people want to show the world and what the world expects to see. This isn't the newsroom."

Miss Westcott was heard to give a huge sigh of relief when I turned in the story on time.

At the end of each day, I dragged myself home on the Underground, ate a little supper, and went to bed. By the end of the week, my cupboard and my closet were getting bare. "When do you find time to go to the shops?" I asked Jane.

"Oh, I take care of any errands before I walk in the door at home or I'd never get them done. Since we're out half the day, run your errands after going to your assignments or during lunch. Just give yourself extra time and learn to write faster so no one notices. All they care about is getting the copy in time to make up the paper."

I was thankful I was going to Summersby Lodge for the weekend. I was also thankful I hadn't been given a Saturday night assignment, so I didn't have to stay in town and work.

I turned in my last story to a frowning Miss Westcott on Friday evening two minutes before deadline. At least I'd followed all of Jane's tips and turned in a crackerjack article with plenty of detail on a talk at the museum, mentioning all the female notables in attendance and what they wore. My notebook was beginning to fill with notes and sketches.

Miss Westcott's red pencil came out immediately as she waved me away, but at least she didn't wince.

Relieved, I picked up a few things for my kitchen, put away my laundry delivery, shook off my weariness, changed into a smart black frock, and took a cab to Lester and Mary's flat. He was Reggie's favorite coworker; Mary was my first friend among the "Whitehall wives," as I thought of them. I'd been invited to their party shortly before Reggie died. With the mandate Mr. Colinswood had given me for my job, attending the party was important for my continued employment.

Heaven knew my work on the society page wouldn't keep my pay packets coming in.

Lester Babcock opened the door to my knock. Beyond his stunned, jaw-dropped expression, I could hear the party was already swinging. "Livvy! I didn't think—"

"It's all right," I told him, putting a hand on his arm. "You and Mary have been good friends. I wanted to come. Please, you don't have to treat me like a fragile widow. That went out with Queen Victoria."

"You're doing all right? Really?"

"I miss him." A little stab in my heart reminded me of how true that statement was. Then I forced on a brave smile and said, "But I also enjoyed your parties more than Reggie did. I hope that doesn't sound disloyal. And I'll hear people talk and I'll be able to imagine Reggie's responses and it'll make him seem—not yet gone. Does that make sense?"

Lester nodded. "I had the same reaction after my father died."

"Is it all right for me to come in?"

Lester realized he was blocking the door and stepped aside. "Of course. We're glad you came."

"Lester? Who—?" Mary saw me and rushed over to give me a hug, nearly spilling her drink. "Oh, Livvy, I'm so glad you came. I don't like the idea of you sitting home alone."

"I don't, either." I hugged her back. "You don't think this is too callous of me, do you? I wanted to see our friends. Well, my friends now, I hope."

"Definitely your friends. Lester, pour Livvy a drink. White wine as usual?"

"Please."

Lester went into their cramped kitchen while Mary and I

walked into the parlor. There were more than a dozen familiar faces in the room. Every one of them stopped talking and stared when I came in.

"Livvy." Carol Hawthorn whispered as if she'd seen a ghost.

"It is indeed," I said and smiled. "You're my friends as well as Reggie's, and I wanted very much to see you again."

"Well, I for one am glad," David Peters said and gave me a boyish grin. Reggie couldn't stand David, referring to him as a lightweight and a dim bulb. However, he was great fun and an excellent mimic. I liked him.

"How have you been, David?"

"Are you up for ridiculous tales and scandalous antics?" He wiggled his eyebrows.

"I love your stories."

Lester handed me a glass of wine and I settled in for a delightful evening. The aches and pains of my unaccustomed workweek disappeared in the gaiety of being among charming friends. Even Sir George Rankin could be mildly diverting when he tried, pointing out a governmental mix-up on a line for the king's speech for the upcoming state opening of Parliament that would have produced peals of laughter and a few red faces in that august assembly.

I found myself alone with Sir George for a moment. "How is Lady Margery?"

"I'm afraid her health is deteriorating. She wants to go to the south of France again this winter. It's expensive, sending her and a companion for months in the sun."

How was Sir George raising the money to provide his wife with her time on the Riviera? "Was she there last winter? I didn't realize she was in such poor health."

"Yes." He gave me a grim smile. "We all do what we must

for our loved ones."

I nodded. I was here to hunt for Reggie's killer, which meant I couldn't let the opportunity pass. "That's why I'm trying to find out what really happened to my husband. Who do you think murdered Reggie?"

A shocked look passed his lined face. "I'm sorry, my dear. Reggie murdered Reggie." Shaking his head, he walked away from me.

I went out to the dining room and found Carol Hawthorn there. She and Edward were in their mid-forties and gossiped with sharp tongues, and I rarely knew what was safe to say to her.

"Oh, Olivia, I was so sorry to hear that Reggie planned to, er, leave you."

I immediately knew what I wanted to say to her, but I found myself biting my tongue. Supposedly no one else knew about the divorce papers. It hadn't come out at the inquest. "Where did you get that idea?"

"Edward told me after Reggie, ah, died. He'd confided in Edward, you see."

I decided to brazen it out. The papers weren't signed and had now been consumed by fire. My position with these people would be seriously weakened if Carol spread this story around. I grabbed a plate and began dropping tasty-looking snacks on it. "I wish he'd confided in me. I know nothing about any plan to leave me. So as far as I know, your husband misunderstood."

"No. No!" She bobbled her plate. "Reggie told Edward if anything happened to him, that there were certain papers that were to go to you. I guess to prevent a scandal after he was gone."

"And Edward told you. How kind of him." My voice

dripped sarcasm. I decided I would carry out my assignment for Sir Henry while avoiding Carol. "So where are these papers?"

"I don't know. And it doesn't matter now, does it? Now that he's killed himself."

I gave Carol a cold stare, speechless at her cruelty.

She put on a sympathetic expression I didn't believe for a second. "I didn't mean to upset you, Olivia. Everyone likes you, and everyone liked Reginald. But he must have been a good fifteen years older than you. No one expected it to last, certainly not after Mrs. Simpson. You're still a girl of what, twenty-five? No one's blaming you. Not really."

I shook my head, unable to figure out where Carol's conversation was leading. Reggie and I got along fine. We never fought. So there couldn't have been any rumors about us. "What are you talking about?"

"This affair that you had. The one that Reginald was divorcing you over. And killed himself over."

I drew myself up, my cold stare replaced by white-hot anger. "I've never had an affair, and Reggie knew I was faithful. What you are saying is cruel and untrue. And if you dare repeat this slander, I will tell Sir George that Edward is spreading rumors around the office concerning a colleague who isn't here to defend himself. Or me."

I took my plate and stalked out of the dining room, my hem tangling around my ankles. Carol had ruined my party spirit. Paul Chambers jumped out of my way when I reached the hallway. "Don't pay Carol any mind. She's just jealous."

"Jealous? No, she's just cruel." I took a deep breath and pasted on a party smile. "So what have you been doing lately?"

"Mountains of paperwork. I don't know how Reggie

stood it." He gave me a grimace. "I'm filling in for Reggie until they decide on a permanent replacement. Not that anyone could replace Reggie. He could find his way through all the records and requests to give the correct response."

"I'm sure you're doing a great job." I was shocked they'd already replaced Reggie, but I shouldn't have been surprised. Life was progressing without him. That thought drove a lance into my heart, leaving me aching and a little breathless.

Chambers peered closer into my face. "Damn. No one had told you, and then I had to go and put my foot in it." He led me to an alcove near the front door where we were out of the way of traffic to the food and drinks.

He balanced my plate while I took a deep breath and dabbed my eyes. First Carol and her knowledge of those terrible papers, now Paul telling me the office had moved on. "I was surprised, that's all. The desk can't be left without a leader, and I'm sure you're doing splendidly. You have as much experience as Reggie."

Paul handed me back my plate, but I had lost my appetite.

"I was two years ahead of him at Oxford, but he was back working in civilian life before I was demobbed. And then it took me a while to find my feet after the war."

Paul had been a handsome man, tall and athletic, before he'd let himself go to seed. He'd landed a wealthy wife and a good job on the basis of his looks, according to Reggie, but he'd never lived up to his promise.

"That happened with so many people." I probably shouldn't have pushed, but I did. "Tell me, after Annabelle died, how long did it take you to find yourself again?"

"It's been two years, and I'm not sure that I have yet." He gave my shoulder a sympathetic squeeze. "Not what you wanted to hear, I suspect."

"No. But I appreciate your honesty." My breath stung in my throat.

"Don't let Carol Hawthorn bother you. She spread some nasty tales after Annabelle died."

I shook my head, unable to remember anything Carol might have said at the time. I'd quickly learned to head in another direction when I saw her coming. I'd have to practice that again.

"She tried to tell everyone that Annabelle was murdered. Pure rot. They weren't sure if it was gastritis, but they were certain it was natural. Who'd want to murder Annabelle?"

"Who'd want to murder Reggie?"

"Exactly."

"But Reggie *was* murdered."

His look of shock reminded me of Abby's when I'd told her the news. "Good Lord. You're joking."

"No. It's obvious."

I had his full attention. "Obvious? How?"

"Reggie couldn't shoot right-handed. The fingers on his right hand wouldn't bend. Whoever shot him and staged it to look like a suicide didn't know that."

"Well, I'll be dashed. He wrote right-handed."

"Yes, but he held his pen in an odd way."

Paul scrunched up his face in thought. "You're right, he did hold his pen funny. And you say he couldn't shoot right-handed." He looked a little pale. "What are the police doing?"

"Nothing. They maintain it was a suicide."

"Did he leave a note?"

"There was a note in his pocket." I decided to keep pushing. "Weren't you one of the people from the office who went to the Windmill Theater with Reggie that night?"

"You mean the night—? Yes. Yes, I was. It was Reggie, me, Edward Hawthorn, Lester Babcock, David Peters, and Blake Fielding. When we all left and went our separate ways, I never thought—"

He'd soon be dead. I shivered. "Yes. Lester said he saw you wave to Reggie as you went toward Charing Cross and he went down Haymarket."

"Yes. I finally sold the house and took a flat near Charing Cross. Quite a relief, I can tell you. Annabelle loved that house. With her not there—" He took a large gulp of his drink and then coughed.

"Are you okay?" I patted his back, more in sympathy than to keep him from choking.

Chambers coughed again and then smiled wryly. "It's odd. I don't want to think my wife was murdered, and you're happy to think your husband was." Shaking his head, he walked off.

As the evening wore on, the flat grew more crowded with laughing, chatting people. I had my back to another group when I heard someone say, "Where's Fielding?"

"He traveled to France to spend time with his wife," a man's voice said.

"Imagine." Carol Hawthorn's voice cut easily through the chatter. "Such a dark-skinned man, and his father-in-law is a senior member of the Nazi party."

"They won't let his wife into Britain because of her father," another woman said. "That's so sad."

"I doubt his father-in-law would let him into Germany," Carol said. "What is he? Indian?"

"I heard Spanish," a man offered.

"Probably Anglo-Indian," another man said.

"I've heard he's about ready to chuck it all in and move

to France so he can be with her all the time."

"He can't have much loyalty to England if he'd do that."

"Well, he's not English," Carol said. "You can see that. So why would he have any loyalty to England?"

"Maybe our secrets are going to his wife and then her father," a man said.

"Hush. You can't say anything like that. Not even here. Not even as a joke," someone else hissed. The conversation quickly changed, but I was left wondering if that was what Reggie discovered. Was that why he was killed?

I was the first to leave Lester and Mary's party. Carol's poisonous words left me wanting to throttle her to keep her from spreading tales. Reggie's death and his legal papers from beyond the grave still stung. And then I'd heard reasons why some of his coworkers might be passing secrets to the Nazis. Could it be for love or money?

I had rescued my hat and purse from Lester and Mary's bedroom and was heading for the parlor to say my good-byes when male voices coming from the kitchen stopped me in my tracks.

"Do you think she came here to find out how Reggie died?" the first one asked.

"If she did, she certainly hasn't learned anything," the second one replied.

I paused by the closed door, but before I could hear any more, Mary came out of the parlor and said, "Leaving already?"

"I'm tired. I'm not used to putting in a full workday." I glanced at the swinging door that led into the kitchen. The voices could have belonged to any man at the party.

Mary came over and took my arm in hers as she led me to the front door. "Feel free to call anytime. And we'll be sure to invite you to the next office party."

"Oh, I hope so." I went through all the usual compliments to my hostess as I hoped the door would open and I'd have a face to put to a voice from that surprising conversation. The kitchen door stayed firmly shut, leaving me with well over a dozen possibilities for the two voices. Finally, I had to leave.

All I had was a suspicion that two people in Reggie's office knew more about his murder than I did.

CHAPTER SIX

I GOT UP early the next morning and threw a few things into a suitcase. Then I made my way through the crowds and the drizzle to Charing Cross station, where I purchased a badly needed coffee to keep me awake during my journey into Sussex to visit Abby and Sir John.

By prearrangement, John picked me up at the station. I was not thrilled to find my father was also in the car.

"We expected you last night." My father could never just say hello.

"I had a party to attend."

"Livvy. You're recently widowed."

"The party was with coworkers of Reggie's. I hoped someone would let slip something useful."

"Useful?"

"Pointing to his killer."

"Oh, Livvy." My father sounded annoyed and astonished that I would attempt such a thing.

John said, "Did anyone?"

"No." I didn't see any point in telling them what I heard when I left, since I didn't know who was speaking.

"Because Reggie committed suicide." My father looked out the window at fields ready to harvest.

I saw no point in responding. Once my father made up his mind, nothing as unimportant as facts could shake his assurance that he was right.

Then my father faced me. "You're not wearing mourning. That a dull tweed, but still—"

"I'll wear mourning when the courts find Reggie's murderer guilty."

"You'll have a long wait. He killed himself," my father snapped as we glared at each other.

John gave a weary sigh.

When we arrived at the house, Abby and I went out into the mix of clouds and sunshine to enjoy the garden. The day was warm and the air carried a hint of fragrance from the flowers. I could shake off my worries and tell Abby stories from my new life as a working girl.

John and my father closeted themselves in the study. Except for a brief period at luncheon, we didn't see them again until dinner, when another guest appeared at the table.

Captain Redmond.

I hadn't expected to see him again so soon. I turned to my father and said, "Is this why you were inside hiding with Sir John all day?"

"They were debating whether or not to introduce me to you," Captain Redmond said. If he smiled, it was too quick a motion for me to catch.

"They must have decided you're acceptable."

"They said you've probably been introduced to worse rogues than me." Now I did see a hint of a smile. What had he told my father?

I glanced over at my father. "When have I been introduced to rogues? I wouldn't have thought you'd allow it."

"Someone introduced you to Reggie," he grumbled.

That was so unlike my father I was speechless for a

moment. I slammed down my wine glass, splashing a little on the immaculate ivory tablecloth as I snapped at him, "How can you say that? He was my husband, and he was recently murdered. That wasn't his fault."

"Are you certain of that?" my father asked, staring at me.

"Yes. Why would you ask?"

At that moment, the footman and the housemaid entered to take away the soup bowls and serve the fish course. We all remained silent until they left the room, even though they were probably listening outside the door and would hear every word.

"He may not have been a rogue, Olivia, but he worked for His Majesty's Foreign Office despite the fact that he could easily have been blackmailed. That was a dangerous position to put himself in. For himself, for you, for His Majesty."

I stared at my father. "What do you mean, 'easily blackmailed'?" Reggie was a kind, gentle man, generous with his time and compliments. The Reggie I knew never took a step out of line. He wasn't here to defend himself, so I felt I must, especially from my father's slanders. "That's preposterous."

My father held my gaze. "Olivia, Reggie was a homosexual."

I dropped my fork. It clattered in the sudden silence. I looked at each face. No one would return my stare except my father.

A pain started in my solar plexus as my brain went numb. My father was not the type to say anything so bold about anyone without proof. Reggie would have been fired if this had come out, even arrested. It would have caused a scandal. He'd have been an outcast and I would have been the subject of pity and ridicule. Suddenly, I wondered if I'd known my husband at all.

Then Captain Redmond glanced from my father to me and said, "We also spent the afternoon discussing how much you should be told."

I stared at him in disbelief. "Don't you mean, would she believe this story? It's impossible. I mean, we were married. Completely married." This couldn't be true. Reggie could never have deceived me so completely.

Abby's voice softly cut the thickening atmosphere. "But you said there wasn't much passion in your marriage."

"Well, that's understandable," I snapped at her. "He worked hard. He was tired. He got those awful headaches from all the close work he did. He—"

"His boyfriend's name was Derek Langston," my father interrupted. "The faggot admitted as much under questioning. Privately, of course. He doesn't want notoriety. Or a jail term."

"If what you say is true, Reggie wouldn't have wanted that either. So why would he have gone to the very public trouble of filing for divorce without evidence?" I was astounded, shocked, struck blind.

"What are you talking about?" My father's voice went dangerously quiet.

"Shortly before he died, Reggie went to a solicitor named McDowell to draft a divorce pleading and a new will. A fact known to at least one of his coworkers. And Captain Redmond."

My father slammed his fist on the table. China, silver, wine goblets, the vase of flowers from the garden, everything quivered. Abby and I both flinched and she shot a worried glance around her table. My father set both hands on the tablecloth and leaned toward me. In a murderously quiet voice he said, "That queer was going to divorce you? How dare he?"

Telling my father about this had started a headache in addition to my stomachache. "He hadn't signed the papers, and I burned them. He had no grounds for a divorce. It wasn't in his best interests. It makes no sense."

"Why do you think it should make sense? His guilt, his desire to be with his lover—"

"No. You're wrong," I interrupted. "Reggie didn't have grand passions."

"Not for you, he didn't." My father took brutal aim at my feelings. "It's scandalous enough that he was a poof without adding the shame of divorce. His death has allowed you to escape disgrace. But just barely."

In my anger at Reggie's betrayal, I grabbed the moral high ground and blasted my father. "Do you hear yourself? A fellow human being, your son-in-law, has been killed, and all you think about is what the men in your club will say." I didn't need a mirror to know steam was rising from my ears.

"It's not only the men in my club. What about your girl friends? Your whole social circle? You'd be laughed out of London." Scorn filled my father's voice.

I plunged on, refusing to give in. Refusing to give up on Reggie. "I wasn't the wiser and so unlikely to upset his arrangements. Why would he act so rashly when it wasn't in his nature? He was in no danger of losing his lover or his position in society. And why now?" I couldn't believe it. Nothing made sense.

"She does have a point," John said. We all turned and looked at him. I, for one, had forgotten anyone else was present for this wretched argument. "But not one we can solve tonight. I suggest we have a pleasant dinner and discuss something else. Anything else. Things will look better in the morning."

Abby gamely began a discussion of our unseasonably beautiful weather. If the staff was surprised to see harmony at the table when they brought in the next course, they didn't show it.

We finally finished dinner and moved into the parlor for coffee. By mutual agreement, we all had brandy instead. When I turned to my father and opened my mouth, John stepped in.

"No. Not another word tonight. There will be plenty of time to discuss this after breakfast."

I looked at Abby, who appeared to be silently begging me to keep quiet. I nodded.

Instead, we played Whitehall's favorite game, what will Herr Hitler do next? Our guesses were as good as the cabinet's.

In less than an hour, our brandies were finished and Abby suggested we all retire for the night. As everyone rose, my father said, "Olivia, I forbid you to see Langston."

My father and I glared at each other. He knew that now I had this information about Reggie's lover, I would visit him as soon as possible. And I would, too. I just wouldn't tell my father.

At least he still hadn't heard about my job.

John grumbled and led my father by the arm to the doorway leading into the main hall. He hated any disturbance to his country life, and my father and I had brought it to his door tonight in spades.

The others followed. I stayed where I was. "Olivia, are you coming?" My father's words were a command, not a question.

I turned to Abby. "Would it be all right if I walk in your garden for a little while? There are some things I need to work out for myself."

She came over and gave me a hug. "Of course. I'll tell the staff not to lock up in here until you've come in. Good night."

They left me then and closed the door behind them. I opened the French doors to the garden and walked outside to the smells of newly turned compost and the snap of dead leaves.

Almost immediately, I found myself wishing I'd worn my coat. It had been a warm day for this time of year, but once the sunlight disappeared, so had the heat. I walked fast, rubbing my hands up and down my bare upper arms as I tried to puzzle out what the Reggie I'd known had in common with the Reggie I'd just learned about.

"Quite a lot to swallow in one evening," a man's voice said behind me.

I swung around as he stepped into the moonlight, all white shirtfront and bland features. "Captain Redmond, why am I not surprised to see you join me?"

"You want to know the truth about your late husband. So do I."

"Why would you care? And no stories this time. Sir John let slip you work for Army Intelligence."

He gave a single, short chuckle. "The colonel's a good man, but not cut out for clandestine work."

"Agreed. So tell me what is going on. And believe me when I tell you nothing else will shock me tonight."

"I was surprised your father decided to tell you Reginald Denis was a homosexual."

I drew back, furious he had learned about this before I had. Apparently the whole world had known Reggie's secret.

Why had I been so blind? Had I ever paid attention to him? "You knew?"

He nodded. "A few months ago, we discovered a leak in Whitehall. Details of our conversations with other governments were being discussed in Berlin. Von Ribbentrop is an ass, but he has his uses. He told us things he shouldn't have known in an effort to impress us."

"Why would anyone give him secrets if he's such a pig?" Reggie had used several barnyard names for the ambassador.

"Some of the men under him at the embassy are brilliant and ruthless. Either they found someone in the Foreign Office who needs money, or has a secret, or backs Herr Hitler. We've been following several men, hoping to learn who the mole is."

"Have you found him?"

"Not yet."

"And Reggie was one of the men you suspected."

"Yes. He had access to all the secrets that were divulged, and he would have been easily blackmailed."

"He'd do this to protect me?" After all I'd heard I was flattered to think Reggie would care about me.

"No. To protect Langston and himself."

That hurt. "You are frank."

"I don't have time to tiptoe around the truth." His voice held a note of sympathy among the chord of sternness.

"Why are you telling me this?"

He stepped forward and took my hand, which had turned to ice. He held both of mine within his larger ones to warm them. They were rough and callused, nothing like Reggie's hands. "I want your help. Last night you attended a party at the home of one of your husband's coworkers. I want you to stay in touch with those people. I want you to watch them and report back to me."

"Spy on them." I'd already agreed to repeat their private conversations to Sir Henry Benton. Could this get any more convoluted? And distasteful?

"Call it what you will. Will you do it?"

I was already planning to keep friendly with them for my job with the newspaper. I wasn't certain what I would report, if anything, to Redmond, but I saw a use for saying yes. "If you'll do something for me."

His scowl in the moonlight showed caution. "What?"

"Get me Derek Langston's address and telephone number."

"Done. Do we have a deal?"

"Yes." Maybe. It depended on what I learned. "Are you still looking for the mole in the Foreign Office, or did you decide to pin everything on Reggie since he can't defend himself?"

There was that flash of a smile again. "Whitehall is satisfied for the moment. However, Army Intelligence finds Denis's death too convenient. Especially since his wife keeps telling everyone that Denis couldn't shoot with his right hand."

My hands were toasty now due to his kind act, but he continued to hold them, and I was glad. Sparks of warmth shot up my arms from being so close to this rugged man. "Why did you come up to me on the street that day and why did you know so much about the legal papers Reggie requested from McDowell?"

"That was a piece of luck. Edward Hawthorn went to his boss, Sir George Rankin, and said your husband told him he'd gone to McDowell to file divorce papers. Rankin abhors any kind of scandal, so he asked us to find out the truth. We entered McDowell's office after hours and read the documents for ourselves. What's happened to them?"

Why is he asking me this? "They were never signed."

"We know. Denis was already dead before we heard the rumor. So what happened to them?"

"The copy mailed to me was burned."

"There was only one copy."

Thank goodness. No one, meaning Carol Hawthorn, would ever be able to prove this shocking aberration in our marriage. "How many people knew about Reggie's supposed boyfriend?"

"Only the people directly involved in the hunt for the traitor. It was a closely guarded secret." He gave my hands one final squeeze and let go. "One other thing. Did your husband ever mention St. Asaph's Hotel?"

My blood froze for an instant. "That's next to where he died. I don't know if he'd ever set foot inside."

"Oh, he had."

"Why?" All I could think was Captain Redmond would tell me it was a place people like, well, people like Reggie would meet.

"Not only do our diplomats meet there for discreet conversations, it being so close to Whitehall, but so do agents for a dozen different countries."

"Reggie wouldn't go to a place where spies gathered."

"Of course he would. In the last few weeks of his life, Reggie Denis appeared to be on his own personal hunt for the leak in his office."

Spies. Something else I never believed Reggie would get involved in. Who was my husband, and what had he been up to?

CHAPTER SEVEN

THE NEXT DAY, I found myself forced to travel from Sussex to London by train with my father. I kept my nose in a magazine the whole way. I don't know what he did because I avoided looking his way.

Actually, I didn't see any of the words on the pages. I was trying to reconcile Reggie the civil servant, Reggie the husband, with what I'd heard of homosexuals. Deviants. Child molesters. Greasy, sweaty men in alleyways.

Reggie didn't like alleys. He found them dark and dirty.

I turned down my father's offer of dinner and went back to the flat, feeling gloomier than the rainy evening around me. I was in trousers, an old pullover, and wooly socks with my makeup off when the buzzer sounded at my door.

Standing in the foyer, the locks still in place, I called out, "Who is it?"

"Captain Marshall. Army Intelligence." Through the peephole, all I could see was his tie.

"Can this wait? I'll speak to you tomorrow."

"I just need a few minutes of your time. I won't come in. It's about your husband's death."

"Tomorrow would be better. I'm not feeling well." Actually, I was feeling angry and sorrowful over what I'd learned from my father. That should qualify for not feeling well. Technically, not a lie.

"Please, Mrs. Denis. This won't take long. It's important. It's about new evidence in your husband's murder." He was standing too close to the peephole for me to make out more than that he wore a trench coat.

"Hold on a moment. I'm going to call someone to verify your identity."

"Who?"

Was that a note of panic in his voice? I definitely wasn't letting him in now. "Someone you work with."

I hurried to the telephone on a small table in the hall and dialed the number Redmond had given me just in case. A man answered by reciting the number.

"I'd like to leave a message for Captain Redmond."

"Go ahead."

"Do you know a Captain Marshall? Sign it, Olivia Denis."

"I'll give him the message when he comes in."

Thinking this must be Redmond's work number at Army Intelligence, I asked, "Do you know a Captain Marshall, by any chance?"

"I'll give him the message." The line went dead.

I counted to ten and walked back. When I looked out the peephole, he was still there.

"Do you know a Captain Redmond?" I called out.

He was standing farther away from the peephole now and I could see him smile. He was clean-shaven and had a boyish grin. "It would be hard not to know him. He shows up everywhere and anywhere, has a keen sense of humor, and is very popular with the ladies."

He certainly knew Redmond.

I opened the door just enough to talk through. Captain Marshall was standing on the landing, twirling his hat around one finger and watching the elevator that ran through the open center of the staircase creak along.

Under his beige trench coat the lapels of an ordinary gray suit peeked out and he carried a gray fedora with a brown band. His brown hair was too close-cropped to be fashionable. Ordinary looking, just like Redmond, down to the gray suit. Did they have a cookie cutter to create these men?

"Captain Marshall."

He immediately stopped twirling his hat and gave me his full, polite attention. I opened the door a little further, my head pressed against the wall.

What I hadn't realized looking through the peephole was Marshall was well above six feet in height, all arms and legs. He left his rainproof coat on with three buttons fastened, I guessed to assure me he'd leave quickly.

Annoyed at his arrival since all I wanted to do was to lick my wounds, I said, "What is so important about my husband's death that it can't wait until tomorrow?"

"We're investigating your claims that Reginald Denis was murdered. I just have a few questions in light of some new information."

"New information?" Wonderful! Someone was looking into Reggie's death and had discovered a clue. "What new information?"

"I don't want to shout it in the hallway where we might be overheard. Perhaps I should come back another day."

I was desperate to hear his new information. It might prove Reggie wasn't a queer. "No. Just whisper it through the crack."

"Why don't you open the door? I'll stay on the landing, but that way we won't need to shout. And this information is of a very sensitive nature." The man gave me a sincere look as he continued to speak quietly.

I was becoming frustrated. "I can hear you right now, and if you lower your voice, I'll still be able to hear you."

"This may sound unreasonable, but I need to be sure you're the only one on the other side of the door listening to this information. I'm going out on a limb sharing this with you, but as his widow, I think you have the right to know."

I took a deep breath, wanting to be reasonable. "I don't want to open the door. I know you didn't come here to argue with me—"

"No," he readily agreed. "I came to share information with you. But only with you. I must be certain of that."

I wanted to hear what he had to say. "You promise to stay on the landing?"

"Of course. I didn't come to frighten you, Mrs. Denis."

I opened the door completely. "Now, what have you learned?"

He lowered his voice to a murmur. "There are some papers missing. We believe your husband may have handled them."

It must be the Foreign Office papers passed to the Nazis that caused Reggie and others to be under scrutiny. Old news. "You'd have to ask his office about papers. He didn't talk about his work or anything to do with it except in the broadest terms. And he never brought work home."

"Your husband confided in a few people that he was working on something dangerous, but not what it was. Do you know, Mrs. Denis? He was head of the Northern European desk, and the Germans are involved."

Not what I expected to hear. "Reggie? Dangerous? You must be mistaken. Germany was part of his responsibilities, but he only dealt with credentials and setting up meetings."

"He didn't bring home any papers? Anything he hid away in his study?"

I shook my head. "Do you really think this flat is large enough for Reggie to have had a study?" At least, not after we married. Somehow my things spread out over most of the flat. "Besides, he couldn't bring home papers from Whitehall. It's not allowed. You should know that."

"These aren't papers from the Foreign Office. We suspect they were stolen from the German embassy and passed to Mr. Denis by a member of the German underground. We need to find them before the Nazis do. It's vital to our national security." Marshall leaned forward. His boyish eagerness was contagious, but his cold blue eyes seemed at odds with his smile.

Reggie in possession of stolen Nazi documents. In league with resistance workers. How extraordinary. It certainly was new information, but I wasn't sure I believed it any more than the horrible news from my father. "How in the world would Reggie have ended up with stolen Nazi documents? He was a very quiet, studious man. And very honest."

"We have reason to believe he at least saw them. He was in contact with a member of the German underground at the time of the theft. As a patriot, he would know it was his duty to take and hide these stolen documents. An action that could have led to his death."

"Reggie wouldn't take stolen papers. At least not without immediately turning them in. I'd check with the Foreign Office."

"We'll follow up with them again, but so far, no one has seen the papers. I was hoping you might have seen them or know where your husband would hide them. You must see how important it is we find them."

"I'm sorry I can't help you, but my husband brought home nothing relating to work. That was a rule of his as well as Whitehall's policy."

Marshall towered over me. Even though he was standing on the landing, his height meant that his arms were long enough to strangle me in my flat. "I'm sorry to have bothered you. And again, you have my condolences. I trust you won't mention this to anyone. We don't want to tip our hand to the Germans in case they don't know we know the papers are missing."

"If they're stolen, surely the Germans must suspect we know they're missing." Did he think the Nazis were stupid? I was certain they weren't.

"Of course, but they don't know who we believe handled the papers after they went missing. That's why you need to keep quiet about this conversation. Someone might overhear."

"And the Nazis have ears everywhere."

My sarcastic tone didn't tell him what I thought of his warning, because he replied earnestly, "It only takes one spy to hear about your husband's connection to the missing documents to ruin all our efforts and put you in danger."

I felt the cold breath of this unknown Nazi on my neck. I'd already had my flat ransacked and with all the revelations about Reggie... I wanted to crawl under the covers and hide.

I started to close the door. "Good night, Captain Marshall."

"Good night, Mrs. Denis. Again, thank you for seeing me at such an inconvenient time. I really appreciate it." His boyish grin broke through his serious expression.

I couldn't resist asking, before I shut the door, "What should I do if I discover these papers?"

"Save them for me. I'll be in touch." He nodded and started down the stairs at a good clip. Smart man. He must have waited for the elevator on his trip up.

As I shut and locked the door, I realized his overcoat and fedora hadn't been dampened by the rain. I walked down the hall and into the darkened dining room to peek out of the draperies at the rain-splattered street below. I watched a figure in a man's hat and the same type of overcoat climb into the back seat of a waiting dark automobile.

"Oh, Reggie, what have you gotten me into?" I asked my empty apartment.

* * *

All night, I dreamed of being chased by homosexual Nazis in dirty raincoats and shiny black boots. I woke up angry with Reggie, Captain Marshall, and anyone else I crossed paths with.

My assignment that day for the *Daily Premier*, handling birth announcements, was guaranteed to annoy the most placid of temperaments. I had spoken to more vapid, love-besotted grandmothers in a few hours than I previously believed could exist in London in a year. That day I learned to hate making the often necessary follow-up telephone calls in reply to the incomplete notices mailed to the paper.

Blast Reggie. He hadn't even left me with a baby to love in his place. Just rumors that said he really didn't love me. That said I'd been wrong about who he truly was.

When no one was paying attention, I called the number Redmond had given me. No answer. Langston was probably at work. I'd call him that night at home.

No. He might refuse to see me. I'd drop in on him after work. If nothing else, I could leave my calling card.

I nearly burst out laughing. There was no way my visit

could be construed as a social call.

* * *

Captain Redmond came up to me as soon as I stepped outside the *Daily Premier* building at lunchtime. "Would you like to have lunch with me and tell me why you called last night?"

Yes to both. With proper decorum, I said, "There's an Aerated Bread Company around the corner."

He took my arm and we strode off along the windy sidewalk. At least the wind was blowing away the smoke from the millions of coal fires in London as well as the previous night's rain. We walked into the ABC and managed to snag a table in the busy restaurant.

As soon as the waitress took our orders, Redmond leaned forward, took my hand, and said, "We seem to have attracted the attention of two men who just walked in."

When I began to turn my head, he said, "No. Don't move. Just look lovingly into my eyes and tell me what happened last night."

I was aware of his warmth and the calluses on his hand as I said, "Do you know a Captain Marshall of Army Intelligence?"

I saw a flash of something, irritation perhaps, before he said, "Why?"

"Last night, an hour or two after I reached home, Captain Marshall of Army Intelligence dropped in on me. He thinks Reggie possessed stolen German papers. What haven't you told me?" Probably a whole lot, but I'd be happy if I at least received answers to my questions.

Redmond scowled. "Captain Marshall?"

"Yes."

"What did he look like?"

"Ordinary looking."

"You can do better than that," Redmond said, scoffing.

"Fine. Blue eyes, brown hair, well over six feet with long legs."

"Captain Marshall is shorter than either of us."

I shook my head. "Not the man I met." Redmond was about six feet tall, and I was about four inches shorter without heels.

He eyed me for a second before dropping his bombshell. "And he was with me last night. I don't think he could have been in two places at once."

Shuddering, I shut my eyes. I'd opened the door to let someone, anyone, into my flat. I could have been murdered like Reggie. Is that what had happened to my husband? And was the fake Captain Marshall Reggie's killer?

When I opened my eyes again, Redmond was staring at me as if he were trying to read my thoughts. "Don't fall apart on me now." Then he gave me his quick grin. "At least not until we find out who those two men are and why they're watching us."

"I never had anyone following me until I met you," came out through my clenched teeth.

"Maybe you never noticed before. Maybe your husband didn't notice and that's how they were able to kill him." He gave my hand a sympathetic squeeze.

Scowling, I leaned forward. "Do you know what they're after? Are there missing German documents? And did Reggie have anything to do with them?" I wanted answers. It felt like the world would turn right side up again if I knew what was happening and why.

He abruptly dropped my hand and sat back as the waitress brought our lunches. Meatloaf, potato, and peas for him, fish and salad for me. Despite trying, I got nothing from Redmond until we'd almost finished our meal. Finally, he said, "I wonder if those two men behind you have the answer to your questions."

I gave him a hard stare. "Right now, I'd like to know if you do." He was difficult to pin down about anything, and I thought I'd scream if I didn't get answers soon. At the very least I wanted to find someone in this business that I could trust.

"We believe something's missing. We don't know if your husband had it or not. But I'd bet those two men know precisely what's going on."

In that case, I wanted to start questioning those two men immediately. "How do we find out?"

"First we finish our lunch. Then we'll split up outside. If I'm right, only one of them will follow you."

"What will you do?"

"Don't worry about that." He wiggled his eyebrows at me and took another bite of his meatloaf.

"How much do you know about this business Reggie might have been mixed up in?"

He swallowed and said, "Not nearly enough."

I speared a piece of fish and leaned forward. "You know more than I do. Spill."

He studied the diners at the other tables and the staff without seeming to do so. Then he leaned forward and, in a voice so soft I could barely hear him, said, "Something was rumored to have gone missing from the German embassy the night your husband died. They were in great confusion, running back and forth and shouting, sending people racing around in autos. So far as anyone can tell, the Germans haven't gotten it back. Yet."

"Maybe Derek Langston knows."

"I'd leave that alone if I were you."

"You gave me his address and phone number. Didn't you think I'd call on him?"

"What do you hope to gain?"

I looked him straight in the eye and said, "I don't know. Maybe I'll understand Reggie better? I just know I need to do this."

We continued to eat in silence until he said, "We still have to get rid of the two following us."

"Those two men. German?"

He grinned briefly. "*Ja*. But I don't think they'll admit it."

"What do you want me to do?"

"Outside, when I give you the word, start walking quickly back to work and don't turn around. Don't stop. Just go back to your office."

"You sound like Reggie. He taught me a lot, but he also protected me. From his secrets. From his job. From life. Well, I'm through with that. You want me to be a decoy, fine. But don't expect me to not look back. To not get involved. I'm already involved." Since I couldn't raise my voice above a murmur, I made my points by jabbing his hand with my finger.

"I have orders not to involve you."

"Whose orders?"

I had to wait until he finished his bite of meatloaf. "It's not bad. You want to try some?"

"No. Whose?"

"I don't know. But the message was delivered by General Alford. I'm more afraid of him than I am of you, so please, be a decoy. And don't look back."

This was beginning to sound like some of my

conversations with my father. I dropped the subject. What I didn't drop was my refusal to follow directions.

We finished lunch discussing neutral topics and then walked to the front where the cash register was. Redmond exchanged pleasantries with the cashier as the line backed up behind us and then we stepped out onto the sidewalk.

"Go." Redmond bumped me into motion in the direction of the newspaper building. Before I could object, he hurried off in the other direction.

I turned and started toward the office at a quick pace. I could hear footsteps running toward me as I turned the corner. The building here was solid brick, so I stepped back against the wall. A moment later, a dark-haired man in a worn suit raced around the corner and passed me by a step or two before he came to a surprised halt.

"Looking for someone?" I asked.

He swung around, saw me, and turned pale. "No. I am late."

"Why have you been following me?"

"No. I swear—I wouldn't follow you, madam." I heard a hint of a German accent. He was studying my face, my clothes, my stance. For what, our next encounter?

I couldn't let him know I suspected him of being part of whatever plot killed Reggie. "You were going to steal my purse." I clutched it tightly to my chest as I moved to confront him, raising my umbrella to strike. "Get away from me, you brazen thief."

The look on his face clearly said he thought I was crazy and he did not want to deal with the police and a crazy woman. "I am sorry, madam. I do not want to steal from you."

He turned on his heel and ran smack into Redmond. The captain shoved my stalker against the wall and demanded,

"Why are you following the lady?"

"I swear. I am not." But his frantic gaze roamed the area. Was he looking for his accomplice or for a passerby to rescue him?

"Your friend from lunch won't be joining us, I'm afraid. Now, who sent you?"

"No one." He pulled his crumpled hat away from the bricks.

"You might ask him about his German accent," I suggested.

"Why is a German following an English lady on London streets?" Redmond asked.

"I am not German." His pronunciation of "German" gave him away. His head jerked as he scanned the area.

"If I hauled you over to the German embassy, would they claim you as one of their own?" Redmond shifted his body so from the street, it would look like two men in close conversation. Nevertheless, he had a tight grip on the German's shoulder.

"No. I have nothing to do with embassies. I am a printer." His nerves made his accent stronger and he was starting to sweat along his hairline.

"Where?"

"Where?" The V sound was very strong.

"Yes. Where are you a printer?"

"At Thompson's. Off Ludgate Hill."

"And your name?"

"Georg Schmidt."

"Get out of here, Schmidt, and don't let me catch you around this lady again." Redmond stepped far enough away that the German could leave but close enough he didn't have room to strike hard.

Schmidt, or whoever he was, straightened his hat and rushed away from us in the direction from which we'd come.

"You let him go?" I was a little disappointed. It must have been the adrenaline still pumping through my body after watching Redmond's masterful handling of the man.

"I didn't have any reason to hold him, and neither would the police. He didn't strike you, did he? Or try to steal your purse?"

"No." The grudging admission showed in my voice.

He grinned at me for an instant before straightening his own hat. "And while his name and address are probably fake, it gives us something to check. Maybe we'll be lucky this time and he slipped up."

"But why would they be following me?"

"Only one of them was. The other followed me." He seemed proud of being chased.

I found it alarming. "What happened to the other man?"

"Probably coming to about now." He held out his arm. "Shall I walk you back to the office?"

"Please." I took his arm and we walked the block to the newspaper. Now that the excitement was over, I discovered I was afraid of another attack. "Will I see you again? And will I see those two again?"

"You'll see me again. Unless someone finds what's missing from the German embassy first." He dropped me at the door, tipped his hat, and said, "I hope they don't."

I didn't know whether to be flattered or frightened.

CHAPTER EIGHT

I WAS FOLLOWED home that night, but the man kept his distance. Happily, the next morning, I didn't notice anyone tailing me.

I spent the morning on the wedding desk as I opened notice after notice. The smile drooped from my face as I thought of Reggie and our wedding.

At lunchtime, I took a walk, eventually finding myself in St. James Park. Reggie had passed by there on his last night. Had he been followed? Now I asked myself, was he following someone?

I looked around, almost expecting to see Reggie there as he'd been so many times when we met on his lunch hour. I'd bring a picnic, sandwiches and a Thermos of tea, and we'd sit and discuss our plans for the weekend, or which operas and classical plays were scheduled for the months ahead, or people walking past. It didn't matter what the subject was. It was the sound of his voice, the smile in Reggie's eyes, the touch of his hand, that still warmed my heart.

Was the man I'd loved the real Reginald Denis? Patriot or traitor? My husband or another man's lover? Trustworthy friend or lying scoundrel?

I needed to know. And I knew it was time to confront Derek Langston.

Movement by a bench made me notice Edward

Hawthorn when he rose and started in my direction. A folded newspaper fluttered on the bench next to where he'd sat. As much as I didn't want to talk to anyone, there was no polite way to avoid him.

He looked surprised for a moment before he smiled. "Livvy," he said as he reached me, "what are you doing here?"

"Remembering Reggie. We used to meet in this park at lunch time in good weather."

"It's a good place to clear the cobwebs after dealing with the mayhem across the street." His glance swept past me to the Foreign Office. "I have to head back inside. Good day, Olivia."

"Good day, Edward."

As I walked forward, I saw a man sit down on the bench where I'd seen Edward, pick up the newspaper, and begin to read. I idly wondered if it was the *Daily Premier*.

* * *

After work I approached Derek Langston's building, and then his flat, with my thoughts in a muddle. I pictured him as a slimy, reprehensible man, someone who had jumped in and stolen my husband away. For all I knew, he was the one who was giving Germany our diplomatic secrets. He could even be Reggie's killer.

I was ready to strike out at him. To tell him he was hateful, diabolical, evil. With my hands in fists, I pounded on the door.

He answered wearing his suit coat, his tie slightly loosened. He wasn't what I expected. He looked like an accountant or a civil servant of Reggie's age and my height. He was slender and good-looking with a receding hairline.

I thought I'd better speak before I lost my nerve. "Mr. Langston, I'm Olivia Denis. May I come in?"

He looked terrified for a moment, but then he offered his hand to shake, which I briefly touched. He ushered me into a small, book-lined parlor and offered me a chair. "Would you like tea or something stronger?"

"What are you having?"

"Tea."

"That would be nice."

He disappeared into what I guessed was the kitchen. I could hear him moving around, and then the kettle whistling. I had trouble pulling off my gloves. The cloth stuck to my damp skin.

Langston reappeared with a tea tray that rattled before he set it down on the table between us. He poured a cup and offered it to me. Liquid had swished into the saucer by the time I added sugar and milk. He loaded his with sugar.

I had to set my cup down as my breath shuddered through my body. I was still angry, but slowly curiosity was taking its place. We sat across from each other and stared at our teacups. For a full minute the only sound in the room came through the closed curtains from the traffic in the street below.

I gritted my teeth and tried not to think of him with Reggie. I did anyway. My face heated and my skin crawled. "Mr. Langston, ah—"

He straightened his spine and without looking directly at me said, "I'm very sorry for your loss, Mrs. Denis."

"Thank you." Despite my determination to be calm, my voice was cold.

Fear flashed in his pale blue eyes.

This was my one chance to learn the truth. I wasn't about to waste it. I wanted to know who my gentle, scholarly husband truly was. And it seemed that I'd have to find out from the man with whom he shared his proclivity. "Did you love him? And did you kill him?"

He leaped up and strode to the mantel, picking up a tall, narrow vase. With his back to me, he said, "I don't know what you mean. Reggie was a good friend, had been for years. And I don't make a practice of killing friends." His voice was unsteady.

If my father was wrong, I was going to strangle him for making me embarrass myself. I couldn't see any other course but to be honest and hope for the best. At that moment, I didn't know if any outcome could be good. "I didn't come here to fight with you, Mr. Langston. I came here to meet you because I was told you and my husband were lovers."

And then I said the most honest words I've ever spoken. "It would make me feel better if I knew you loved him. Since I learned about you, I've come to doubt he loved me."

He turned to face me. Fear still cried out from his eyes and from the stiff way he held his body. He appeared to be a quiet man, a gentle man. The same qualities I appreciated in Reggie. I could easily believe they were friends.

And because he reminded me of Reggie, I hated to see him suffer more than I suspected he already was. "I'm not going to cause you any trouble. Your secret is safe with me. But I will warn you that because of state secrets traveling from the Foreign Office to the German embassy, a lot of security people know about you and Reggie."

He glared at me. "That's preposterous. He had nothing to do with giving away secrets."

"I know. But that's not what Whitehall believes."

Something inside him seemed to give up and the defiance in his eyes vanished. His slumped posture proclaimed defeat. He held my gaze for another second before he looked down. "We tried to be discreet. We couldn't let anyone know. We'd both have been ruined. And Reggie worried about you finding out. He didn't want you hurt."

I tried to smile, but my face couldn't decide if I wanted to smile, frown, or scream. "Thank you for telling me that. It means a lot."

"Reggie was a good man."

"Yes, he was. A good man and a kind one."

He set down the vase and sat across from me. Leaning toward me with a guilty expression, he said, "I attended his funeral. I sat in the back and slipped away before the end of the service. I hope you don't mind."

Twisting my fingers, I took a deep breath and tried to relax. This man loved my husband. I was now sure he understood Reggie better. Still, I replied by rote. "I'm glad you had a chance to come to the funeral and say good-bye."

And then I had to ask what I'd wanted to know since I'd learned about this man. "How long had you and Reggie—?"

"Almost eight years."

Long before I'd met Reggie. "Then why did he marry me?" My voice rose on a wail and I was immediately embarrassed by my lack of control.

He gave me a wobbly smile. "I asked him that. I needed to know. I felt used. Betrayed. Much like you must now."

I nodded, too overcome for words.

"There was a big promotion coming up, the head of the Northern European desk for credentials and ceremonies. Apparently, someone named Sir George said he could have the job in a moment if he were married. They considered unmarried men not to be as reliable."

Reggie had gotten the job shortly after we'd become engaged. I'd been obtained to check off a box on his curriculum vitae like a language skill or a degree.

I was not pleased. If Reggie had been there at that moment, I would have killed him myself.

Langston gave me a brief smile as if he were trying to cheer us both up. "He had recently met you. He found you interesting, enthusiastic, intelligent. And he was ambitious. He wanted that job. He told me his marriage would keep us both safe from suspicion."

"That was hardly fair to either of us." Damn Reggie. I never guessed he was a heel. A low-down, sneaky, rotten bastard. I thought he loved me.

And then my thoughts jerked me to reality. Hadn't I used him to escape my father and his never-ending rules and our never-ending arguments?

Derek apparently didn't notice my anger as he answered, "I don't believe Reggie saw it that way. He was never content with our relationship. I think he would have preferred to love women. He struggled against his nature, and in the end, I think he liked having things both ways."

I tried to smile as my fury slid away. "Sort of like men who keep a wife and a mistress." That had to hurt, too.

Derek's smile was kindly. "I suppose so."

I asked him, anguish in my tone, "Did he ever love me?"

"It was important to me that if he was going to cheat on me that he love you. He told me he did." He patted my shoulder. "He was very happy with you."

Somehow, Reggie had failed to keep his secret safe. Perhaps he'd only kept it hidden from me. "But in the end, our marriage wasn't enough of a disguise to keep you two safe."

He looked puzzled, probably mirroring my expression. "What I don't understand is why Reggie would be suspected of stealing government secrets. It's absurd. He was a patriotic Englishman."

"He was one of many suspected simply because they had specific knowledge that was leaked to the Germans from the Foreign Office. That's how you came to the attention of the people who look into these things."

He grimaced. "Bad luck, that."

"And somehow, it led to his murder."

"What?" For the first time, I saw hope on his face. "You mean he didn't kill himself?"

"No. He was shot in the right temple. He couldn't have fired that shot. While Reggie was right-handed, you do know about his fingers?"

"The first two fingers of his right hand were stiff. Childhood accident, I think he said." Langston burst into nearly hysterical tears. He pulled out a handkerchief and breathed deeply as he wiped his eyes. When he had recovered, he said, "I'm in your debt. I've been so miserable, thinking I was the cause of Reggie's death."

"No, you weren't. If Reggie had learned who the traitor was, he would have turned him in. I think his murderer shot Reggie to protect his identity."

He leaned forward eagerly, ready to leap in at my command. "Are you hunting his killer? I'll help you in any way I can."

Who knew? Maybe he could. I'd certainly committed myself to finding Reggie's killer. "What is your occupation, Mr. Langston?"

"Please, call me Derek. I'm an accounts manager for a bank in the City. Do you have any idea who the killer could be? Anyone you want me to look into?"

I sighed, wishing it were that easy. "No. Reggie's job put

him in the path of other nations' officials. He worked with foreign embassies, organizing ceremonies and keeping records of diplomatic credentials. Not the sort of information I would expect the Nazis to be looking for."

He studied his tea for a long moment. Then he looked up and said, "There is something."

"What?"

"We frequently met for dinner at the Metropolitan Hotel. It's a common location for business dinners, and we knew how to play the part of associates. At least I thought we did until you told me someone discovered our secret. Anyway, we were having dinner when a man passed by our table and suddenly stopped. He had a German accent."

"When was this?"

"Two days before Reggie died. He came up to our table as if he were passing by, but I got the sense Reggie was his target."

"What gave you that impression?"

"I couldn't tell you. His furtive gaze, perhaps?" He gave me a wry smile. "Anyway, he looked surprised and stopped, thanked Reggie for straightening out the problem with his credentials. Reggie said he was glad to be of assistance. Then the man lowered his voice and said, 'Perhaps you can assist in one more matter.'"

I found I was leaning forward. "What else did he say?"

"Nothing. Then the man looked away and he paled, as if he'd seen someone. It's such a cliché, I know, but he did. Reggie said, 'Tomorrow.' Then the man hurried away."

"Did you learn his name?"

"Reggie called him Manfred. I don't know if it's his first or last name."

"What did he look like?"

"Blond, blue-eyed. Mild German accent. Slender build. Face like a Greek god. And I shouldn't say this, but I think he's one of us."

"What do you mean?"

Langston had the grace to blush. "I believe he preferred the company of men."

"How can you tell?" I was getting quite an education. I wished Reggie had told me some of this so I wouldn't be getting so many surprises now.

"There are a hundred little signs. Things that wouldn't mean anything to anyone else. There isn't anything specific I could point to, but because we all have to be so careful, we develop an extra sense."

"I shall have to find this Manfred and learn what he knows." And I knew someone who could find out his full name and what kind of problem he'd had with his credentials. Someone I wouldn't mind seeing again.

"Oh, thank you, Olivia. May I call you that?"

"Of course, Derek." I smiled at the man I was beginning to think of as an ally.

"There is one person you'll have to be very careful of. I don't know his exact position, but he would like to see me hang. Sir Ronald Harper."

Of course. Somehow I wasn't surprised that he'd suddenly appear like the heavy in a gangster film. "Don't worry about him. He's my father."

Derek blinked and bit his lip. Then he said in an expressionless voice, "Oh. I suppose that explains it."

"Explains what?" What had my father done now?

"He came here a week ago and threatened to have me charged with sodomy and thrown in jail. If my employers find out..." Derek wrung his hands.

"He won't. I won't let him."

"He's being a father trying to protect his daughter. Don't think I can't have sympathy for him." Derek gave me a weak smile.

I returned one equally weak as I thought of my father. "If you're a person Reggie could love, then you must have boundless stores of sympathy. Something my father will never understand."

He opened his mouth, shut it, and nodded. "Thank you. I could pay you the same compliment."

"If I hear anything that might explain why Reggie was murdered, I will tell you. I hope you'll feel free to do the same."

"I'll be glad to. Although the police will keep you informed if they make an arrest. They won't tell me. I hope you will."

"Yes, Derek. I will." I held out my hand.

He took it and gently squeezed while I expected a handshake. "Thank you, Olivia, for—oh, dear—your consideration."

"It's what Reggie would have wanted." He had broadened my horizons and my sympathies during our marriage. Now I knew why, and I found it helped.

"I believe you're right. I'm honored you see it that way."

I stopped in the doorway. "What I can't understand is why Reggie would have gone to St. Asaph's Hotel so late on a weeknight. If he hadn't gone there—"

"Didn't you know? I don't know why, but recently, Reggie had taken to dropping in there at odd hours. The middle of the afternoon. Late at night. It made no sense to me, and Reggie wouldn't tell me why."

CHAPTER NINE

I LEFT FEELING drained from my conversation with Derek. Rain had begun to fall while I'd visited with him, and the cold sting quickened my steps. There were few people about, and they all hurried head down to avoid the worst of the stabbing chill and the wispy fog that rose out of gutters and alleys. Derek lived perhaps ten blocks from my flat, so there was no point in catching a bus.

The strain of my upcoming meeting with Derek had left me out of sorts all day. It wasn't until I finally talked to him that I could begin to forgive Reggie.

Now that it was over, I hoped the walk would make me feel better. My heels clicked on the pavement, out of sync with the steps of other office workers I heard growing louder as I passed and then fading away. Except one.

Those steps stayed even with mine, following me across the street and up the next block. I sped up, gripping my umbrella tighter.

The footsteps, a man's due to the lack of a sharp click from high heels, kept an even pace at a constant speed. Since I could hear his steps, he couldn't be more than ten or twenty feet behind me. He could catch up at any time.

I peered over my shoulder as the fog thickened. There were three men at various distances behind me. All wore their hats pulled low over their faces and their coat collars turned up. Which one was following me?

Perhaps it was the presence of the other pedestrians that kept me safe. I approached another side street. Maybe he'd turn off there.

Had Reggie heard someone following him the night he died? I was sure of one thing. I didn't want to die tonight.

My breath hurt as it scratched past my cold throat. My feet were numb from the cold rain and my legs were tired from the long day. I ran across the side street, dodging a taxi, and hurried on.

If anything, the footsteps sounded closer now. And there was no one approaching me on the pavement. The fog was beginning to devour whole buildings. A glance behind me showed only an indistinct shape in the gloom.

I began a slow run on weary legs. After a block I was gasping for breath. He had sped up, but he hadn't caught up. I wondered what he wanted and when he'd make his move. And if there was anything I could do to stop him. The fog hid most of the road, but I didn't hear any passing traffic. There was no one around to help me if I were attacked.

I gasped with delight when a bobby materialized on the pavement a few yards ahead.

I sprinted the last distance to the policeman and said, "Terrible night out, isn't it?" as I spun around to see my stalker.

The pavement, at least what I could see of it, was empty. And I could no longer hear footsteps.

The bobby nodded to me. Then he peered more closely at my face, scowled, and said, "Something wrong, miss?"

Sounds were now swallowed by the fog, and no one had appeared out of the cloud. "Nothing now. The fog is making me fearful. Could you walk the last block with me, constable?"

He walked with me to my apartment building, where I thanked him and hurried inside my building. Looking back out through the glass front doors, I found the street and the bobby had been swallowed in a gray blanket. I sighed, relieved to be home.

"Terrible night out, Mrs. Denis," Sutton, our building doorman, said.

I jumped a foot before I turned and faced him. "Yes, it is." I didn't take a deep breath until I entered my flat.

Despite my hopes, the next night I was again followed home from the Underground after work. This time, the man was obvious about it, but he didn't approach me. I didn't recognize him, but with his trench coat collar turned up and his hat brim tilted down, it would have been difficult to recognize anyone.

I clung to the string bag I'd begun to take to work nearly every day. Today it was weighted down with groceries I'd picked up while out on assignment with Jane.

I'd learned from her the joys of carrying a string bag every day when I left for work. It could be rolled up and hidden from Miss Westcott when not filled with shopping, and I soon discovered everyone in the office had one. Mine was a stylish beige with pink strands running through in a daisy pattern. I loved the bag, but there was no way I could run while carrying it, loaded down as it was that night.

Maybe he was afraid I carried a weapon in the bag. My follower kept his distance and so I didn't feel the need to run or scream.

I entered my building and looked around. No Sutton. Then I glanced back at the street. My "escort" had disappeared. Traveling home from work was starting to make me anxious. I began to appreciate the crowded London streets and Tube carriages for the safe havens they presented.

After I reached my flat and locked the door behind me, I dialed the number I had for Redmond. Once again, a man's voice answered with the number.

"Please have Captain Redmond call Olivia Denis."

"Will do." This voice was cheery in a first-rate public school way. It was the kind of voice that found everything a delight, and if something wasn't satisfactory, someone would surely take care of the problem.

"Thank you." I hung up, unwilling to find the world as wonderful as the voice on the phone seemed to.

I was still standing by the phone, wondering what to do next, when it rang. I picked it up and said, "Hello?"

"What can I do for you, Mrs. Denis?"

"Captain Redmond?" After everything that had happened, I wanted to make sure.

He must have heard the rising panic in my voice because he said, "What's wrong, Olivia?"

"I was followed home tonight by a man who made no secret of it. The same thing happened last night. Was that your doing?"

"Stay in your flat. I'll be there as quickly as I can." The line went dead.

It took Redmond half an hour to show up. "I didn't see any sign of him when I arrived" was his greeting.

I was relieved to see Redmond despite how irritating he could be, like a knight who'd defend the castle in a few days after he returned from a golf match. "He isn't yours?"

"No. We try to be more discreet."

Redmond walked me into the parlor and told me to sit. When I didn't move, he sat on the couch and patted the seat next to him.

His good looks and easy grace flustered me. A month ago I was still married. I sat as close to the edge of the seat as possible.

In a quiet, solemn voice he said, "Now, tell me everything."

Heaven help me, but I had to trust someone. I hoped trusting Redmond wasn't a mistake. I told him all.

When I finished, he said, "Langston didn't know what your husband and Manfred were talking about?"

"No."

"Whatever it was, it must have been important. Manfred was murdered the same night as your husband."

I stared at him in shock before I said, "What is going on?"

He ignored my question. "And you have no idea who the two men from your husband's office were that you eavesdropped on at the party?"

"No. And I wasn't eavesdropping." Not really.

"And Captain Marshall mentioned that he was searching for missing German documents?"

"Yes."

"Do you think it's too soon for you to have a boyfriend?"

I blinked at the sudden turn in our conversation. "Good heavens, yes." Heat shot through my body. I suspected danger and passion simmered beneath Redmond's bland shell.

I knew I might be persuaded. And that would be scandalous. And very wrong. I was sure he could be trusted with state secrets, but I didn't know if he'd be faithful with my heart.

Faithfulness had taken on more meaning since I'd learned Reggie had failed me.

"We need a reason to be seen together frequently. For me to be invited to your late husband's friends' parties."

"If I showed up with a new beau, I'd never be invited back." My tone was a bit priggish, but his suggestion would destroy the reason I worked for the *Daily Premier*. The real reason I was employed.

"You're right. A boyfriend would upset the old tabbies in Whitehall."

I stared at Captain Redmond in open-mouthed surprise at his blatant disrespect before I shut my mouth and considered what I'd learned. "You think those two men from his office are involved with the leak of information from Reggie's office to the German embassy. And they know something about his death."

"Yes. And so do you. Unless you think that conversation at your friends' flat was about cricket scores?"

"No. Of course not. But it's still too soon—" It was too soon, and even thinking about it made me feel guilty. Still, I knew Redmond might be the perfect Watson to my Holmes for learning who killed Reggie and why.

Finally, an idea came to me. "Wait. You could be a cousin of Reggie's, just arrived in London for your new post. No one in Whitehall knows you, do they?" No one would be shocked to see me with a relative of Reggie's.

"Some people in Whitehall might know me, and it would be easy to find out about me if someone wanted to dig. We could say I visited the flat to see my cousin Reggie, but I've been too busy to be very social. Since I'm family, you're keeping up the connection."

"Then you could play up the fact you know some of them when we go to parties. Have you met any of them?" It might make this whole travesty easier if his office worked with

Reggie's.

"I'll make sure I do. I'm officially assigned to a ceremonial unit in the War Office under General Lord Walters. Since your husband's office handles ceremonies, it would seem likely I'd work with them from time to time." He stared into middle distance for a moment. "Yes, that might be the answer to a lot of problems, Cousin Olivia. Now, have you eaten?"

"No. I dashed in and called you."

"Let's try the chop house around the corner, shall we?"

My fears kept me in my seat. "Do you think that man is still out there?"

"He won't bother us. And I don't know about you, but I'm famished." That seductive lazy smile flashed across his face for an instant. How could he appear so relaxed and then immediately look ready for battle?

I took a deep breath as if preparing to jump into cold water. "Let's go."

The restaurant was a two-minute walk from my building, or a minute and a half if I was walking with Captain Redmond. If the man who followed me was still lurking about, I didn't have time to notice him.

Nothing about Redmond was slow, including his reaction when we sat down and I said, "You might become habit forming, Captain."

"I hope so, Cousin. We must stick together at this sad time."

"Don't lay it on too thick," I warned him.

We lingered over our meal, enjoying each other's company. Redmond turned out to be a charming conversationalist and no fan of Mrs. Simpson. Not surprisingly for someone in the military, he believed the former king committed the cardinal sin of shirking his duty. He admired our present king and queen and we compared notes on what we'd seen of the coronation parade. Reggie and I'd had a special viewing spot. I suspected Redmond was part of the security force.

When we finished our meal, he paid and we walked out onto the street. "I'll walk you to your building. And if you find yourself being followed again, call me. I'll come as quickly as I can."

I feared I was already relying on Redmond too much. And I worried I was trusting him more than I should.

* * *

After another night spent restlessly tangling myself in the sheets while being chased by faceless men in my dreams, I could barely drag my body out of bed when the alarm rang. Running cold water over my head shocked me awake, but it left my hair damp and curly. After I brushed my hair into some sense of order, I barely had time for tea and toast and a dab of lipstick.

Once I left my building, the pulse of London traffic gave my heart a jolt. The energy of pedestrians hurrying past and the raucous noise all around me sped my feet. Going out to work in the morning hadn't yet lost its thrill. The bustle of hurrying down into the Tube, riding to Chancery Lane Station with a carriage full of businesspeople, and then walking the distance to the *Daily Premier* building amidst a sea of commuters woke me more than caffeine.

I reached my desk with a few minutes to spare and was immediately sent up to Mr. Colinswood's office by an icy Miss Westcott. Glancing in, I saw Colinswood seated behind his desk. "Mrs. Denis. A moment?" he called out.

I stood by the door, expecting to be fired. My typing was

not improving. I seldom failed to disappoint Miss Westcott. I was being paid more than I could possibly be worth.

"Come in and sit down. And shut the door."

I entered and shut the door. This wasn't going to end well for me or my bank account.

"You remember my mentioning some irregular assignments in your job duties?"

"Yes, of course." *Here it comes. My last chance to save my job.*

"There's a diplomatic reception being held at the German embassy this Friday evening. Quite a large do. We'd like you to manage an invitation and tell us everything you can about what occurs. Who talks to whom, who snubs whom. That sort of thing. Particularly among the members of the German embassy staff."

"That's tomorrow night. Why do you want me in there? Surely you have reporters who cover this sort of thing."

"From the outside. We need someone on the inside."

"Why? Nothing newsworthy will happen."

"We want a report on von Ribbentrop."

"Why do you want a report on him?" Reggie had nothing but disdain for the egotistical man.

"He's been the German ambassador since poor von Hoesch dropped dead. Our first real Nazi ambassador." He started ticking points off on his fingers. "Seeing how other ambassadors treat him should be a hint to their governments' reaction to Hitler. Seeing whom von Ribbentrop keeps close to him at the reception should tell us who the powers are in the German embassy. Who we should keep an eye on. Find out which of the Germans have wives or girlfriends here and whether they're British or German."

Maybe it was all the strange happenings lately, but I was

suspicious. "Why is the *Daily Premier* interested in collecting all this information?"

"You do realize we'll be fighting the Nazis sooner or later."

"That's the government's decision. Not the newspapers'." I had been raised to a life of privilege, not the life of a typist. I'm afraid I sounded rather snotty.

My boss leaned back in his chair and stared at me. "Mrs. Denis, you must realize your typing is deplorable. The newspaper hired you for reasons having nothing to do with your ability to write a coherent article. We need you to get into that reception and we need you to note all these things. Can you do it?"

His message, at least, was clear. Do this, or lose my job. Reggie hadn't left me well provided for, my father wasn't as wealthy as he or I would like, and I liked money and all the things it bought. "Does Sir Henry know about this?"

"Sir Henry suggested it. He thinks you'd be perfect for the job." Colinswood shook his head. "He sees more in you than I do, but he's the chairman."

"And you'll pay my expenses?"

His eyes widened. "Within reason. Finance has to accept all expenses. Not me."

"Tomorrow night is short notice to procure an invite. Let me see what I can do." I gave him a smile with more confidence than I felt and rose from my chair.

"That's the spirit. Thank you, Mrs. Denis. I'll expect you to report in by the end of the day to let us know if you'll be attending the reception."

I understood that to mean I had a deadline to find a way in to the German embassy party or lose my job.

CHAPTER TEN

I TOOK MY handbag and headed straight for the ladies' room. The woman staring back at me in the mirror looked like a worn-out drudge. I applied a light powder and some eyeliner, then redid my lipstick. No one came in to ask what I was doing. They were all doing what they'd been hired to do.

I, on the other hand, had been hired with a view to doing some clandestine work for the *Daily Premier*. Sir Henry, for personal reasons, wanted to make use of my access to official London. I hoped I could turn this situation to my advantage.

Once I'd tidied my hair and straightened my hose, I went back to my office. Miss Westcott glared when I repinned my hat at a jauntier angle and picked up my coat. I could only hope Mr. Colinswood would put in a good word for me as I waved to her and left.

I caught a cab to the Foreign Office. After explaining whose wife I had been and where I was going to the guard on the desk, I signed in and was escorted to the overcrowded set of offices on the second floor where Reggie had worked.

Sir George Rankin met me at the entrance to the "Credentials and Ceremonials" section. Nodding to the retreating guard, he asked, "Mrs. Denis, what brings you here?"

Past him, I could see David Peters, the handsome lightweight I'd enjoyed laughing with at Lester and Mary

Babcock's party, talking to Paul Chambers, who'd taken over Reggie's job. Both worked on the Northern European desk. Either could have been one of the voices I heard in Mary's kitchen discussing Reggie's death. It only took me a second to make my choice. I hoped it was the right one. "I'd hoped to have a word with Mr. Peters."

"Peters? By all means." He spoke to David as he walked past into the office and I remained by the door.

I pasted a smile on my face while I waited for David and Paul's conversation to end. Once Chambers stalked off I said, "David?"

He looked at me, shot a glare in Paul's direction, and then turned back to me with a big smile across his face. "Livvy? What are you doing here?"

"Come to ask you a favor. One your sense of humor will appreciate."

His handsome face took on a clownish expression. "Oh, good. We never get to have any fun around here."

"I want an invitation to the German embassy reception tomorrow night."

The clownish expression died away, followed by surprise and then caution. "It'll be a crashing bore. I've just been told I'm stuck representing the office and I'm dreading it. But why do you want to attend?"

David attending the reception was better luck than I'd expected. I knew I had to put his fears to rest immediately or he'd never help. "The clothes, of course. I'm a society page reporter now, which means they pay me enough money to keep me going since Reggie died, but only because I told them I could report on the latest fashions at the biggest dos. And this reception qualifies as a big formal-dress do."

"You're kidding. You're a reporter." He still looked

uneasy as he backed a half step away from me.

"Not the kind you're thinking of. I bet you've never read the society columns." I gave him a teasing grin and hoped he bought my version of the truth.

He held up both hands, palms out. "Not me. All that nonsense about skirt lengths and who married whom." He shuddered.

"That's why I want to get inside. I can't see skirt lengths and colors and fabrics if I have to stand outside. Do this favor for me, please."

When he hesitated, I continued, "I do know how to behave at these things. Please?"

"On one condition."

"Anything." Well, that wasn't quite true, but I figured I could find a way out after I got into the diplomatic reception if his one condition was too ghastly.

"You go as my guest. I have to go to the blasted thing anyway. Might as well have someone along who'll find it as ridiculous as I will."

"Excellent." I grabbed his hand and squeezed it as I grinned like a crazy woman. Relief made me giddy. "I can't think of an escort I'd rather have. What time will you pick me up?"

"It starts at six. Say, on the hour and we can be fashionably late."

"Perfect." And since it would take me hours to get ready, Colinswood would have to let me off work at lunchtime.

I turned around and was nearly knocked over by a man in a baggy business suit. Unsmiling, the man gestured to me to go first. He was good-looking, but what caught my attention were his dark eyes. I felt as if he could see through me. I walked away, but I looked over my shoulder when I reached the door. The unknown man was deep in conversation with David.

When I returned to the *Daily Premier* building, I went straight to Colinswood's office and told him the reason I'd given David for begging an invitation and the condition to my success. His response was a smile that took years off his face. "You'll have someone there to tell you who everyone is while you make note of their frocks. You couldn't have planned it better."

"There will have to be a society page article on those frocks."

"You think your escort will be suspicious?"

"Wouldn't you be?"

"You won't get a byline."

"I don't need one. I'll make sure to throw in a detail or two he'll furnish. Enough so he'll know my excuse was on the up and up." I started ticking conditions off on my fingers. "I'll need a new pair of stockings and some sort of ornament for my hair. I'll need to get off at lunchtime tomorrow to get ready. And I expect to be paid for my time and my purchases."

"You need five hours to get ready?" Colinswood sounded scandalized.

"Obviously, you've never been to one of these affairs. And I don't have a maid, which means it takes me even longer."

Colinswood pursed his lips. "Sir Henry expects you to deliver. I'm sure he'll allow it."

The editor had bought it. I released a breath I hadn't realized I was holding. "If he asks any questions, tell him to check with Esther."

Colinswood's expression smoothed. "Ah. You went to

school with his daughter."

"Yes. We're quite good friends. Sir Henry knows I can handle any social situation. But what I don't understand is why he is so interested in the Germans."

Colinswood looked around me to his open office door to make sure no one was loitering. "He has, uh, interests in Germany, Austria, and France as well as England. He's trying to learn all he can to protect them."

"Protect them from what?"

"Being taken by the Nazis."

* * *

The rest of the day went quietly. I covered a charity tea attended by several duchesses and one of Victoria's remaining daughters. The fashions were outdated and the colors dreary. A string quartet played gloomy music in the background. I used "charming, regal, and gracious" a great deal in my report. I never used the word "elderly." I turned in my story and watched Miss Westcott's face cringe in horror as she read it. Let others search for synonyms. My mind was already on my clandestine assignment.

On my way home, I made a detour to a milliner's I knew, where I picked up the perfect little dark blue wisp of net with silk flowers and a silver butterfly to decorate my hair. The *Daily Premier* would have to pay for it. The dainty wisp would put my bank account in arrears.

That night, Abby called about the weekend. I promised to come down on Saturday without telling her where I'd be Friday evening.

Then Esther called. "My father said you're going to the German embassy tomorrow night to spy on them."

"Well, not exactly spy. More 'learn the lay of the land.' Esther, what is this all about?"

"Can I meet you tomorrow? Say, at lunchtime?"

"I'm getting off work then to get ready. Sure, if you'd like to help me make myself attractive."

"Absolutely. Like we did at school."

I rang off, wondering what Esther would tell me.

The next day arrived and I left work at lunchtime. Mercifully, my figure hadn't changed during the time I was married to Reggie, so I could reuse evening gowns I'd worn to diplomatic receptions in the past. Changing a scarf or jewelry or my hairstyle would make any of them do.

I was partial to a shimmery dark blue gown that glided down my body. The back was low; the front had a diamond cutout that gave a peek of my décolletage. The dark blue slip of a hair ornament matched my risqué dress perfectly. I hoped Colinswood would think of it as a bonus for doing such a grand job at the reception.

I'd just laid out my outfit when I heard a knock. I opened the door to find Esther there with bags from Fortnum & Mason. "I was sure you hadn't had time to eat, and neither had I. They do a good picnic lunch there. I told them we didn't need a hamper. We can just use your plates."

She set out the containers on my dining room table while I brought in the table settings. When we finished the goat cheese salads and truffles, I said, "This is most impressive. Why such extravagance?"

She leaned closer and murmured, "I want you to have a big sendoff. I want this to be a success."

I'd been to diplomatic receptions with Reggie. They were low-key. Everyone was dreadfully polite as they watched the clock and wondered how much longer they'd have to stay. In a word, boring. "How can it be a success if I don't know what the result should be? If it's even possible to learn anything about the Nazis from something as sedate as a diplomatic event."

Esther walked over and looked out my window to the street below. "How much do you know about me?"

What an odd question. "I know you're Sir Henry's daughter. That you're bright and lovely and kind. And that you never told Miss Humphries about the lipstick."

"Or the stockings. Don't forget the stockings."

"How could I?" It was not my finest hour. "You're a loyal friend. And we were the same age when we lost our mothers. Five years old." It hadn't stung in a long time until I lost Reggie.

She continued to look out my window. "Your mother was a well-bred Englishwoman. Mine was a research chemist." She lowered her voice. "She was also a German Jew."

I hadn't known that. "Are you? Jewish, I mean."

"No. I was baptized as a baby. Otherwise, I doubt I could have attended Saint Agnes. Even my father's not rich enough to get around that restriction."

"True. Would have been a laugh if you hadn't been baptized. On Saint Agnes, I mean." Far outpacing any of my childish pranks. "Still, I don't understand. What do you hope to gain by my attendance at this embassy reception?"

"My mother's family is still spread all over Europe."

"That's terrible. Can't they get out?" I'd heard the desire of Jews to leave Germany far outstripped the willingness of Great Britain and the Western Hemisphere to accept them.

"My grandparents refuse to leave. They can't believe it will get worse. And then it does, and they say it can't get any worse than that." I saw a shudder run through her back.

"Can't the family prevail upon them to leave?"

"Do you have grandparents?"

"I have my mother's mother. Point taken."

Esther turned and gave me a smile. "We need a warning system set in place to tell them that now they must sell up and get out. In time."

"And you want me to look and listen and see if the time is near? Or if anything is planned?"

"Yes. In fact, I may ask you to go over there to help get them out. I can't. They'd count me as a Jew. But you're so Aryan with your auburn hair and blue eyes that no one would give you a second look."

"Men often don't." I was still hurt by Reggie's duplicity.

Esther gave me a skeptical look, but I wasn't ready to share Reggie's preference with her. Or anyone.

I'd been to Germany with Reggie and hadn't liked it, except for the opera. I spoke fairly good German. Was this the real reason I'd gotten the job on the *Daily Premier*? In that case, I couldn't say no. "Let's hope it doesn't come to the point that they must get out."

"Yes. But I'm not sure my grandparents would leave, no matter what."

She sounded so upset I gave her a hug. "I'll do what I can. Now, help me do something with my auburn hair and blue eyes."

We went to work in earnest. Dangling silver earrings with silver sandals and bag completed my ensemble. What with curling and styling my hair, it took us every second to get me ready. At five, Esther said she had to leave, but assured me I would be a knockout.

I wish she could have stayed around to see the final result, because she was right. Once I finished all the details, I looked terrific.

When David arrived, his whistle told me he approved. I

had already slid on my white shawl and my long white gloves and put my essentials in my purse so I didn't have to let him inside the flat. We rode downstairs in the poky elevator, my high heels making the stairs risky, and went out to the taxi.

Once we were on our way to the German embassy, David said, "Are you sure you don't want reporters writing about your gown?"

"No. What I've learned is if I look like I belong, people don't question whether I'm a guest and I can ask them about their frocks as if I'm considering stealing away their dressmaker." I gave him a knowing look. "Women find other women wanting to steal their dressmaker very flattering. As long as no one mentions it. Then it's considered crass."

He shuddered. "I'll leave before I have to be a part of those conversations."

"David, just getting me in there is a big-enough favor. And if you happen to introduce me to some of the fashionable women at this party, I would be thrilled." My enthusiasm was genuine; the reason wasn't quite what I'd led him to believe.

"I'm sure I can introduce you to a few." He grinned. "Lucky I was assigned to attend."

"Pure genius on your part."

"Did Reggie ever introduce you to anyone at the German embassy?"

"Yes, but I don't believe any of them are there any longer. They were part of von Hoesch's administration." Gone, like Reggie. Shaking off my now-gloomy mood, I said, "You must know most of the new ones."

He drew away slightly. "I try to stay away from them. All physical stamina and Aryan superiority. The Scandinavian embassies are more to my liking."

"It sounds like Paul Chambers doesn't much care for

them either, since he assigned you the task of attending tonight. This is an important affair, isn't it?"

"The German government has spent the last several months redecorating the inside of the embassy. They're showing the building off tonight. Strange." David looked out the taxi window.

"Strange?" If I had redecorated anything, I'd want to show it off.

"Chambers. This is a big event. The last couple of weeks, he's been avoiding any contact with the Germans even though he's the new head of the desk. Strange."

"Why strange? Will it affect him getting Reggie's job permanently?"

I knew the answer to my question before David told me, "It might. And I believe he's ambitious. I guess he had more important things to do tonight."

"What could be more important than keeping his bosses happy? Reggie asked me that a time or two when I didn't want to go to some boring dinner with him."

"Paul's gone through most of the money he made from the sale of the house and he's desperate for a big win."

I looked at David, perplexed. "A big win?"

"At the card table. I swear he'd do anything for money."

I felt an ominous weight settle on my shoulders. If Paul would do anything for money, did that include selling secrets to the Nazis?

I already thought the traitor in Reggie's office might well have murdered Reggie. Paul Chambers could be the leak, and he had been with Reggie at the theater the night he died.

Paul Chambers was now on my list of potential killers, along with Sir George Rankin and Blake Fielding.

CHAPTER ELEVEN

I CHANGED THE subject as I ran the news about Paul Chambers through my mind. "You must know almost everyone in London, at least by reputation, by doing their credentials. I appreciate you escorting me. I imagine there are a lot of girls you'd rather take tonight."

"No. This is work. I know you won't distract me."

"Thank you," I said with ice in my tone.

"Oh, no, Livvy. You're a lovely girl. I don't mind being seen with you. But you'll always be Reggie's wife to me. And I can be sure you're not using me for some ulterior motive."

I thought of Sir Henry and immediately felt guilty. "I'll always consider you a good friend, David. But you know I have an ulterior motive. I need to report on ladies' frocks."

"That's nothing." He shook his head and looked like someone had run their nails over a chalkboard. "It's the attempts to meet someone they admire, or worse, try to apply for a job or a visa."

At least I wasn't doing anything so blatant. "So tell me all the latest juicy gossip."

He kept me entertained the rest of the ride with a rollicking tale involving a member of the French embassy trying to keep both of his girlfriends and his wife from meeting. The French could always be counted on to carry out their misconduct with style.

Once we arrived at the German embassy, David presented his invitation and we walked right in. The reception was held in the grand foyer, a huge hall just inside the front doors. The open space was busy with people seeing and being seen. Noise bounced off the high ceiling and pounded down on our heads.

From one hall on the left, waiters arrived carrying flutes of champagne; on the right I could see the cloakroom. The other hallways and the grand staircase had large, squat-nosed men in tuxedos standing by them acting as gatekeepers. Or bouncers.

We were in the middle of the crush to pass through the receiving line. As unimportant people, we were barely acknowledged as we were sped through our bow and curtsy.

Once through the line, a waiter came by and David grabbed two flutes for us. Meanwhile, I stared at a tuxedo-clad man as he strolled by. It was the man who'd spoken to David when I left Reggie's office the day before. I held my breath, frightened when he nodded.

Then I remembered I had as much right as anyone to be there. I'd been invited. As a guest on someone else's invitation, but still, I wasn't a gatecrasher. I lifted my head and nodded in return. His mouth curled up in a cynical smile before he marched up to one of the bouncers and whispered in his ear. The man was good-looking, but his expression was brooding.

The bouncer stepped back and the man walked past him down a hallway. Then the bouncer signaled a man across the reception area, who ambled over without appearing to have a destination.

Their casualness seemed forced, making me wonder why.

I took a flute from David and nodded my thanks. The champagne was chilled and quite nice. French, probably. "David, who was the man I ran into as I was leaving your office yesterday?"

"Did you run into someone? I really didn't notice."

"He spoke to you just as I left."

"I don't know. I guess he was looking for Chambers. I don't remember."

Now wasn't the time, but I was going to have to look more closely at David and his connections to the Germans. He'd been one of those with Reggie shortly before he was killed. Still, I couldn't picture jolly, never serious David as a traitor and murderer.

A rather stiff blond man came up to David. "I see you made it, Herr Peters."

"Yes. May I introduce Mrs. Denis?"

For an instant, I was afraid he'd give me the Nazi salute like von Ribbentrop had to the king not long before. The ambassador had nearly knocked the king over. Fortunately, he took my hand and bowed over it in vague homage to gentlemen kissing the back of ladies' hands. The image was ruined by the militarily precise click of his heels.

"Your embassy is lovely," I said. "Herr—?"

"Schreiber. You like what we have done to renovate the inside?"

"Yes. The ceiling is impressive." John Nash, the famous classical architect who'd designed these buildings, was probably turning over in his grave. While the outside had been spared by regulation, what I could see of the gutted and rebuilt inside oozed money. Marble, glass, paintings, mosaics, carpeting, and the detailed ceiling two stories up were all put together to make a display. From the number of swastikas, I suspected a display of Nazi bad taste.

"We've been working on this for months. Tonight we are showing off our efforts. We even imported a string quartet from Berlin for the event." Schreiber looked pleased. There was something familiar about the man, but I couldn't place him.

The music formed a lacy backdrop to the Nazi display. "I hope the ambassador is here tonight to enjoy his party." Von Ribbentrop traveled to Germany frequently. The rumors said he couldn't stay away long before running home to make sure he was still Hitler's favorite.

"Yes. Would you like to meet him?" he said in a tone that reminded me of a school headmaster. Had he been one before the Nazis came to power?

I didn't want to, but I had a job to do. "That would be kind of you, Herr Schreiber. David?"

I saw an impish gleam in my escort's eyes. "Yes. I'd love to greet him."

We followed the stiff German back across the room. Ambassador von Ribbentrop was taller and paler than I expected. The two Germans "heiled" each other and then Schreiber introduced us. Mercifully, von Ribbentrop must have decided the Nazi salute wouldn't go well in diplomatic receptions, because he gave us a curt nod and we bowed and curtsied in response.

"I hope you're having a nice time," the ambassador said.

I smiled and said, "Yes. This is a lovely reception."

"We are sharing what we've done with this old building to make it tasteful and modern."

In my imagination, Nash stopped spinning as he made an angry leap up from his grave to wreak havoc on the damage done to his building by Nazi decorators. "All of diplomatic

London appears to be here to see your new decor."

"That's hardly surprising. We have the largest embassy in London and where we lead, others follow."

There was nothing tactful I could reply to that. Switching topics, I said, "You speak English with no noticeable accent."

"I spent some of my younger years in Canada, and even lived in London for a time. I learned to speak it like a native. Something we try to foster in our diplomatic corps."

Again that superior tone. I tried another topic. "Is your wife enjoying her time in London?"

"My wife is the woman in the green dress over there. You should ask her," von Ribbentrop said, gesturing to a nearby blonde talking to a dark-haired couple with streaks of silver in their hair.

"And your wife, Herr Schreiber?" I said, turning to him.

"My wife is at home in Potsdam with the children."

"How lonely for you."

"Not at all. I bunk with the military attachés at Number Seven. There's always someone to talk to."

"Certainly makes life in foreign cities less uncomfortable," David said, "to have fellow countrymen around." I wondered what his experience had been in his foreign postings. He was only a few years older than I was. I hoped he'd made lots of friends.

"Mmm." Schreiber turned to his boss. "Mrs. Denis is the widow of the Foreign Office official who, er, died recently."

"My condolences," the ambassador said. "I had expected Herr Denis to attend tonight's gala until I heard of his untimely passing."

"Yes. I'm sure he would have enjoyed it." So why was David, an underling, attending tonight rather than Paul Chambers, who replaced Reggie? This would be obvious to the upper echelons in Whitehall. If he hadn't killed Reggie, I hoped Paul had a good excuse.

"And despite his death you came out for our little party." Von Ribbentrop sounded suspicious.

"David is an old family friend and he asked me to join him." I gave the ambassador a smile.

"Hmm. If you'll excuse me?" He left, giving us a short bow with the heel snapping the Germans were so good at.

"Of course." I walked over and greeted his wife, getting a good look at her dress and nabbing a quote for the paper. I was introduced to the couple, the Italian ambassador and his wife, and looked her dress over as well. David greeted the Italians in their language and they gave him a warmer reply than I received. The couple walked off talking to David, which left me alone with Frau von Ribbentrop.

"How are you enjoying life in London?" I asked.

"I look forward to going home."

"Those must be the favorite words of every diplomat and his wife. 'Going home.'"

We shared a smile. Hers was sad. "You have had to live away from home?"

"No, but I've talked to enough wives at diplomatic receptions. They all say the same thing. Nothing looks or smells or tastes like home. Do you have children here?"

"Yes. They say their classmates taunt them because they are German. We are all beginning to hate Britain."

"I am sorry." I wasn't going to report that in the society page. However, Colinswood might find this interesting.

"Good evening, Mrs. Denis." Frau von Ribbentrop walked off, and I went in search of other dresses while keeping an eye on von Ribbentrop. The French wives were exquisitely gowned. The Russians were dowdy. The English had the best headgear, all net and feathers and jewels. The American women were loud and daring, and the German bouncers watched them with a cross between amusement, lust, and disdain.

Partially concealing myself behind a potted plant, I pulled out my notebook. I jotted notes on various women and their dresses along with quick sketches of their gowns that would aid my memory. Then I focused my attention on the massive staircase that split and turned in an oddly uneven way, all the while keeping an eye on the bouncer at the bottom of the steps.

"Frau Denis. We can't have you being a wallflower, can we?" a thick German accent said from behind me.

How had someone sneaked up behind me? I spun around, holding my notebook tightly against my side. And found myself looking into the mesmerizing dark eyes of the man I'd seen in Reggie's office the day before. "H-how do you know my name?" I stammered.

"If only you knew how much trouble you have caused." When I started to object, he said, "Now, now. Don't be shy. Let me see your book, please." His tone told me this wasn't a request.

I held it out to him.

He glanced at the open page. "You find the staircase Speer designed bold, magnificent. Frau von Ribbentrop's dress is green silk with a bias cut and a low-draped back?" He flipped back a couple of pages and then looked at me. "What are you doing? If this is spying, it is not what your handlers will want to know."

"I'm not spying." Well, not the kind he meant. Oh, I hoped this wouldn't get David and me thrown out. I needed his friendship, and my ability to enter places like this, to keep my job.

The German looked like he might laugh before his dark-eyed gaze pierced me. "Then what are you doing, Frau Denis?"

"Not spying. Just making sure I remember the details." I bit my lip. My heart was racing and I was beginning to tremble.

"Then I suggest you remember with your mind and rejoin the party." He handed me back my notebook and indicated with one hand that I should precede him toward the center of the room.

As I stepped away, he added, "I like your sketches. You put a lot of detail in very few lines."

I hurried away toward David. When I looked back, the man had disappeared.

Keeping my assignment in mind, I watched as Schreiber came and went from von Ribbentrop's side frequently, as did another man. That man had earlier been signaled to follow the man I spoke to about my notes. "Who's the man with von Ribbentrop now?" I asked David.

"Liestran. Von Ribbentrop's right-hand man and a nasty piece of work," he murmured in my ear.

I glanced at David, since he seldom said anything negative about anyone. Diplomatic training, I suppose. "Now you've made him interesting."

"Stay away from him, Livvy. Von Ribbentrop is full of hot air, but Liestran is dangerous. He not only believes in the invincibility of the master race, he believes it allows him to be a thug."

His tone sent a shiver up my bare back. As I watched, Liestran turned away from von Ribbentrop and walked over to a man in a British army uniform. I sucked in my breath.

The soldier was Captain Redmond.

"Come on, David. I want to meet this Herr Liestran." I took David's arm and half-dragged him toward my quarry.

"This isn't a good idea," David said through a clenched-teeth smile, but he had no choice but to come with me. Anything else would have made obvious the grip I had on his sleeve.

And I wanted to see Redmond in action with this German thug in a formal setting.

When we had made our way through the crowd to the pair, Redmond turned toward us and said, "Cousin Livvy, what are you doing here?"

"You two know each other?" David asked.

"He's Reggie's cousin." I hoped David would buy our tale.

"Adam Redmond," he said, shaking David's hand.

"David Peters, an office mate of Reggie's."

"How nice. A family reunion," Liestran said, an amused smile playing on his thin lips.

"May I introduce Major Liestran," Redmond said. "Head of embassy security."

"So nice to meet you," I said. "Are you and your wife enjoying your time in London?"

"My wife lives in Berlin with the children. I stay here in the embassy, since I wouldn't have time for my family if they had traveled with me."

"I hope you make frequent trips home to see them," I said.

"I assure you I do. Do you like to travel, Mrs. Redmond?"

"It's Mrs. Denis, and yes, I do."

Liestran glanced at David, made the connection, and his face lost all expression. "My condolences on your loss, Mrs. Denis." He bowed slightly and clicked his heels together.

"Thank you."

Past him, I saw a thin, fair-haired man in his late thirties arguing with Schreiber. Their voices were like the buzz of angry bees over the hum of the party. Herr Schreiber seemed agitated as he made swift gestures with his replies. The unknown man turned redder with each exchange and his voice grew louder.

Two of the bouncers closed in on him as he clearly said in German, "He was my brother. And you and Rickard killed him. I'll hunt you down, Schreiber." Then he turned on his heel and stormed off, bumping into David as he passed ahead of the bouncers.

"I say. Sorry," David said as the man passed without a word of apology.

"I wonder what's gotten into him," Redmond said without any interest in his voice.

"I find you British full of surprises," Liestran said with his sly smile. British? I had heard the unknown man speaking German like a native. Maybe it was David's warning, but Liestran gave me the creeps.

"I suppose I could say the same for the Germans," David said, icicles dripping from his words.

The sly smile widened on Liestran's face.

Herr Schreiber joined us. He nodded to us and then murmured a few words in Liestran's ear.

I couldn't make out Liestran's reply. The one thing I did hear was Liestran call Schreiber "hauptmann." *Captain*. Why was he in civilian clothes at a diplomatic reception where all military officers were expected to wear their dress uniforms? And why didn't he correct my use of "herr"?

Whatever Liestran was up to, Schreiber was right behind him, helping.

Schreiber nodded to us again, wished us a pleasant evening, and walked away. "If you'll excuse me," Liestran said and left in the opposite direction, heading for the hallway I'd seen him enter before.

I looked at the two Englishmen with me. "Where does that lead?"

David gave a small sigh. "I don't know, but we've put in enough time here. Ready to go, Livvy?"

"It leads to some offices and then to the next building where the military attachés reside. Why?" Redmond asked.

"I was curious. A man I saw David talking to at Whitehall went down there, followed by Liestran."

We both turned to look at David.

"I don't know who you mean. Livvy mentioned him, but I don't remember speaking to anyone in particular yesterday. Can we go now?" David was obviously uncomfortable, and I had no idea why.

"I'd guess there's another exit down that hallway?"

"Several," Redmond assured me.

There was no reason why the man in the tuxedo wouldn't exit through the party, but why had he entered this way? The crowd at the reception was thinning, so I guessed nothing more would be learned that night. "I think I've seen enough, thank you. Good night, Captain Redmond."

He took my hand and bowed over it, then gave me a heated look, the kind of look that makes women swoon. He and David shook hands before David took my arm and hustled me toward the door.

Before we made our exit, a woman in a silver metallic-cloth gown with bleached blonde hair in a curling upsweep parked herself in our path. "Why, David," she said in a loud American drawl, "I didn't know you'd be here tonight."

"Well, here I am," he said with a tight smile and a tighter voice.

"It's so nice to see you again. And in such impressive surroundings."

Here in the center of the building, the room was two stories high to accommodate the enormous German flag. I pictured John Nash rising from his grave with mayhem on his mind. If the building burned to the ground, the fire brigade would have to look for a ghostly arsonist in Regency attire.

The slender American woman was impressive, too, in a dress that left little to the imagination. If my dress was sultry, hers was shocking.

David, looking like he had suffered a beating, said, "Livvy, may I present Mrs. Claire deLong. Claire, this is Mrs. Olivia Denis."

"Olivia. What a mahvelously English name," she said in a voice that was suddenly grating on my nerves.

Given this heaven-sent opportunity, I had to learn more. "I believe you knew my husband. Reginald Denis." My voice was frosty. According to that crooked lawyer, Reggie was going to leave this woman all his worldly goods. I couldn't believe it. Reggie had better taste.

But if the legal papers were fakes, why bother to write them up and send them to me?

"Denis? Ah, yes, Reggie. We've been introduced. Delightful man. So English." She wrapped her fur stole closer around her.

"He's dead," I snapped.

"So I've heard. So sad. It doesn't bear thinking about." She turned to David. "Be a dear and find me a glass of champagne."

David gave me a look, raised his eyebrows, and scanned

the room for the nearest waiter. They all seemed to have vanished. "I'm afraid you're out of luck. Perhaps one of the Germans can help you. Major Liestran, maybe?"

"Such a helpful man, the major. I know you've made his acquaintance in the past."

David turned an unhealthy red.

I decided to be as unhelpful as possible. "It was nice meeting you, Mrs. deLong," I said with an emphasis on the *Mrs.*

She gave me a nasty smile, the kind I'd want to rip off someone's face. "I find having an ex-husband in the background to be so useful. Rather like being a widow. Oh, there's darling Adam." She slinked off.

When I turned, it was to see her air-kiss Captain Redmond's cheeks. He greeted her with a warm smile and then she snaked an arm around his body and whispered into his ear with her blood-red lips. His smile widened.

In all our discussions, he hadn't told me he knew the woman my husband was supposedly leaving me for.

I walked off with an image of an intertwined Captain Redmond and Mrs. deLong in my mind and a sour feeling in my stomach.

CHAPTER TWELVE

AFTER THE reception, David and I went out for dinner, dressed to the nines, at a Corner House restaurant. We got a few looks when we walked in, but then the other patrons forgot all about us.

It wasn't until our meat, potatoes, and the courgette and aubergine mixed in tomato sauce had arrived that David's flow of joking chatter stopped. We both dug in. Once he'd eaten about half of his, he looked at me and said, "Don't you have to rush off to a telephone and call in your report on everyone's frocks?"

"What?" I started to laugh. "I don't work on the news desk. I can stroll in tomorrow morning and write up my report. It should appear on Sunday. By then I'll be off in the countryside." I had to keep up my pretense that I'd wanted to attend the German embassy party only for the society page. Was David seeing through my excuse?

"Visiting your friend Lady Abigail?"

"You know the Summersbys?"

"Reggie used to talk about how close you two are. Like sisters, although she was his cousin. I think he always felt a bit left out."

I set down my fork as my appetite drained away.

"Oh, dear," David said. "I didn't mean to upset you."

"It's all right. It's only—I thought we had the perfect

marriage."

"I'm sure you did."

"No. If we'd had a perfect marriage, I wouldn't feel so…" I was going to say angry, but that would mean sharing Reggie's secret. "Guilty. I didn't want him to feel left out."

It wasn't until we were drinking our coffee that I asked, "David, what did Claire deLong mean when she said you found Major Liestran helpful?"

"She was being nasty. The man nearly got me fired a couple of years ago." His face reddened as he glared at his coffee cup.

"Good grief. No wonder you don't like the man. What happened?"

He looked at me and visibly relaxed. "Nothing, really. A tempest in a teapot, as they say. But it left a sour taste in my mouth. The man is a troublemaker."

"He must be if he tried to get you fired. What a terrible man."

David's only response was a weak smile.

I wished Reggie were here to tell me David's secret. Reggie thought he was foolish, but he never told me why, blaming it on David's gossipy stories. But were David's complaints about Liestran a disguise for his real dealings with the Germans? Or did Liestran have a hold on David that forced him into being a traitor? Was he Reggie's killer?

I had a fourth name from the office to add to my list of potential murderers.

"Tell me about Claire deLong."

"There's little to tell. Like many bright young things, she likes German gods in uniform." His lips clamped shut in a thin line as he snatched up the bill and rose from the table.

When we walked outdoors, I said, "You obviously don't

like her. Did Reggie know her?"

"Forget it, Mrs. Denis."

When I opened my mouth to speak, he shook his head.

We strolled from the restaurant in silence. When we got to my block of flats, David and I shook hands outside by the front door. Then he walked off into the night.

Sutton opened the door for me and said, "Your cousin has gone upstairs to wait for you, Mrs. Denis."

"Abby is here?" Well, she was Reggie's cousin, but I thought of her as mine.

"No. The military gentleman."

Captain Redmond. Not the person I wanted to see right now after finding out he knew the deLong woman.

I took the lift up to find Redmond still in his dress uniform sitting in my parlor. "How did you get in?" I asked, tossing my bag to the side and sitting down to remove my high-heeled sandals before I unpinned my chic hair ornament.

"You looked lovely tonight." He smiled at me as if he desired me. Reggie had said similar things to me many times. Now I knew he'd meant it in an abstract way, not to indicate any passion. Was it the same with Redmond, or was the heat I saw in his eyes genuine?

My tone was cold. "Thank you. How did you get in?"

"Your lock is easy to pick. There was evidence it was picked before, too. Probably by your burglar."

Refusing to be distracted, I said, "You know Claire deLong."

"Yes."

"Quite well?"

"Not as well as she'd hoped." His raised eyebrows infuriated me.

"I don't feel like putting up with your ego tonight, Captain Redmond. Go away." I walked back into my hallway in my stocking feet and opened the front door.

He joined me in the doorway. "Why were you there tonight?" he asked in a low voice.

"Why were you? Was it to see Mrs. deLong?"

"Partially."

"Get out."

"Livvy, it's not—"

"Get. Out."

His eyes darkened and his lips thinned for an instant. Then his face relaxed and he left, twirling his brimmed uniform hat as he jogged down the stairs.

I slammed the door and locked it. I undressed and climbed into bed, but I couldn't sleep. Captain Redmond had deceived me about knowing that awful deLong woman. I listened to the London traffic a few floors below my window and wondered why it mattered.

He wasn't anything to me. He had given me information in my quest to learn who killed Reggie. He was friends with Sir John, he made a respectable addition to a dinner party, and I had to admit he'd been honest with me. Some of the time.

But he hadn't told me he knew Mrs. deLong, and that hurt.

* * *

I hauled my suitcase with me to the society page office early on Saturday morning, where I wrote and handed in a lengthy description of the dresses worn by various diplomatic wives at the reception at the German embassy the night before. I had several bland quotes and included Frau von Ribbentrop's praise for the new interior. I had no idea what Miss Westcott and the rewrite editors would do with it.

Then I went upstairs to Colinswood's office. I wasn't surprised to find him there on a Saturday morning.

"Going somewhere?" he asked.

"A friend's for the weekend. My story from last night is turned in. Remember you promised to run some of it to keep my cover intact."

"I remember. What did you find out?" He gestured to a chair but I remained standing. I wasn't going to stay a second longer than I needed to.

"It was a typical diplomatic reception. Full of diplomats."

"Meaning?"

"I couldn't begin to guess what other nations feel about Nazi Germany from the words and actions of the diplomats gathered."

"Did you learn anything?"

"Number Seven, Carlton House Terrace houses several military attachés posted here without their families. The head of security, Major Liestran, lives there and very obviously has von Ribbentrop's ear. So does a Herr Schreiber, who may be Hauptmann Schreiber, but he wasn't in uniform last night and wasn't introduced by rank."

"Anything else?"

"Frau von Ribbentrop told me she and her children are beginning to hate England due to our dislike of Germany. Schreiber and Liestran left their families behind because they'd be too busy to spend time with them here. An unknown German had an argument with Schreiber. He said Schreiber and Rickard, whoever he is, killed his brother."

Colinswood just shook his head. "That doesn't sound diplomatic. But why hold a reception now?"

"To show off the new interior of the building. Nash

would be furious if he could see it. There's nothing classical or understated about the building now. Swastikas everywhere."

"Costly?"

"I'd say so. The materials must have cost a fortune. An architect named Speer designed a very modern, very massive staircase."

"Then they must expect to occupy it for a number of years. That doesn't indicate a plan to begin war immediately."

"They don't seem to be the kind of people who consider things like cost. Looking superior seems to be their only concern."

"Still, we can hope."

From what Esther said about her and her father's plans for me, I hoped the Nazis would hold off whatever they had plotted for years.

"Here are my expenses." I handed him receipts for stockings and the little hint of a hair ornament.

"Good Lord. Hats cost that much?"

"Ask your wife."

"I'm not married."

"Then, yes, they do." I wouldn't have dared buy it if I thought I couldn't get the *Daily Premier* to pay for it. It looked terrific on me, but I couldn't afford it on my salary. "Anything else?"

"No." He shook his head before picking up a pencil and a sheet of copy. "Enjoy your weekend."

* * *

When Abby picked me up in the car at the train station, she told me Sir John had gone golfing and wouldn't make an appearance until dinnertime. It was a beautiful Saturday and she suggested we drive to the coast and have lunch at a tearoom overlooking the shingle beach. I picked at my salad, still annoyed at my lack of success at my job at the paper, finding Reggie's killer, and figuring out what Redmond was up to.

Finally, Abby set down her fork. "What's wrong?"

"Nothing's wrong."

"This is me you're talking to. I know you better than that. What's wrong?"

"If someone murdered John, wouldn't you want to find out who killed him?"

"Of course."

"So far I've not had much luck."

"Isn't that the job of the police?"

"They don't believe Reggie was murdered. If I don't find out, no one else will." I sniffed. "Abby, I'm afraid I'll forget the sound of Reggie's voice."

She reached out and took my hand. "How much do we really notice about the people and things around us? What you're describing is perfectly normal."

"And I wonder why he married me. We talked all the time. We were great friends. But why marry me?"

"I'm sure he loved you in his own way."

"I thought we had a normal marriage. Now I'm learning I didn't know him at all. Or I don't understand marriage."

Abby studied me for a minute. "Does that affect how you feel about him?"

"No. I still love him and I'm angry someone killed such a wonderful, kind man. And I'm still determined to find out who murdered him and see them hang."

She nodded. "What have you done so far?"

"I spoke to the lawyer who wrote up the will and divorce papers. Nothing there. I met Claire deLong at the German embassy last night. I know Reggie wouldn't have wanted anything to do with her. Loud, brassy, a flashy dresser. Everything he disliked."

"So we can discount those legal papers as an effort to throw everyone off the trail." Then she blinked. "What were you doing at the German embassy?"

I looked at her over my raised teacup. "Watching Claire deLong drape her body over Captain Redmond."

"He knows her?"

"When I asked him, he didn't deny it."

"The swine." Abby had always been on my side, even when I didn't deserve loyalty.

I took a sip of tea and set down my cup. "She climbed all over him, not the other way around. I got one of Reggie's office mates to take me so I could get a close look at the ladies at the reception and then write about them for the paper. Redmond was there in an official capacity. At least, he was in dress uniform. I have no idea why the deLong woman was there."

"Is she a Nazi sympathizer?" Abby asked, eagerly leaning forward.

"Perhaps. There was an official with the German embassy murdered the same night as Reggie. I wonder if it was for the same reason and by the same people."

"Good heavens. How did you learn about that?"

"Someone told me Reggie spoke to a German two nights before he was murdered. And then Redmond told me about this German's death." I didn't think it would be a good idea to mention Derek Langston to Abby. She was more open-minded than Sir John, but there was no reason to stir up that tempest again.

"You have made progress." Abby dug into her salad

again.

"But not enough." I took a bite of mine. I certainly wouldn't tell her about my only result. Being followed.

After lunch, we walked along the street above the beach. The smell of the sea and the sound of the waves soon relaxed me. London felt far away. No one was following me. The demands of my job, both for the newspaper itself and for Sir Henry, and my investigation into Reggie's death seemed removed from this place. "Do we have enough time to walk along the coast path for a bit before we have to return?"

"Of course we can. It'll only take us a half-hour or so to drive back. I even wore the proper footwear," Abby replied, showing me her flat-soled sandals.

I'd worn lace-up flats for the train ride, so we started out at a brisk pace. The weekend and the good weather had brought out an assortment of hikers, in pairs or small groups. I let my worries blow away on the salty breeze.

We hadn't gone far when we noticed a solitary man farther along the trail looking out to sea with binoculars. Then he glanced down the low cliffs to the beach below. He appeared to jot a note into a small book before slipping it into his jacket. He ignored us as we approached on the winding path.

We greeted him just before we would have squeezed past. He lowered his binoculars and turned a furtive glance toward us. It was the fake Captain Marshall. Had I been followed here?

I felt my eyes widen before I said, "Captain Marshall." I didn't know what else to call him. I had no idea who he really was.

If I could believe Redmond about Marshall's identity, that is. I was having trouble trusting anyone.

Marshall looked stunned for an instant before a polite smile crossed his face. "Mrs. Denis. What a pleasant surprise. What brings you here?"

"Visiting friends for the weekend. And you?"

"Enjoying a little free time away from the bustle of the city. I say, you haven't found the missing item in your husband's things, have you? It's turning into a treasure hunt in London." His wording made him sound like a rather thick public school grad. Odd, he hadn't struck me as that type. His accent, perhaps, or his mannerisms.

I felt a drop of icy suspicion slide down my back. Unfortunately, that was becoming my response to everyone. "No, I've not found anything." I introduced him to Abby and the fake Marshall made some pleasantry.

Abby said, "Are you a birder, Captain Marshall?"

"Why do you say that?"

"The binoculars and the notebook. You certainly appear to be a birder."

"Oh, a birder. A bird watcher. Yes, of course." He looked faintly relieved.

"Are you having any luck?"

"I'm afraid not, Lady Abigail."

"Well, come along with us, then. I've always had good luck spotting birds. And this stretch of beach has two or three uncommon species." Abby gestured down the path.

He looked as thrilled with that idea as I felt. "That is very kind of you, but I'm enjoying a bit of solitude. Nothing but the sound of waves and birds calling. After London, this is a relief. I'm sure you understand."

"Of course. I expect I'll see you in town." I nudged Abby as I made a side step around him to move on.

He tipped his hat to us. "Ladies."

Abby and I continued our stroll. I had an uncomfortable itch in the small of my back as if someone were staring at me. It took all my willpower not to turn around and look.

When we were far out of earshot, Abby said, "He's good looking. Where did you meet him?"

"He's a friend of Captain Redmond's."

"So you've been seeing your captain in London."

"He's hard to avoid." I looked out over the sea and then the fields on the other side, dark green striped with pale yellow in our lovely autumn weather. "It's hard to believe looking at this that anything as terrible as murder and treason is going on in London."

Abby grabbed my arm. "Livvy, you're scaring me."

That wasn't fair of me to trouble her with my concerns. "I don't mean to. But you read the papers, and I'm sure John tells you the rumors out of Whitehall."

"Yes." The fear didn't leave her eyes. Then I thought of her two sons who'd be conscription age in a few years and worried about them, too.

I put on a cheery face at odds with what I felt inside. "I've just been working too hard. Listening to women describe their grandchildren for the birth announcements is wearing on my nerves."

"Because you and Reggie didn't—" she began, wincing as she spoke.

"No. Because they can't all be the second coming of Christ. I'd love for just one of them to say, 'He's a very ordinary baby with the usual number of fingers and toes, but we're very happy with him,' and then only give me the details I need for the paper."

Abby burst out laughing. "I must have sounded like mine were extraordinary when they were little. Most parents and grandparents outgrow that stage once the children start school."

I smiled sadly, knowing I'd have to remember Abby's sons for Reggie now that he was no longer around to be their godfather. "Where are the boys this weekend?"

"Staying at school. They're practicing for the big sports events coming up. We'll be attending next weekend, but if you want to come down here, I can tell the housekeeper to make up a room for you."

"No. I wouldn't dream of coming down here if I can't enjoy your company." I took her arm and said, "Let's head back. John will have fits if we're the ones late for dinner."

When we turned around, Captain Marshall was nowhere in sight.

We arrived back at Summersby Lodge before John, allowing us to wash up before he returned. I heard him come in and then Abby's voice, but I didn't pay much attention as I dressed for dinner and then stared out my window at the rear garden and the fields beyond. The peaceful scene was at odds with my turbulent thoughts.

The German embassy was missing something, possibly documents. Claire deLong was a tart who Reggie would have avoided, not mentioned in his will. Reggie was a homosexual. Someone in the office was giving the Nazis Whitehall's secrets.

Reggie was murdered.

It was growing dark by the time the gong sounded for dinner. I went out my door and immediately crashed into Captain Redmond. "What are you doing here?" I demanded. I wanted to keep the troubles in London separate from the tranquility at Summersby Lodge.

A grin shot across his face before disappearing. "I could

ask you the same thing."

I wished, not for the first time, that he didn't look so trim, so healthy, so good in an evening suit. "Did Sir John invite you?"

"Yes. A weekend of golf and country air."

"That's almost what Captain Marshall said."

Every muscle in Redmond's body seemed to spring to attention. He appeared two inches taller and his face took on hard angles. "You've seen the impostor again? Where?"

"Walking along the coast path outside Hastings. Lady Abigail and I ran into him while we were there."

He scowled and turned away from me as if he'd already forgotten my presence. Before I could say something scathing, I heard my father's voice say, "Olivia. I didn't expect to see you this weekend."

I turned around. "I didn't expect to see you either. Playing golf with Sir John?"

"Captain Redmond and I rode down together early this morning and made up a foursome with Sir John and a neighbor of his." He scooped up my arm and started walking at a healthy clip. "All that exercise has left me famished."

Redmond had already disappeared downstairs.

"How are you, Father?"

"I'm well. And you, Olivia?"

I recognized those words as a tender family moment with my father. "Doing well. I never expected working at a newspaper to be so interesting."

"I've heard about your job. I suppose this is Sir Henry Benton's doing," he grumbled.

"He was kind enough to offer me a chance."

My father slammed to a halt as if he were suddenly glued to the floor. He still had a grip on my arm that sent me spinning around to face him. "Offer you a chance? A chance at what? Making a mockery of your good name? Turning you into a middle-class drudge?"

I stood as straight as I could and stared at his face. "A chance to earn a living. A chance to have a life. An independent life."

"Hmmpf. Marriage should be good enough for you."

"Reggie's dead. Remember? And not even you can bring him back."

CHAPTER THIRTEEN

UPSET AT MY father's thoughtless comments, I pulled away and rushed blindly downstairs. I glanced over to see Captain Redmond on the telephone. He was speaking softly, his hand in front of his mouth so I couldn't hear his conversation.

More secrets. I burst into the parlor at a greater speed than I'd intended. Abby and John looked away from each other toward me. I glanced from one surprised face to the other and said, "Have I kept you waiting? I hope not."

"No, Livvy. You're right on time," Abby said, studying my face and my heaving chest. When my father strode in a moment later, her expression changed to tell me she knew I'd had another row with him.

We walked into the dining room and I found myself next to my father and across from Captain Redmond.

The food was excellent and everyone was hungry. Perhaps that explained the lack of conversation at the table. I caught Redmond studying me across the table. Holding his gaze, I gave him a brief smile, which he returned.

Abby tried to start a conversation a couple of times, but her attempts fell flat. Finally, she said, "Livvy and I walked along the coast path this afternoon and ran into a friend of yours, Captain Redmond. A Captain Marshall."

"Mrs. Denis mentioned it," Redmond said.

"When did you see Livvy?" my father asked in his usual demanding manner.

"Just before dinner," Redmond said.

"What do you think of her working for that newspaper?" Father sounded like he was warming up for an interrogation.

Redmond looked him straight in the eye. "I think it's useful."

My father glanced at me, his eyes wide, and said, "Useful?"

"She gets herself invited to interesting parties." He gave me a brief grin and turned his attention back to his roast.

"Nothing scandalous, I hope." My father's face and neck were turning red and I feared he'd have a stroke.

"I met one of Queen Victoria's daughters at one event I covered," I told him. "A hospital fundraiser."

Abby leaned forward. "Wonderful. Which daughter?"

"Louise. She's thin and doesn't look a thing like her mother despite being older than the queen was when she died. She's a charming old lady who's determined to wring every penny out of contributors for the Princess Louise Hospital for Children. She urged donations with great vigor." I heard her appeals by eavesdropping since I wasn't considered important enough to be introduced. Writing for the society pages had taught me how to word things so it sounded like I was part of the conversation and not an interloper.

"How exciting," Abby said. "She must be ninety."

My father appeared to relax. "How are plans coming for the State Opening of Parliament?"

Sir John gave a ponderous report on his role in a purely ceremonial, very minor function that took us all the way through dinner until we left the table.

When we settled in the back parlor with our coffee and my father lit his cigar, Redmond sat next to me and said in a low voice, "We need to talk. In the garden when the others go upstairs."

I remembered how cold I'd been the last time we talked in Abby's garden. "This time I'm wearing a shawl."

"Do you have a role in the ceremony between the king and Parliament for the State Opening?" Abby asked Captain Redmond.

"No. I'm afraid I don't get to do anything as interesting as that." He sounded sincere.

"But I thought you'd been assigned to General Lord Walters' ceremonial office. They're practically at the center of all the action for the State Opening," Sir John said as he once again fiddled with lighting his pipe.

"I drew a short straw. I have to deal with all the minor ceremonies. Making sure the guard is changed at the palace and all that. Nothing so grand for me as a spot in the parade for Parliament's opening." Redmond gave us all a cheery smile.

"Is it true Queen Elizabeth is going to attend along with King George?" Abby asked.

"That's what I've heard," Redmond said.

"I've seen the procession between the palace and Parliament, but I'd love to see the ceremony inside," I said.

"No, you wouldn't," my father told me. "They march the king in and he sits down in the House of Lords. Then they call the House of Commons to come over and they make a show of being very casual about it. The king reads a boring message written by the prime minister and then they all leave and have lunch."

"Maybe, Captain, you're lucky not to have a role in this,"

Abby said.

Personally, I'd have bet anything Redmond had a vital role to play in keeping our monarchs safe during the parade.

"But you do get to attend diplomatic receptions." I gave Redmond a knowing smile, thinking of the night before and Claire deLong greeting him effusively.

The look he gave me was unreadable. "Some."

After that, I couldn't wait for the others to go upstairs for the night, but the men had to replay every hole of their round of golf. When Abby finally suggested we call it a night, I told her I planned to walk in the garden and went up to get my shawl.

When I came back down, my father and Redmond were deep in conversation. They stopped when I entered the parlor and turned to face me with guilty expressions.

"I know a conspiracy when I see one."

"It's for your own good, Olivia," my father said. Redmond had the grace to look uncomfortable.

"Captain Redmond has nothing to do with my job, so what are you involving him in, Father?"

"This obsession of yours that Reggie was murdered."

"He *was* murdered." My father was impossible. Even if he couldn't see the benefit, I thought it a fortunate thing that I'd been hired by the *Daily Premier* and didn't have to move home.

"Even if he were, there's nothing you can do about it."

My shoulders slumped as I considered the truth of his words. "Perhaps, but I have to try."

"Olivia—" my father began.

Redmond put a hand on his shoulder. "Good night, Sir Ronald. Hopefully we'll reach an agreement in the morning."

"We'll discuss this on the links after church. Good night,

Olivia." My father came over and kissed me on top of the head before he left the room. He used to kiss me good night the same way when I was little. The memory choked me up for a moment.

After the door clicked shut behind him, Redmond said, "He means well, Livvy."

"I know. Unfortunately, meaning well isn't the same as doing the right thing."

"And you think finding out who killed your husband is doing the right thing."

I studied Redmond's face. "Don't you?"

"Yes, but not only because whoever he is committed murder. We have to consider what he has planned for the future." He walked over and opened the French doors leading outside.

I wrapped my shawl around my shoulders and preceded him into the garden. The night was cloudy and I could barely see the path between the flowerbeds. "What do you think Reggie's killer has planned for the future?"

"War."

"Then you think the killer is German."

"Don't you?"

I tugged my shawl closer around me. "No. At least none of the German embassy staff I've met. He wouldn't have gone near them at night in a secluded spot. And Reggie wouldn't have gone out late at night carrying his pistol. He avoided trouble."

"Even if he were going to meet someone dangerous?"

"Reggie wouldn't meet someone dangerous late at night. Well, not if he knew the man was dangerous. And in any case, he wouldn't have brought his pistol. It was his father's. He'd had it since before he left for the war. I've never known him to fire it."

"Your husband was in the war?" Redmond sounded surprised. Surely he had access to records. "But you must have been a baby then."

I'd heard comments about our age difference from my friends and Reggie's coworkers when we married. I had wanted to marry and get out of my father's house, and I'd already grown tired of shallow young men. Reggie's quiet intellect had swept me off my feet.

I refused to acknowledge Redmond's implied question. "Reggie went in at the very end of the fighting as a young man. He didn't see any combat." I faced Redmond. "This doesn't answer how his killer got Reggie's gun."

"The simplest answer is he broke in and stole it, or he tricked your husband into showing it to him and then ran off with it."

"He didn't keep it loaded. I don't even know if he had bullets for it."

"Then it was probably stolen and he was shot at a later time." Redmond shrugged.

"That doesn't necessarily make his killer German."

"He was seen speaking to a German embassy employee and two nights later they're both murdered. We know we didn't do it—"

"Do we?" I raised my brows.

"Yes. So the only other group interested in the reason they met would be the Germans."

"What about the two men I heard talking in Lester and Mary Babcock's kitchen?"

"If they had a hand in your husband's murder, they're working for the Germans. What better place for a turncoat to work than in the Foreign Office? We've been looking for the person who's been passing secrets to the Germans for several months."

"You seem to believe everything revolves around the Germans. Couldn't Reggie have been murdered because someone wanted his job or he found out someone was stealing and was going to report him? That would be the kind of thing Reggie would do. He was terribly honest."

Redmond shook his head. "It's possible, but I'd still bet on the Germans. Their current government contains the nastiest group of thugs I've ever encountered."

I couldn't argue with that. There was something creepy about von Ribbentrop. And Liestran had made my blood freeze. "But Reggie avoided thugs. I've already found four members of his office who might have reason to be doing business with the Nazis and I'm sure there are more."

"Germany appears to be at the heart of this business."

And that made me think back to the embassy party. The dark-eyed man would have needed to sign in at the entrance to the Foreign Office on Thursday morning, just as I had. I saw a way to track the man down.

"I'd like you to be careful around Peters," Redmond said.

"David? Why?"

"There was a question about his loyalty while he was posted to Italy a couple of years ago."

"I don't believe it." Even as I said the words, I remembered my unease after the embassy party in David's company.

"He got involved with a young woman. A pretty young Italian. We know he gave her a visa for a third party, who turned out to be a German spy."

"If what you say is true, they'd have thrown him out of the diplomatic corps."

"He was saved by coming forward with a full account. That and having filled out all the appropriate paperwork concerning the visa when it was issued. That was how we caught the spy. Nevertheless, he was sent back to London in disgrace."

"Poor David." Or poor Reggie. He worked with him and had gone out with him the night he was murdered. Even in the dim light, I made out the scowl on Redmond's face and changed the subject. "What is known about Manfred?"

"He was a holdover from von Hoesch's ambassadorship. Not a Nazi, enthusiastic or otherwise, but a competent paper pusher. That was the only reason he was kept on at the embassy. After his murder, we decided the missing item the Germans were searching for must be a document."

"And if he found some record of something the Nazis did—"

"More likely something they plan to do," Redmond said. "There'd be no reason to kill him over something that had already happened."

"Why would he involve my husband?" Things kept coming back to Reggie. What was he mixed up in?

"Were Reggie and Manfred friendly?"

"I never heard of Manfred, and Derek only met him the once. Derek thought it was by accident."

Now it was Redmond's turn to raise his fair eyebrows. "Derek?"

"Langston." I'd begun to think of him as an old family friend. It made it easier for me to overlook their scandalous relationship. And my ego needed to overlook *that.* "If Manfred had already found this secret, perhaps running into Reggie made him think of Reggie as the person to pass it on to." I shivered in the cooling air. "We saw how well that turned out."

Redmond took off his jacket and laid it over my shoulders. "This secret had to be written down to make it dangerous enough to kill over. And not a copy. This has to be an original document. Anything else would just be a rumor and easily dismissed as a fake."

"I'm sure people have been killed over rumors." Despite the jacket that smelled of aftershave and espionage, I was growing more chilled the longer we stood in the garden. If we discussed this much longer, I expected snow to start falling.

"I'm sure they have, but this had to be something concrete. Otherwise, the Nazis wouldn't fear its disclosure and put so much effort into retrieving it."

"Any idea what we're looking for?"

Redmond shook his head. "We need to find out where your husband could have hidden this thing. We need to follow his trail for the evening he was murdered."

I didn't like the way this conversation was headed, but I felt powerless to stop it. "How will we do that?"

"Did you see him the evening he was killed?"

"No. We were supposed to meet here at Summersby Lodge the next day."

"Reggie never came home that night?"

"I don't know. I wasn't there."

"You weren't there. You weren't here, either. Where were you, Olivia?"

"I had dinner with my father."

"So I heard. But you didn't spend the night at your childhood home."

"You asked him?" Leave it to Redmond to verify where I was when the police just made assumptions. This was going to lead to another argument with my father.

"No. I know better than to ask some things directly. Your father just mentioned it in relation to something else. So where were you?"

"I spent the night at my grandmother's. Her companion had to travel to a funeral and she couldn't find anyone to stay with her that one night. I said I'd do it. I had dinner with my father and then went over there." I stopped and breathed in the strong scent of the chrysanthemums in the border next to the path. Ordinarily, their smell would relax me, but nothing was going to make this conversation easier.

"So you have an alibi for the night." He sounded relieved.

"Only for arriving after dinner and leaving the next morning when I met her next caregiver. My grandmother would remember that I visited her, but it's doubtful she could tell you the date or time without prompting."

"Not a good witness."

"No."

"Likewise, you could have left for a short time and she wouldn't have noticed if she were asleep."

"Yes. She doesn't sleep well because of her arthritis and shortness of breath, but it's possible I could have slipped out for half an hour or so." It felt like an admission of murder. I felt guilty, and I knew I'd done nothing wrong.

"Did your father know you were going to visit your grandmother?"

"Good heavens, no. She's my mother's mother. He hasn't had anything to do with that side of the family since my mother died."

"He took her suicide hard." His voice was a murmur on the breeze.

I glared at him, no longer chilled. "It wasn't a suicide. It was an accident. An accidental overdose."

"Your father doesn't think so."

"My father doesn't have faith in anyone or anything but himself. He holds women in especially low regard. My parents didn't like each other, but my mother didn't have to escape him through death or divorce. She could have just ignored him."

"Like you do." I sensed his quick smile rather than saw it in the poor light.

"Yes."

"Still leaves you without an alibi for the night of Denis's death."

"Yes." *Thanks for reminding me.* John was still worried that I'd be arrested for Reggie's murder and kept warning me of my vulnerability.

"Did you go back to the flat at any time?"

"Ye—es."

He stilled when he heard my hesitancy. "When?"

"After dinner with my father. I went to pick up my bag. It was already packed for my visit here."

"Did you see your husband?"

"No. I could tell he'd returned after work to dress for the evening. He was going to the theater with some men from his office. I have no idea where he ate dinner or with whom."

"So you didn't see your husband at any time anywhere for that entire night."

That was harder to answer. "I don't think so."

"Livvy, either you did or you didn't."

"It's not that easy."

I heard his sigh. "Please try to explain."

"When I left the flat for my grandmother's, I took a cab. It was a miserable night out, and there were few people about. A few blocks from the flat, I spotted a figure walking along the sidewalk. He wore a trench coat, typical bad weather wear. His umbrella hid his face. But there was something about him that made me think it was Reggie."

"How sure were you?" Clouds skimmed away from the moon, letting me see Redmond's expression. His face told me nothing about his thoughts.

I pulled my shawl and his jacket closer around me, shivering in the cool garden air as I thought back to that night. "My first reaction was to think, 'What is Reggie doing there?' Then I looked harder out the window, but a bus pulled up and blocked my view. I couldn't decide if the man was Reggie or my imagination was playing tricks on me."

"Describe exactly what you saw."

"Oh, I'm not sure—"

"Try."

I took a deep breath. "Black trousers for a tuxedo beneath a trench coat. Worn with shiny black shoes. Umbrella angled in front of him against the weather. Top hat. I saw that as we approached from behind. Oh, and he had a thick book tucked under his arm. That must be what made me think of Reggie. That and his stride."

Redmond nodded. "Where was this?"

"Oxford Street, near Regent Street."

"And the quickest way from your flat to the German embassy and St. Asaph's Hotel. You do realize the significance, don't you?"

"Of the hotel? No." It would forever be the spot where Reggie died. Somehow, I didn't think that was what Redmond was referring to.

His voice cut like steel through the air. "It's where the spies of various governments, ours included, rendezvous. Along with gamblers, arms merchants, and purveyors of secrets. In short, a dangerous place."

CHAPTER FOURTEEN

"REALLY? WHY would spies and shadowy people from different countries all meet at the same place? And why the St. Asaph's?"

"Because it's close to the offices in Whitehall, the Admiralty, Scotland Yard. Because it's comfortable, and smart, and anyone could have a reason for being there. Because our government has reason to talk to people unofficially."

"But I saw this person hours before Reggie's body was found and not near the St. Asaph's."

"He could have met someone there later. He didn't expect you to be home. He was free to come and go as he wanted."

"But he was meeting men from work for an evening at the theater. The pathologist said death was before or around midnight."

Redmond nodded. "Which theater was it?"

"The Windmill."

"Oh." He turned a snicker into a cough. Clouds covered the moon again, making it hard to see his face.

The revue at the Windmill Theater featured female nudes frozen in tableaux like statues. Lord Cromer, who as Lord Chamberlain was the censor for the theaters, had approved it as long as the women didn't move.

I'd been told a lot of women attended the revues there, but I had no interest in joining them. Neither did Mary Babcock. I suspected the rest of the Whitehall wives had declined as well.

"And they left at closing?" Redmond asked.

"I believe they did. The police learned about this outing from questioning his coworkers. What we need to do is talk to Derek."

"Langston? Why?"

"Has anyone asked him if he saw Reggie that night?"

"I doubt it. I'll talk to him tomorrow when we get back into town."

"You?" I put scorn in my voice. "Derek will tell me a great deal more than he'll tell you."

"Made friends with your husband's lover, have you?" He conveyed his smirk in his voice.

"Yes." I doubted Redmond would understand, but I had to try. "We both loved the same man. He's been murdered, and we both want his killer to face justice. That's more important than what separates us."

"What divides you is your husband cheated on you with Langston." Redmond sounded furious at Reggie's betrayal, not at the details. In this, he reminded me of Abby, who mentally separated the wheat from the chaff at lightning speed.

"Maybe he cheated on Derek with me. Maybe he loved Derek more." Once I'd said it, pain rose in my chest. I wasn't good enough. As an employee. A sleuth. A wife. A friend. A tiny sob escaped my throat.

"Okay, okay." He held his hands up. "We'll talk to Langston together."

I could insist on going on my own, but I couldn't imagine

Redmond going along with that. He'd just meet with Derek later. "All right. But you will be nice to him."

"When have I ever been less than nice?" His tone proclaimed his innocence.

I wish I could have seen his face when he said that. He said he'd knocked out the man following him after our lunch. He seemed capable of solving all sorts of problems with violence, but to give him credit, he didn't seem like a violent man.

"What were you and my father plotting when I returned to the parlor?"

"He's spoken to my commanding officer. He doesn't want me to see you or help you with your inquiry."

"What did your commanding officer say about his interference?"

"He delivered your father's message. Then he said, 'Just be careful. She's the only daughter he has.'"

I was tired of my father's interference. "Good night, Captain Redmond." I handed him his jacket.

I took two steps toward the house when I heard "Livvy" just behind me. I turned around and found myself in Redmond's embrace. A moment later, I found out he was a very accomplished kisser.

Still dumbstruck by his kiss, I let him end it and get in the first word. "Don't ever think, because of your husband, that you're not a desirable woman. I know I desire you. Good night, Olivia."

The only response I could think of was to run into the house. Then I spent half the night replaying his last words to me. And his kiss.

In the morning, we all squeezed into Sir John's gleaming sedan for church in the village. Redmond sat in front with

John. Father sat in back with Abby and me, showing his displeasure with me by his silence. That suited me well. I was wondering what Derek Langston could tell us that I hadn't thought to ask him before.

After church, the men went off to the links with their clubs. Abby said, "They won't be back until dinnertime. What shall we do?"

"Would you like to do a bit of sleuthing?"

"Livvy." She gave me a look. "Is this something John or your father would approve of?"

"No. How would you like to catch the next train to London and drop in on St. Asaph's Hotel? I've been told Reggie spent odd moments in the bar there. Apparently, it's a meeting place for spies."

"He was meeting with spies? Reggie?" Abby seemed to freeze in place, her complexion suddenly pale.

"That's what I've been hearing. Let's go up and check it out. We're certainly dressed for it." We were still in our church finery.

Abby had always been up for an adventure, unlike Reggie. An hour later, we were taking a cab across the heart of London to St. Asaph's Hotel. When we walked in, I heard Abby murmur, "This does not look like a place Reggie would go."

It was opulent. Gilt worked into the carved furniture. Yellow velvet upholstery on the chairs. Breathtaking plasterwork in the ceiling. The gallery above the back of the lobby was ornate and curved like the boxes in a Victorian theater. And this was just the entrance.

"Come on. You promised me a drink." Taking Abby by the arm, I led her toward the thick blue-carpeted double staircase and we walked up to the gallery level.

It was as if we had entered a different world. The bar area was the way I'd imagine a men's club to look, all paneling and brown leather sofas and chairs. The clientele was mostly male, talking quietly in pairs or reading the newspaper, cut crystal glasses holding brown liquids in front of them. Here and there I spied women in fashionable hats and understated jewelry talking to a man or sitting in pairs. We wouldn't stand out.

I chose a table where we could see people coming or going by the staircase and sat down. Abby joined me, looking around like her head was on a swivel. "This looks more like Reggie."

A waiter came over. Abby ordered white wine. I ordered a martini and said, "My friend will have one, too."

She gave him a weak smile and nodded. When he left, she said, "A martini?"

"I don't intend to drink it. I just thought it would make a good prop." All the other women seemed to have the same wide-mouth glasses in front of them that we would have.

"I imagine it will be ghastly."

She was right. When it arrived, I took a sip. Positively dreadful.

We sat there for a while, nursing our drinks and looking around. None of the other patrons looked familiar. Or suspicious. The acoustics were such that I couldn't overhear anyone else's conversations.

"This is getting us nowhere, and the men could be back from their golf game at any time. We need to go," Abby said.

Just then, I heard a female American say, "I'm so glad you could meet me today."

I put out a hand to Abby's wrist. "Who's behind me?" I whispered.

"A blonde. She's with a man."

I dropped my handkerchief and swung around in my chair to pick it up. I could see Claire deLong clearly, today wearing a demure suit that was slightly too tight and pumps a fraction too high. On the other hand, I'd kill for her bumper-brim, asymmetric crown hat. Definitely one-of-a-kind. Unfortunately, she stood in profile to me, my view of the man Abby had seen her with blocked by a wide pillar done in tasteful paneling.

"I can't see him. Who is he?"

Abby made an "I don't know" face.

"Can you still see him?"

"Yes."

I pulled out my compact and opened the mirror, holding it at an angle so I could see what Abby was seeing. Moving it around, I saw a great deal of ceiling and the back of a chair before I located Claire deLong again and then focused on the man she was with.

It was a rabbity, inbred-looking man. "Probably an aristocrat," I muttered.

At the sound of a voice clearing, I looked up as I guiltily closed my mirror and slid it back in my purse.

"What are you doing here, Mrs. Denis?" Sir George Rankin said. I didn't know the distinguished gray-haired man he was with.

Sir George and that awful deLong woman in the same place at the same time. Was that what Reggie came here to watch? Were they the people he suspected were passing government secrets?

"Abby and I are larking about town while the men are playing golf. Do you know Reggie's cousin, Lady Abigail Summersby?"

"We met at the funeral." We spent a minute or two going through the social ritual while I wondered why Sir George and his friend were there.

"Do you come here often?" I asked. It was clumsy, but I couldn't think of any other way to learn anything.

"This is quite convenient to Whitehall. And a nice change from my club." The other man made a small noise. "Oh, yes, that's right. You've never met Reggie Denis's widow. He was one of my men. Mrs. Denis, General Alford."

"Oh, you were Captain Redmond's commanding officer," slipped out before I thought.

"You know Captain Redmond?" the general asked, staring hard at me.

"He's playing golf with my father and Colonel Summersby today," I said with a bright smile.

"Yes, he was part of my unit. Useful man, Redmond. Almost as useful as this fellow here. Sir George was once one of my men."

"A very long time ago," Sir George said and both men laughed.

I wondered if I should read anything into Sir George working for the same man Redmond now reported to unofficially.

"I thought you might be watching Mrs. deLong," Sir George said.

"Claire deLong?" Abby said, peering around my chair.

"Why would I do that?" I asked, ignoring Abby.

Sir George held my gaze with his dark eyes. "Oh, I don't know. But your mirror was definitely aimed in her direction."

I had to think fast. "I wanted to see who she was with today after her performance at the German embassy party Friday night."

"You went to that?" General Alford asked, suspicion in his tone.

"Yes. I did a story on the party for the society pages of the *Daily Premier*." I made my answer breezy as I watched an inexplicable look pass between Reggie's old boss and Redmond's general. Why were they here?

"I'm sure Reggie would be pleased to know you're doing all right," Sir George said.

"I wouldn't be involved in any of this if it hadn't been for Reggie's death. I wonder why he was here the night he died." I held his gaze and saw a calculating look in his eyes followed by another glance at General Alford.

Abby made a show of looking at her watch and said, "We have to leave now if we want to get back in time for dinner. As it is, we may have left it too long."

We carried out a minute or two of pleasantries. The men returned downstairs, curiously without stopping for a drink. We'd already risen to leave when that blasted American voice said from behind me, "Mrs. Denis. I never thought I'd see you in a place like this."

I turned, pasting on a smile. "Really? Why not?"

"This doesn't look like your kind of place at all."

"Oh, I can be very surprising when the need arises. Good day, Mrs. deLong." I sauntered off, hoping Abby would keep up.

Why was she there? Was it to watch Sir George, or the other way around? And had any of them been here the night Reggie died?

As we crossed the lobby, Abby whispered, "That was Claire deLong? Oh, my." I murmured agreement as I watched Sir George and General Alford head toward an elevator with a man who was dressed as a hotel manager.

Again, why?

CHAPTER FIFTEEN

TRAVELING BACK to London with my father and Captain Redmond after dinner should have been uncomfortable. I suspected I'd rather the trip had been embarrassing or painful rather than what it was. Boring. They replayed every hole of their match in excruciating detail. I would have taken a nap, but my father kept waking me up.

I arrived at the station in London with my nerves frayed. Redmond sent my father off in a cab and then turned to me. "Shall we head to Langston's?"

We went to my flat to drop off our cases and Redmond's golf clubs. I walked into the parlor and noticed Reggie's address book on the desk blotter, not in the pigeon-hole where I kept it. Puzzled, I walked from room to room. The draperies were closed more than I had left them. The large pieces of furniture were slightly out of position.

"What's wrong?" Redmond asked as he followed me about the flat.

"Someone has searched in here again. It wasn't your people, was it?"

"No. Are you sure someone's been here?"

"Yes." At least they had left the place neater than they had the last time.

"Then the document or whatever is still missing and they're certain Reggie had it."

"I need to speak to Sutton."

"Don't bother. These men are professionals. They either told him they were here for another flat or they bypassed him completely."

The safety of moving home appealed for about ten seconds until I thought of living with my father again.

When we arrived at Derek's block of flats, I was the one who gave the doorman my name. He called Derek and then sent us up, his head already bent over his newspaper by the time we entered the lift.

As soon as we knocked, Derek opened the door. When he saw Redmond, his welcoming smile slipped away.

"It's all right," I told him. "Captain Redmond is helping me find out who killed Reggie. We have some questions. Is this a good time?"

He nodded and stepped back to let us in. I walked in first, slipping off my coat and gloves as I went into the parlor. Redmond pulled off his gloves and set them inside his hat as he followed me.

Derek parked himself in front of the mantelpiece, his eyes darting from one of us to the other. He wore a smoking jacket with trousers and plaid bedroom slippers, as comfortable-looking and unfashionable as Reggie looked in the evening in our flat. I immediately felt at home and a little sad.

"We're trying to learn all we can about Mr. Denis's last night. Did you see him at any time after, say, five in the afternoon?" Redmond asked.

"Will this help, Olivia?" Derek asked, looking at me.

"Yes. We've received more information, well, hints of information, that we think leads to Rggie's death and that of another man. Anything, no matter how small, may help us discover the truth."

He nodded, swallowed, and turned to Redmond. "I met Reggie for dinner at a chop house."

"Was he already dressed for the evening when he arrived?" I asked. People might eat there dressed in evening clothes, but only because they were going to the theater afterward and wanted a reasonably priced meal beforehand.

"No. We were both in business clothes. We blended in better that way."

"Which one?" Redmond broke in.

"The Westmoreland. In the Strand. He told me he had a meeting after we ate and then he had to dress for the theater and he couldn't stay long. We ate and parted ways at the restaurant."

Derek began to pace, and I knew we'd learn more. "He came here an hour later, perhaps a little less, and asked to borrow a book. I got it for him and he left. That was the last time I saw him. And he was still dressed in his business suit."

"How did he seem?" Redmond asked.

"Nervous, frightened, exhilarated. He kept pacing and his fingers never stopped moving. He kept tapping them and twisting them and poking them into the cushions on the back of the sofa. And he never looked me in the eye."

"He wasn't like that at dinner, was he?" I asked.

"No. He seemed fine earlier. Just as he always was."

"Did he give any hint as to who he met, or where?"

Derek shook his head. "Not at dinner, nor when he arrived here. I wish he had."

"What book did he borrow?"

"Hardy's *Far from the Madding Crowd*."

"I hated that in school," Redmond muttered.

I smiled. It wasn't my favorite either. I remembered it as

a heavy volume that made my arms and my head ache every time I picked it up.

"Did he do anything with the book while he was here?"

"No. He just thanked me and left. I thought he wanted to reread it for some reason. He certainly never got the chance."

"Did he really like Hardy?" Redmond asked me.

"I think so. I don't remember seeing the book around the flat. I'll look for it and return it to you," I told Derek.

"Not so fast," Redmond said, holding up a hand.

"Do you think it has something to do with Reggie's death?" Derek asked.

"He came to borrow that book after his meeting with someone he wouldn't name even to you, Langston. A few hours later he was murdered. That book may contain a clue as to who killed him and why." Redmond gazed from one of us to the other.

Derek held Redmond's gaze. "Keep the book as long as you need, Olivia."

"And those were the last two times you saw or spoke to Denis or had any word from him?" Redmond said.

"Yes."

"Did you and Denis frequent the St. Asaph's Hotel bar?"

Derek shook his head. "I've never been there."

"Do you know if Denis would have gone there on his own?"

"I doubt it. He wasn't much of a drinker. Hanging around bars wasn't a pastime he'd enjoy."

"And Denis was cautious?"

"He had to be. We both did."

"Did Reggie say anything about going to the theater with men from his office when he picked up the book?" I asked, interrupting Redmond's questioning.

"He said something about going, but he didn't sound pleased. He didn't like revues, much preferring classical plays and operas. But someone in the office invited him and he thought he'd better go. It made for better relations in the office, and he'd told me he'd been having problems there lately."

"What? He didn't tell me." One more secret Reggie had kept from me. Didn't he trust me with anything? Or was I completely dense?

Derek gave me a kindly smile. "He didn't want to worry you. But apparently there'd been some bad feelings over differences of opinion. He wouldn't tell me any of the details. Said he wanted to give the people involved a chance to remember where their loyalty belonged."

"People in the office?"

"Yes."

"Was it because of—you two?"

"I asked Reggie. He said no, that no one knew about me. He said this was political."

I swung around to Redmond. "It sounds like Reggie knew who was leaking information to the German embassy."

Redmond rose and picked up his hat and gloves, his face shuttered.

I turned to Derek. "Have you heard from a Captain Marshall?"

"Yes. I thought he was rather rude."

"He's an impostor. He spent Saturday studying the coast, and I don't think he was hiking or bird watching."

"Why?" Derek asked.

"He didn't seem like someone on holiday. Where did you meet him?"

Derek squinted, wrinkling his brow. "He came here after

work one day last week. He wanted to know if Reggie asked me to keep anything for him before he died." Glancing from one of us to the other, he said, "I shouldn't have talked to him."

"No. You did fine," I told him. "Better not to let him know we suspect him."

"Of killing Reggie?" Derek stood taller, his nostrils flaring. "If he dares to come back here I'll—"

"Do nothing. Tell him you've nothing more to add and don't let him in." I stood and patted his shoulder. "He's not who he says he is. If he's a killer, and we have no evidence that he is, don't give him a chance to physically harm you, too."

"I'll let you know immediately if I hear from him again, Olivia. But why did he come here? Did you tell him about me? About Reggie and me?"

"I've been followed for a while now. Since these people know I believe Reggie was murdered, they must have thought my coming here meant there was a connection between you and Reggie. I'm sorry."

"It's not your fault, Olivia." He held out his hand and I shook it.

He and Redmond shook hands as well and we left. Once we were on the darkening streets, Redmond asked, "Shall we walk?"

"Yes. It'll give us a chance to talk."

"All right. What do you want to talk about?"

"What was our fake Captain Marshall doing walking the coast trail with binoculars and a notebook?"

"He's German and he's studying our beaches. Don't you think we're doing much the same in Germany?"

"Why the beaches in Sussex? East Anglia is much closer

to Germany."

"But the southern beaches are much closer to France."

"They'd take over France first? What a terrible idea."

Redmond stared at me in silence.

"There's a lot of talk of a possible war, but after the last one, I can't believe anyone would want to try it again." Like many people my age and younger, I hadn't any real memories of the war. Our elders had spent the years since then telling us how terrible it was and the newsreels from Spain about the civil war had reinforced their lessons on the evils of fighting.

He reached out and gently stroked my hand as if trying to soften bad news. "There are only so many countries Herr Hitler can threaten without someone starting a fight."

"Surely he'll stop before it leads to war."

Redmond glanced at me and didn't reply. I gave his hand a squeeze.

"I hope all he wants is an alliance with Britain. No one wants to go back to the continent for another bloody war."

"He may not give us a choice."

I gazed into his hazel eyes and the sadness there made my heart sink. Redmond, with his superior knowledge thanks to his job, thought war was inevitable. I hoped he was wrong.

"I learned your commander, General Alford, used to command Sir George, Reggie's supervisor."

"How the devil did you find that out?" He didn't sound happy.

"Abby and I went to St. Asaph's Hotel while you were out on the links. We ran into them there."

He stopped and swung me around to face him. "That's a place you need to stay out of."

I gave him a smile he didn't return. "It's perfectly

respectable."

"Yes, it is. It's the people who meet there who aren't necessarily respectable."

"Such as?"

In the light from the street lamp, I saw a smile hovering on Redmond's lips. "Ask your father about when he worked for General Alford."

"My father? I can see him doing something sneaky."

He grinned. "You're such a loyal daughter."

I was tantalizingly close to one of my father's secrets. And then in a blinding flash of clarity, I asked, "If he pretended to push papers, are you doing anything ceremonial for General Lord Walters?"

"Enough not to raise questions."

* * *

I was ready to climb into bed that night when the phone rang. Expecting sinister men on the other end of the line, I was surprised to hear Carol Hawthorn's nasal, upper-middle class vowels. "I hope I'm not calling too late."

"Not at all," I lied.

"We're having a little party Friday night, and we hope you'll be able to join us."

"Thank you, Carol. I'd love to."

"Wonderful. I'll see you then." She hung up before I could say good-bye.

After I hung up, I decided to take a chance and called Lester and Mary. Ignoring Mary's sleepy voice, I said, "Have you been invited to a party at the Hawthorns' Friday night?"

"No. Why?"

"Because Carol just called and invited me to spend the evening at her house."

"How very strange."

"Especially since I'm not one of her favorite people."

"Lester," I heard her call out, "has Edward Hawthorn said anything about a party next weekend at their house?"

I couldn't make out the words between them, and then Mary came back on the line. "Lester hasn't heard a thing. Shall I let you know if we get an invitation?"

"Please do." I rang off, wondering why a woman who didn't care for me or my standards would invite me to her home before she called sweet, likable Mary Babcock.

CHAPTER SIXTEEN

AFTER THE STRESS of a weekend in the country with my father and the fake Captain Marshall, followed by the gloom of war talk with Captain Redmond, coupled with secrets I couldn't uncover, I was glad to be back in what was becoming the familiar world of the *Daily Premier* society page offices. I received my first compliment from Miss Westcott and congratulations from Jane Seville for the report I'd turned in Saturday morning about the German embassy party.

Apparently I'd balanced the mix of quotes and dress descriptions and put them in the right order. I'd have to look at my story again to figure out how I'd done it.

Finally, a success. That was enough to make me smile.

In the afternoon, I was sent to cover the opening of a library in the northern suburbs by a minor royal while Jane took photographs.

"What do you think?" I asked. "Will I pass as a library patron from the new housing estates?"

"The area is all sports grounds and cemeteries. I don't think you need to worry about your outfit in the land of young mothers with the newest electric appliances," Jane told me.

Since she always wore rust or brown suits with cloche hats and clunky shoes, I was never sure if I could trust her fashion sense. I grabbed my purse and my notebook as well as my string bag and followed Jane, with her brown and rust string shopping bag and myriad bags and satchels of camera gear, to a waiting taxi.

When we arrived, I saw the man who'd argued with Schreiber at the reception sitting on the stage with the dignitaries. He was introduced as Hans Manfred, the head librarian of the new facility. Remembering the way he stormed out of the German embassy on Friday night, I took notes from the back of the meager crowd until near the end of the presentation. Then I whispered to Jane not to get me in any of the pictures and worked my way along the edge of the gathering.

I blocked his way when he left the platform. "Mr. Manfred? You're head librarian here?" I said, holding up my notebook.

"Yes." He gave me a polite smile.

"And it was your brother, employed by the German embassy, who was murdered by his coworkers?"

His smile vanished. "Excuse me—"

I shifted to block his path. "My husband was murdered the same night. He worked in the Foreign Office and knew your brother. I heard you threaten Schreiber at the embassy reception Friday night."

"Why were you there?" Distrust poured out of him.

"I was trying to learn who killed my husband."

He glanced around. "We can't talk now. Contact me here later."

"I'm Olivia Denis." I held out my hand. "I'll be in touch. Your library is quite grand."

He shook my hand. "Thank you."

I lowered my voice. "Who is Rickard?" Manfred had

mentioned the name at the reception.

"A very tall SS officer. He appears pleasant, but he is vicious. A killer."

I pictured the man I suspected of being a German spy talking to me on the south coast path. I had one last question; the one that was most important to me. "What was your brother going to give to my husband?"

"Later." Manfred looked past me and then darted away.

I walked off to gather some quotes for the paper, but inside, I was cheering. I felt sure I finally had a name for my fake Captain Marshall.

And then I realized the German's search of our coastline was so important he'd been sent there instead of attending von Ribbentrop's party.

After that, it was hard to focus my attention on the minor royal or any of the guests for the opening. I was lucky. For once, they all seemed to want to give me a quote.

The audience began to break up. As I glanced toward the door looking for Jane, I spotted a familiar face in profile. Schreiber.

A woman in a flowered hat walked between us, obscuring my view. When she moved, he was gone. Was he following me, or was I seeing things?

When I left work that night, I was glad to see Captain Redmond waiting for me by the entrance to the Tube. He tipped his hat and said, "Let's ride over to your neighborhood and have some dinner."

He didn't have to ask twice. I'd missed lunch and was starving. I held up my string bag. "I'll have to take this home first."

"What have you got in there?"

"Odds and ends. Jane and I were sent on assignment to

the north side of town and managed a little shopping on the way back."

"Does your boss approve?"

"Miss Westcott? I'm sure she knows, but as long as all the deadlines are met, she turns a blind eye to whatever else we get up to."

Redmond waited in the lobby while I took my shopping up by the lift. Remembering the fake Captain Marshall's admonishment that the Germans had ears everywhere, I waited until we were seated in the restaurant before I murmured, "I think I learned Captain Marshall's real name. He might be Herr Rickard." I was sure the clink of dishes and the rumble of voices would hide anything I said.

"How did you learn that?" Redmond asked.

When I told him, he nodded. "You learned more from the brother than we did. He refuses to speak to us."

"I'm going to call him at the library in a day or two. I'll see what else I can find out. Now, do you know Herr Rickard?"

"I know the name from the list of German military attachés. He's also housed in Number Seven, Carlton House Terrace. We only have a copy of his passport photo. No height mentioned."

I'd pictured all of the Germans living in that row. "Manfred didn't live there. Why not?"

"Number Seven is basically a barracks. The clerks live in mansion blocks or residential hotels in the city. Very convenient for work."

"Is it convenient to the docks where Manfred's body was found?"

"Yes. And Denis was there the night he died. Probably before he saw Langston the last time."

"And you've known this how long without telling me?"

"Not long."

"I need to tell Derek. See if he can think of any other details of that meeting."

"Why is he Derek, and I'm Captain Redmond?"

I took a bite of dinner to give myself time to consider my conflicting emotions. I'd love to call him by his first name, but I wasn't sure I could trust him. Not that he lied to me. It was more his sins of omission. After I swallowed, I said, "Perhaps someday you'll be Adam."

He smiled at my words. "I'll go with you to speak to Langston."

"Tomorrow after work."

"Have you forgotten what tomorrow is? The opening of Parliament. I'm afraid I'm going to be rather tied up."

I pictured him doing something heroic and dangerous. A little flutter of pride and admiration sped my pulse. "The day after, then. After Reggie left the restaurant with Derek, he could have taken a taxi to Manfred's, received the papers, taken another taxi to Derek's to get the book, and then—well, we know he dressed for the evening. We know he went to the theater." My imagination wouldn't take me any further.

"It wasn't far, and if he didn't know what Manfred was going to hand him, Denis might have walked over. Once he saw it, I think he would have taken a taxi away from there in a hurry."

"Yes. It would have taken Reggie a few minutes to accept whatever Manfred wanted to pass on to him. He didn't approve of theft for any reason."

"We can be sure he overcame his scruples this time," Redmond said in a dry voice.

"Can we? Could Reggie have been murdered after he

refused to play any part in whatever this is?" I stared at Redmond, horrified at my thoughts.

He held my gaze. "Was he killed not for what he did, but what someone suspected he did? That seems unlucky in the extreme."

We were quiet the rest of the meal. I was picturing Reggie trying to accept stolen property over his very strong personal objections. Whatever this secret document was, it had to be a doozy. Or he had refused it, and as Redmond said, been extremely unlucky.

Except for Redmond's comments on our fair autumn night, our walk to my building was also quiet. By the time Redmond took me up to my flat, saying he was worried about burglars and he wanted to see if I had Derek's book, I was feeling guilty about being bad company.

The moment I opened the door, my phone began to ring. I walked forward to answer it in the scant light slipping in from the landing. Redmond thumped his hand against my wall looking for the light switch.

"Hello?"

"Mrs. Denis. Olivia. Is that you?" Derek gasped out his words.

"Yes. Derek?"

"Yes. Oh, Olivia. I came home to two men ransacking my flat." He sounded close to tears, and then a moan escaped.

I felt like I was spinning back in time to Reggie's killing and my burglary. My throat constricted as I whispered, "Did they hurt you, Derek?"

"They beat me. They tore my home apart. Oh, Olivia, it's awful."

"Have you called the police?"

At this point, Redmond was standing by my shoulder,

trying to hear the conversation.

"No. They warned me not to."

"Nonsense. Call the police. I'm on my way over."

"But Olivia—"

"Call them, Derek. I'll be there soon." I hung up and grabbed Redmond by the sleeve. "Let's go."

CHAPTER SEVENTEEN

I SWUNG Redmond around to push him out my door. When he resisted and put on the brakes, I told him what had happened. Then he rushed downstairs with me on his heels, passing the elevator going up. He flagged down a cab within seconds and we were on our way.

The police were already there when we arrived. I rushed past them while Redmond commanded the attention of the officers in the lobby. They were questioning the doorman whose bloodied head was half-hidden by a towel.

I made it up to Derek's floor before I was stopped by a constable. "Miss. You can't go in there."

"How is Derek? Is he all right?"

"He's talking to the sergeant, miss."

"He called me and said someone had broken in and beaten him. I'm going in to see him." I dodged around the constable and stepped carefully through the debris to find Derek in his destroyed parlor. "Are you all right?"

Despite bruises rising on his face, a bloody nose, and scraped knuckles and hands, he nodded.

"And you are?" the detective asked.

"Olivia Denis. My husband was recently murdered and my flat was also torn apart. You have a report on it."

This interested the square-shaped man enough that he walked up to me and looked me over. "So you think these events are related?"

"Yes, I do."

"Did they take anything in your burglary?"

"No."

"That's what Mr. Langston claims, too." Disbelief dripped from every syllable.

"If we knew what the burglar was looking for, we'd have a better idea if anything were missing from this mess." I walked over to Derek and put a hand on his shoulder. "Do you need to go to hospital?"

"No. How did you survive this, Olivia?" His words came out as a groan.

"I didn't come home to be beaten by thugs. All I had to do was put my place back together. Do you want me to help with cleaning this up?"

He gave me a wan smile. "Perhaps tomorrow. Right now I just want to curl up in a tight ball and pretend this never happened."

Redmond strode in, took one look at Derek, and said, "You need a slug of brandy. Where is it? Kitchen?"

"It's in a puddle on the kitchen floor with pots and pans and tea leaves."

"Olivia, wait here with Langston. I'll be back in a bit." Redmond turned and marched out of the flat, leaving the detective in open-mouthed surprise.

"Who was that?"

"Captain Redmond, British Army," I told the policeman. "Are you going to check for fingerprints?"

"They wore gloves, Olivia. Leather gloves. And masks," Derek told me.

I said to the detective, "Then I'll get out of your way and start cleaning up the kitchen, if that's all right with you."

"You're a dear. Thank you," Derek said when the officer didn't reply.

From the experience of cleaning up my own kitchen, I had a plan. Pots and pans were shelved, china was washed or swept into the dustbin, and I was mopping the floor when Redmond stuck his head in from the hall. "Any glasses in one piece?"

I handed him one from the cabinet. Then I dumped the dirty mop water down the drain and returned to the parlor.

The police were gone and one corner of the room was now picked up enough to move around in. Derek was sitting with a glass of brandy clutched in both hands. Redmond leaned with one elbow on the mantel, staring through the wall opposite.

I sat across from Derek. "What's our next step?"

Derek shook his head forlornly. Redmond ignored me.

"Does anyone but the three of us know you lent Reggie the book?"

"No."

"When you finish your drink, why don't the three of us go over to my place and see if we can find it?"

"Can't hurt." Redmond pulled away from the mantel and headed out the door.

Derek and I scrambled into our jackets and pulled on gloves and hats as we followed him down the stairs. When we reached the lobby, the doorman, who still sported a white bandage on his forehead, said, "Blimey. You got the worst end of that fight."

"Thank you for your help in getting the police," Derek said stiffly.

The doorman blushed, and once we got into a taxi, I asked, "Didn't he call for help?"

"Not until they turned on him."

"I'm glad you're all right," I told Derek. Redmond was still ignoring us, looking past the driver's head at the oncoming headlights.

Once we reached my flat, I went into the kitchen and put together an ice-packed towel for Derek's face. When I returned I heard Redmond say, "You're sure he left your flat with the book in his possession."

"Completely sure." Derek winced as he put the cloth against his cheek.

"Do you have any idea of where he went after dinner? A street? A neighborhood?"

Derek slumped even more than before. "None. If I'd known what was to happen, I'd have pressed him to tell me."

We began a search of every book we could find. There was no *Far from the Madding Crowd*.

We ended our quest in the parlor. Derek and I dropped into chairs while Redmond paced.

"There aren't many people Reggie could have left the book with. Someone in his office. Sir John, had he been in London. Do either of you know of anyone else?" I asked.

Redmond shook his head.

Derek said, "He had his family, acquaintances from work, and a few old classmates. That's how Reggie and I met. I don't think there was anyone else in his life."

"What about a club?" Redmond asked.

I was beginning to see a way forward. "He belonged to the Corinthian. He might have stopped that night and left the book behind. Captain, will you check there?"

He nodded.

"Derek, can you get in touch with your classmates? See if Reggie stopped by to see anyone and left your book with them? Don't mention anything else, just that you lent Reggie a book. You've checked and I don't have it and you'd like it returned if anyone is in possession of it."

"I'll say it's part of a set. And you, Olivia?"

"I have a plan. I'll check with the men from his office—"

"You realize in some cases we'll be talking to the same people. How do you want to split this up?" Derek asked.

"He's known some of the men from his office since public school?" If I'd known that, I hadn't paid any attention.

"Yes. Hawthorn, Chambers, Fielding, and Babcock all went to the same school that Reggie and I did. We weren't close, since we were in different years with little in common. I remember Fielding loved Germany."

Could he be a closet Nazi? His wife was the daughter of a high-ranking one. "Did the rest of you have political interests?"

"Not really. Chambers was always doing card tricks, Reggie was busy finding a way to sneak off to the theater, Hawthorn was out on the sports grounds, and I had my nose in a book. I don't remember what Babcock was up to. He was younger than the rest of us. Scrawny little kid."

"I suppose it won't make any difference if our efforts overlap. Captain, have you—?"

Redmond whirled around to stare at me, finally paying attention to the conversation going on around him. "You have a plan? No, Livvy. This isn't a game. These people have killed two men and beaten up another. There's nothing to keep them from killing you."

"What do you think their goal is?" I asked. "It certainly isn't murdering me. I'm not that important to them."

"War. Sabotage. Treason. If you get in their way—"

"Sabotage?" So that's what had been worrying Redmond.

"You think Manfred passed on plans for sabotage to Reggie?"

"Possibly. And if anyone in the German embassy is involved, you'll be dead long before you discover what they've planned." He glared at me, and I felt my enthusiasm dim.

"All I want is to find out who killed Reggie. And I believe it was the traitor in his office. Either one of the men who went with him to the theater or someone who knew their plans and waited outside. They'd be the only ones who knew where Reggie would be at that precise time."

"You think Reggie found out the identity of the traitor before anyone else in the government?" Redmond asked.

"Yes. He was well positioned for the task. Good Lord. It might even be Reggie's boss, Sir George Rankin." Air leaked out of my lungs as I revisited that possibility. "His wife travels for her health. That must cost him plenty."

Redmond frowned. "Even if you're right that it's someone from his office, someone you know, the traitor is now a murderer. It's easier to kill the second time. Or a third."

"I'll be subtle. And I'll tell you what I learn. What could go wrong?" Even as I said it, I felt myself tempting fate.

"Plenty. If you're wrong about the killer's identity, you have to remember these Germans are ruthless. They've been sent over here on a mission. Either make us allies or make preparations to conquer us."

Impossible. I couldn't believe it. "The Germans at the embassy are diplomats. Just as the men in Reggie's office in Whitehall are diplomats. If the Germans are trying to make us allies, they wouldn't go around killing people. You're talking complete rot."

"I wish. These German diplomats, as you call them, are

consorting with thugs and criminals known to the police. Some of their diplomats are themselves thugs. That's probably who tore Langston's flat apart."

I stared at Redmond, unable to believe diplomats could be involved with criminals. Reggie certainly wouldn't. My father probably wouldn't. Well, maybe.

"There's a leak in Whitehall and it's probably in Denis's office. We've known that for months, but we can't find the traitor. We've followed the German diplomats around, and learned that besides the thugs, they've been meeting with some politically untrustworthy characters. Oswald Mosley, for starters. Unfortunately, we haven't yet uncovered a secret meeting with one of our diplomats." Redmond's face tightened with anger.

"That doesn't mean Reggie didn't discover which of his coworkers was passing secrets to the Nazis."

"It's possible. It's also possible whoever it is killed him. Olivia, this is dangerous."

Derek said, "I agree it's dangerous, but I'm going to follow Olivia's directions in an effort to help. I think you should at least consider it."

I jumped in. "I've been invited to a party at Edward and Carol Hawthorn's this Friday evening. You need to spread the story that you're Reggie's cousin so you can come with me. I plan to ask about the book there."

"I've been working as an aide to General Lord Walters, at least officially, for a few months now. How do you think I found myself at the party at the German embassy last Friday? Deputizing for him. And yes, I've started telling people that I'm Reggie's cousin."

"Then you're welcome to come to the party with me." I turned to Derek. "You'll excuse me if I make you sound very rude about the loss of that book?"

He shrugged. "Whatever helps."

I went out to the kitchen and brought back more ice for Derek's bruised face. He handed me the soggy tea towel with the remnants of ice in it and I returned the dripping mess to the kitchen.

When I came back into the parlor, Derek said, "This is very kind of you."

"You needed help. And Reggie dropped us both into this." How I wished he hadn't.

"He didn't mean to, Olivia," Derek quickly admonished me.

"I know. I just meant it wasn't any fairer to you than it was to me. I know it's not Reggie's fault. It's the fault of whoever killed him and beat you up and tore apart our flats." I realized I was pacing the floor and stopped, only to begin wringing my hands.

My opinions criticized by Derek. My efforts belittled by Redmond. Ordinarily, this wouldn't have bothered me. Tonight, I was tired and frustrated at my lack of success and more than a little scared. Derek's burglary brought back every fright I'd had since Reggie was killed. Redmond had now listed all the dangers and I was terrified.

Redmond held my hands between his. "Can I do anything for you?"

I shook my head, unable to speak without crying or screaming. I felt like everything that had happened was crashing down on me and I had no strength left.

Redmond guided me into a chair and set a glass of brandy between my hands. "I'll take you to the party on Friday and we'll see what we can learn. Langston, are you ready to share a cab back to your flat?"

He rose. "Thanks for the ice, Olivia. Try to get some rest." He took the tea towel out to the kitchen.

"You too, Derek." Then I gave Redmond a weak smile. "Thank you."

Everything that had happened seemed to take its toll on my nerves all at once. I managed to keep my composure until they had left and I locked and bolted the door behind them. Then I rushed into my bedroom, threw myself on the bed, and fell asleep as tears streamed down on my pillow.

* * *

The next day, 26 October, was the State Opening of Parliament. I became part of the crowd as I made my way to work. Jane, along with every photographer the *Daily Premier* could scrape up, would spend the day out on the parade route and lurking about Parliament. Reporters were speaking to every source they could think of.

I thought the pageantry would be anticlimactic after the coronation just a few months before. Reggie, using his position, had procured us a special viewing spot for that spectacular procession. I'd enjoyed the perks that came with our marriage. Now I found myself at the newspaper on typing duty for the day. Fortunately, after a few weeks working for the *Daily Premier*, my copy was no longer terrible.

When I finally left the building that night, my fingers aching, I saw a dark sedan loitering by the curb near the door. Redmond's warnings struck home. If I disappeared now, no one would miss me until the next morning, and by then I might be dead.

With the spectacle over, the streets were surprisingly empty. I might be overly cautious, but I was scared. I quickly flagged down a taxi and quietly cursed the cost as I kept glancing out the back window.

The dark sedan stayed right behind us, not hiding the fact they were tailing me. "Is that a friend of yours, miss, in that car behind us?"

"No. It's no one," I lied.

"Here now. I don't want any trouble. Maybe you should get out." He started to change lanes, cutting off a lorry, to reach the curb.

"No. There won't be any incidents as long as there are witnesses. Just take me straight to my address. Then I'll jump out of your cab and run indoors. The doorman will see I'm safe then." I hoped so. Sutton took so many tea breaks.

The cabbie dropped me by the building's front door, tires squealing from the car behind us. I paid the driver before I jumped out. Then I dashed to the entrance, my purse banging against my knees.

Footsteps ran behind me. For once, Sutton was there to open the door. I dashed inside and looked through the glass doors. A man, muffled up in a scarf with his coat buttoned up and his hat pulled low, walked in right behind me. He stood frighteningly close as he said, "Where is it, Mrs. Denis?" His accent was East End. His nose was bent and flat from breaks. He had to be one of the English thugs Redmond had mentioned.

"Where is what?"

"You know. Don't play dumb. We know you have it."

I kept backing up. "Then you know more than I do. What do you want?"

"The letter. Where did you hide it?" He grabbed my arm with a meaty fist.

"What letter? I didn't hide any letter. And who are you?" I moved to pull down his scarf to see his face, but he struck me. I fell onto the floor, my cheek burning.

"Now see here!" I looked up to see Sutton confronting the man, a length of lead pipe in his hand ready to strike.

The man pushed by Sutton and raced out of the building.

Sutton was helping me up as we heard an engine race away. "Are you all right?"

I suspected I'd have an angry bruise, but nothing felt broken. "Yes. Thank you. That was quick thinking."

"I try not to let too many people know I keep that at my desk. Do you want me to call the police?"

I remembered Redmond's warning the night before and the beating Derek received. Then I pictured the demands of my father that I move home. "No. They must have mistaken me for someone else."

I didn't draw a deep breath until I locked and bolted the door of my flat behind me.

I called Redmond's number and left a message. He called back in a few minutes.

"I had a car follow me the whole way home tonight," I told him. I didn't try to hide the hysteria lurking in my voice. "It was waiting outside the building when I left work."

"Did someone try to grab you?" His voice sounded lethal.

"I took a cab from in front of the paper and came straight home. The car followed us the whole way. When I got out and ran inside the building, a man followed me in and demanded to know where I'd hidden the letter."

"Did you get a good look at him?"

"No. He was all covered in a hat and coat and scarf. Sutton came at him with a pipe and he fled."

"Good for Sutton. Are you all right?"

"Yes." Relatively. "The man was English. East End accent. A real brute."

"You noticed all that. Good girl."

The phrase annoyed me. "Don't be patronizing."

"I'm not. I don't want to see you hurt. I'm glad you took precautions to stay safe. I can't come by to take you to dinner. Too much to do after opening Parliament. Do you have anything to eat in your flat?"

"Of course." Did he think I was completely helpless?

"Good. Take care of yourself."

He rang off before I could say good-bye.

CHAPTER EIGHTEEN

THE NEXT morning, I was back on the society desk opening announcements. Fortunately, that put me in close proximity to a telephone and a reason to use it in search of more details on bouncing babies and blushing brides. No one would notice if I called a library.

After a minute, Hans Manfred came on the line.

"It's Olivia Denis. I spoke to you Monday about my husband and your brother. Now, what do you know about what your brother was involved with?"

"I read your husband's obituary. It said he died of an accident." His tone sounded cautious.

"I'm sure your brother's did, too."

A grunt of agreement. Then, he said, "Friedrich was my younger brother. I wanted him to stay here. Not to go back to Germany. Already they were suspicious of him."

"Why?"

"It doesn't matter. His posting was over. He decided to take something so your government would allow him to stay. So they'd be grateful to him."

"Why do you believe Schreiber and Rickard were his killers?"

"We shouldn't be talking on the telephone. They could be listening over the lines."

"Why do you think they're his murderers?" I pressed.

A sigh. "They are thugs. Hoodlums. SS officers. They take care of people who are problems." I heard a small noise. "I can't talk now."

"Can you meet me at noon?"

"There's a tea shop one street over from the library. The Bluebird. At noon." He was whispering now.

"All right."

He hung up without saying good-bye.

Short on time, I took a taxi to the tea shop and waited outside in the sunshine. At ten after, I became impatient and started to walk toward the library. A wide alley opened onto the street from the direction of the library. I glanced along it to see an ambulance and some bobbies.

Fearing the worse, I turned down the alley. A bobby stopped me after a few steps. "I'm afraid you can't go down there, miss."

The hairs on the nape of my neck stood up. "There's been an accident?"

"A robbery that went wrong. You be careful how you go, miss."

"You haven't caught the robber?"

He shook his head.

I tried to glance around him as a flashbulb went off, lighting up the area. "I was supposed to meet a Mr. Manfred at the tea shop. He's late. It's not him, is it?"

The bobby's shocked expression told me before he said, "You'll need to speak to my guv'nor."

There went my lunch hour. I admitted who I was and said I was doing a follow-up interview on the library with Hans Manfred. This detective was a carbon copy of the one who hadn't investigated Reggie's death: overworked, tired, and jaded. He took down my story, assured me it was

Manfred, and allowed me to leave. I knew he wouldn't follow up.

I saw no point in telling him about the attack on me the night before or my suspicion someone had overheard our phone conversation.

In the taxi on the way back to the newspaper, I mourned a man I barely knew and wondered what Manfred could have told me about the document everyone seemed so intent on retrieving. Now I'd never know.

I returned in time to go with Jane to the opening of an exhibit of Roman artifacts put on by the Italian embassy for the benefit of a charity. A little makeup hid the bruise from the night before enough that Miss Westcott didn't hesitate to send me on this assignment. I found the choice of charity, a cycling competition, odd, but the event was well attended by embassy wives and antiquity-loving locals. Perhaps it was the excellent red wine that was the draw.

Jane, with her cameras, was obviously with the press, but I was dressed to blend in as a guest in an autumn russet-colored dress and jacket with a navy hat, belt, shoes, and purse. Since her role was obvious, I had her carry my string bag as well. We presented our tickets and snagged our wine glasses. "This is good," Jane said, tasting her wine.

"Don't be so surprised. It's Italian, and as they're putting on this show, they want to serve the best. Oh, dear."

"What is it?"

"The flashy bottle blonde over there. Claire deLong. I'd rather she didn't see me."

"Not a fan of yours?"

"I'm not a fan of hers. I'm surprised she's here. There aren't enough men around." She was dressed to attract them, nonetheless. Her navy dress was just that much too tight and low cut, and her heels that much too high. The veiled visor hat was, in my opinion, just a ploy to appear demure. That might not be an opinion I could put in the paper, but I did have the right to consider her too tacky to mention in my article.

"Pull your claws in and go do your job," Jane advised before finishing off her glass.

I scanned the room. "I see Frau von Ribbentrop over there by that frieze. I don't know the woman she's talking to."

"The Countess of Cheltenham. Hold this while I get a photo." Jane handed me her glass while she approached her quarry. She called out, "Smile, ladies," and a flash of light caught the two dour-looking women.

The wife of the Italian ambassador was much happier to have her picture taken with clusters of invitees. While Jane was busy, I set down her glass on a passing tray and walked over to Frau von Ribbentrop. "Enjoying the collection?"

"Yes. Some of these pieces are lovely."

Good. That could be used in the society pages. I pressed on. "Has the Italian government put on this display of antiquities in Germany yet?"

She pulled her fur stole tighter around her shoulders. "Last year, they put together a far larger show in Berlin to coincide with the Olympics. Of course, we had a grander space, more opulent, in which to hold it. We have an arena worthy of a truly magnificent show. There are a number of grand pieces missing from here," she finished with a sniff.

I looked around the two-hundred-year-old marble temple and wondered how any location could be a grander setting for this show. I wasn't supposed to enter into a disagreement with the people I should be interviewing, but I couldn't resist. I was proud of my heritage. "I've always thought this is a well-proportioned classical gallery. And the Italian government has sent a lovely display of antiquities."

"That's the problem with the British. They have no sense of grandeur. And don't think the Italians have sent the best of their collection to share with you." Frau von Ribbentrop sneered and walked away.

I had a description of her outfit and a quote I could use for the paper, along with the assurance that the wife of the German ambassador hated the British. I saw the Countess of Cheltenham talking to the Duchess of Tayle and strolled over in their direction.

"My dear, she is so full of herself," the countess said. For a moment, I was afraid she was talking about me. Then I realized she hadn't noticed me.

"She's not as bad as her husband. And I've heard it said he wants to come back as our overseer once we sign an alliance with them. Make Britain a colony of Germany? Whatever are they thinking?"

"We'd never do that. Just imagine," the countess said. "Curtsying to that woman as if she were the queen."

"I've heard the government—" The duchess stopped and glanced at me as if I were a malingering servant. "Yes?"

"Your Grace. My lady." I gave them a deep curtsy. "The antiquities are lovely, aren't they?"

I got good descriptions of their dresses that I sketched into my notebook while standing behind a particularly large piece of ancient sculpture. I could use their quotes for my article. But now I had a question about what I'd just heard. What was the government doing about the German desire to be our masters?

I talked to a few of the more illustrious guests at the exhibit's opening and thanked the Italian ambassador's wife for arranging to send the lovely statues to London for a showing, gathering quotes as I went. I stopped once as I toured the exhibit and jotted more notes. Finished with my last quarry, I headed toward the huge entrance where I'd arranged to meet Jane. I'd almost reached her when Claire deLong stepped into my path.

"I wondered why you were here," she said in her loud, grating American accent.

"I wondered the same." Already we were attracting attention. A little circle was beginning to form around us. Women appeared to talk to other attendees, and while not looking directly at us, endeavored to eavesdrop on our conversation. This had to be because of Claire deLong. I never attracted attention.

"You work for that dusty little rag, the *Premier*."

My temper flashed. The *Daily Premier* wasn't a rag. They tried to be truthful on the news pages. Society pages had always been for self-advertisement. However, I didn't want this crowd knowing I was here specifically for the paper. Claire deLong was noticed wherever she went, and the circle around us was drawing more spectators.

Might as well give them a good show. "We all have a day off on occasion. Even you must. You're out before the sun set."

"It's not nice to be catty, Mrs. Denis."

"But it's so much simpler than having to keep all the lies straight, isn't it, *Mrs*. deLong?" Out of the corner of my eye, I saw Jane nod to me and walk outside. With a smile, I strode past that odious creature and left the building.

Jane had already flagged down a taxi and climbed in. I slid in after her. I scribbled more notes for my story as we maneuvered through the late afternoon traffic.

Once we were back at the *Premier* building, I went upstairs to write up my notes on the showing and hand them in to Miss Westcott before going to Mr. Colinswood's office. As usual, he was behind his paper-strewn desk. He barely looked up when I knocked. "Come."

"I've picked up a story, or gossip really, about an offer to make Britain a colony of Germany, or a protected state, or something, and our government's plans to respond to this offer." As I tried to articulate what I'd overheard, I realized how fantastic it sounded.

"Where did you hear that?"

My cheeks heated as I admitted, "It was a duchess and a countess talking at a reception for the show of Roman antiquities put on by Mussolini's government."

He bit his lip, no doubt in an effort not to laugh at me. "Now there's a source."

"I'm not saying it's gospel. I'm passing this on as a lead for the news reporters." When I realized Colinswood couldn't look me in the eye, I added, "You know about this already."

"We've also heard rumors. From more reliable sources, I might add."

"What have you heard?"

He sighed and tossed down his pencil. "Von Ribbentrop is pushing for Britain and Germany to sign a bilateral alliance. Rather like the one they signed with Italy."

"We wouldn't, would we? Is this just von Ribbentrop's idea or is Hitler behind it?"

"I can't imagine the ambassador would try to work out an alliance without orders from Herr Hitler. Just like I can't figure out why von Ribbentrop has been talking to us about getting their old colonies back. Surely a German Africa isn't part of Hitler's master plan. It doesn't make sense."

Colinswood shook his head.

"What is our government saying?"

"Privately, they think they're dealing with madmen. Publicly, they're trying to negotiate an agreement that keeps Hitler satisfied without letting him take over half of Europe or that encourages him to start another war."

I leaned on the door frame. "It always boils down to that, doesn't it? Keeping Hitler happy so we don't have another war."

"We can't afford it. Not in money. Not in lives. You probably don't remember much of the last war, but I tell you, it devastated us without bringing the fighting to Britain. Think of the technological advances since then. If there's another war, our country will be at the center of the destruction."

Not something I wanted to consider. "I was little, but I remember how happy people were on Armistice Day. I believe I actually saw my father smile. He was sent home from the front early because there was no one to take care of my mother and me. She died a few months later, an accidental overdose compounded by influenza, but a strong wind would have carried her away before then."

I shook away my memories. "But that's neither here nor there. I suppose what you're trying to tell me is the government is walking a fine line with Hitler, trying to keep him in check without getting him so angry he starts a war. And the newsroom is well aware of what's going on and doesn't need to hear rumors picked up by the society page."

He leaned back in his chair. "Ordinarily, that would be true. However, Sir Henry Benton hired you for your access. Whatever you hear, we want to hear."

I nodded. "I'm going to a Foreign Office party on Friday.

If I hear anything, I'll pass it on."

As I turned to walk out into the noisy newsroom with clattering typewriters, ringing telephones, and men's loud voices, I heard Mr. Colinswood say, "Good job on picking up on that rumor."

My step was lighter as I walked away.

* * *

Redmond took me to dinner again at another busy chop house, this one in Holborn. Once we had our dinner and were sure no one was eavesdropping, he leaned forward and slid a small, square photo toward me.

"That's the man I know as Captain Marshall," I said in a small voice. The icy gaze in an otherwise boyish face was unforgettable.

"That's Rickard's passport photo. I heard about Hans Manfred. Tell me what he said about Rickard."

I told him, and then said, "He said he would tell me more, but Manfred was killed on his way from the library to meet me for lunch."

"Meet you? Good grief. You need to be careful. Hans Manfred was stabbed twice. A professional job made to look like a robbery by taking his watch and emptying his wallet."

"Germans again?"

Redmond nodded. "Or English thugs for hire. Manfred wouldn't tell us anything about his brother. I wonder what he would have told you if he had lived."

"He sounded so uneasy. Frightened." Sickened, I fell silent. I couldn't believe there was a secret worth so many lives.

"I went by the Corinthian Club," Redmond said after finishing some of his dinner. "Denis left nothing there, including Langston's book."

Another avenue blocked.

"I don't want you to look around or worry, but we were followed here from the *Premier* building. Someone is building quite a dossier on us."

I was suddenly cold despite my warm and cheery surroundings. "Germans?"

"Probably. You haven't come to anyone else's attention, have you?" His smile was brief.

My glare was longer. "I hadn't come to anyone's attention until I met you."

He shook his head, then speared a piece of his dinner with a quick, lethal thrust. "You came to their attention the moment your husband got mixed up in something much bigger than he knew."

If Redmond was trying to scare me, he had succeeded.

CHAPTER NINETEEN

FOR THE REST of the week, I was followed, but at a discreet distance. The evenings were always misty, so I'd put up my umbrella and head for the closest Tube station. I was always aware my "bodyguards" were there lurking beneath their upturned collars and low-brimmed hats, but there were so many men who fit the description I didn't know which ones to fear. When did they plan to strike again?

Nevertheless, their constant presence wore down my nerves.

Friday evening, Redmond came by to take me to the party at the Hawthorns. He wore a new, decidedly well-made evening suit. The single-breasted style with wide lapels drew attention to his broad shoulders and the slimmer cut of his trousers made me discreetly glance at his backside as he walked past me into the flat. Oh yes, the ladies would all thank me for bringing Reggie's cousin along.

I put on my black slant-brim hat and black gloves, picked up my matching purse, and ushered Redmond out the door. We took the lift down and Redmond let Sutton summon a taxi. While we waited, my so-called cousin positioned himself so he could watch the entrance and the street.

The only person to enter the building was the grumpy old lady on the first floor. A taxi stopped and we climbed in, Redmond tipping Sutton outrageously.

"Why so generous?" I asked him as we drove away.

"The tip? Depending on how this case goes, I may need his help. If I tip well, he'll be more likely to remember me and do as I ask. And he did rescue you."

We spent the trip talking about the war in Spain and the upcoming Guy Fawkes celebrations until we pulled up in front of the Hawthorns' detached house in the suburbs at Wimbledon. As we walked up the short cement walk, Redmond said, "Who knows where we'll find a taxi around here."

I had no time to worry about that. I had to face Carol Hawthorn and her disapproving frown. Her expression would freeze in horror when she'd discover I'd brought a man with me. Reggie hadn't yet been dead the requisite time.

With Carol, I wasn't sure there would ever be a requisite time.

Fortunately, it was Edward Hawthorn who opened the door. "Well, hello, Olivia. Glad you could make it."

"I didn't remember that Wimbledon was so lovely. Oh, this is Reggie's cousin, Adam Redmond. He came by to check on me, so I brought him along. He's in an office around Whitehall, too. Maybe you two know each other."

"No. Sorry. But you're welcome. I'm Edward Hawthorn." He held out his hand.

Redmond shook it. "Adam Redmond. I brought a white wine, hope it fits in."

"I'm sure it will. Come on, I'll show you to the kitchen. Carol's around here somewhere, Olivia." Edward led Redmond off to the back of the house, leaving me standing in the front hall.

I opened up the first door I came to and walked into the front parlor, glad I hadn't removed my hat and gloves first.

Everyone stood around a little stiffly, perfectly attired. They had drinks in their hands, and there were dishes of nuts on the doily-covered end tables, but a layer of frost was settling in the room.

"Olivia," Carol said, taking one step toward me and sounding a little too bright. "I'm so glad you could make it."

Mary Babcock rolled her eyes and then winked at me. "We are glad to see you. And you certainly look smart." She rose and walked over to me. Taking my hand as she maneuvered me back into the hall, she said softly, "How are you doing?"

I answered in an equally quiet tone. "His death still wakes me at night." During the day, I kept busy enough that his passing didn't twist my insides too often. "Keeping you in my life has made this easier. Makes me think that Reggie is still remembered by all of you."

I couldn't say, "I'm spying on you for my boss at the newspaper and bringing a spy from Army Intelligence into your midst because someone here is a traitor." Mary would have found that shocking.

Dear, sweet, innocent Mary gave my hand a squeeze and said, "You'll always be welcome. You're a part of this group, no matter what some people say." Behind her, I could hear Carol talking loudly to two couples.

"I'm not welcome tonight?"

"Some people are a little too worried about exactly what stage of mourning you should be in."

"So I shouldn't visit with old friends?" My voice took on a hard tone. "Carol called and invited me."

"Who is he, Livvy?"

"You mean Captain Redmond? This is about him?" At that moment, Redmond sauntered down the hall with Lester,

Mary's husband, and Edward. "Mary," I said loudly, "this is Captain Adam Redmond, Reggie's cousin. He works in the same neighborhood as Lester."

"Right down Whitehall from us as it turns out," Edward said.

Redmond handed me a glass of white wine. "I've heard it's good. Tell me what you think."

At that point, the mood changed and we all began to talk and laugh. A couple of times, I mentioned Reggie borrowed a book from a friend who wanted it returned. Everyone laughed because Reggie was always reading, always borrowing books, and several people found the fact that only one was missing a miracle. No one had seen him with *Far from the Madding Crowd* nor did they have it, including the men in the theater party that night.

I heard someone call "Fielding" and I turned around to see a tanned, dark-haired man I'd met once or twice. Blake Fielding. The new man in the office who'd gone to the theater with the group the night Reggie died.

"I've not had a chance to give you my condolences, Mrs. Denis. He was a good man. I wish Peters and I had talked your husband into walking to the Underground station with us."

I wish they had, too. "Why didn't he?"

"He said he had something to check on first. I thought he was headed back to the office." He shook his head. "We all miss him."

"Do you and David live near each other?"

"Good heavens, no. Different rail lines. We split up as soon as we got inside the station."

I decided to try a shot in the dark. "I was told you went to boarding school with Reggie."

"He was a year ahead of me. Lord, we were so silly then. Reggie's favorite possession was his theater programs." Fielding laughed.

"They stayed his prized collection. He hadn't changed where they were concerned."

A deep blush appeared under his tan.

I wasn't concerned with whether he found Reggie's program collection amusing. "Are you fond of anything from your school days?"

"Not really. I was an admirer of the kaiser back before the war. I don't know if it was his overcoming his withered arm or his blondness. With my dark skin and being so terribly ill with scarlet fever when I returned to England after my early years in India, you can imagine the rumors that flew through the school, that I was a gypsy or an untouchable Hindu. Actually, my mother's Spanish and I got my coloring from her, but you can imagine how cruel boys can be."

I nodded. "They so often are." And then I chanced a shot in the dark. "I imagine the Nazis wouldn't think of you as part of the master race."

Fielding grimaced. "Then let's hope they don't come over here. Some of my happiest memories were hiking in the Black Forest in the late twenties and early thirties, but once the Nazis rose to power... Eck. Swines. They've ruined the place."

"Weren't you posted to Prague? You must have felt surrounded by Nazis there."

"More than you can imagine. They made my life a living hell, but things have just gotten worse since I came home. I almost wish I'd stayed in Prague."

"Have they been threatening you? I know Reggie found them difficult."

"If they were only threatening me, it wouldn't be so

damnable. But my wife—Excuse me, Mrs. Denis." Wincing, he hurried away.

A couple of hours after we arrived, Carol came over to me in the dining room as I put tiny sandwiches on a plate and said, "I didn't know Reggie had a cousin in town, much less working with him."

"Between the difference in their ages and a coolness between the older members of the family, they didn't see much of each other as youngsters. Adam looked Reggie up a while ago and the two became friends as adults." I should have talked this over with Redmond first, but the story wasn't too detailed. "Speaking of youngsters, how are your boys doing?"

"Andrew will be going to Oxford in the fall, following in his father's footsteps, and Mark is captain of his rugby team."

"You must be so very proud of them."

She smiled, and for the first time, I saw a happy, rather than a censorious or cruel, Carol Hawthorn. "I am."

"Does Andrew want to follow his father into the Foreign Service?"

Back came the strained face I often saw on her. "I'm so afraid he won't get the chance. If these warmongers have their way, he'll have to go into the military. I lost a brother to the last war. I don't want to lose a son in another."

"But if it comes down to Hitler coming here, to England, surely—"

She leaned forward, vehement in her half-whispered words. "Hitler has no interest in fighting Britain. Not if we don't interfere with what he does in Europe. He'll leave us alone. He promised."

I leaned back, blinking. "When did he promise that? Everything he's said has been combative."

"Don't believe the English warmongers." Then Carol straightened and raised her voice to a normal pitch. "I need to check on the hors d'oeuvres. Can I get you anything?"

She walked off, leaving me to stand there, puzzled in her wake. *Hitler promised*? If the Hawthorns were Nazi supporters, I had another suspect for the traitor who killed Reggie.

"Mrs. Denis. How are you doing?"

I swiveled around to find Sir George Rankin behind me. "Doing well. Reggie had a wonderful group of coworkers."

"And schoolmates. A lot of these men have known each other a long time."

I was nearly fifteen years Reggie's junior and never paid much attention to who he went to school with. "He went to Oxford, and I suspect at least half of the credentials and ceremonies office staff was there together."

"In the years following the war." When I looked blank, he said, "The earlier classes were nearly obliterated in the war. I'm one of the few from before the war to survive and go to work in the Foreign Ministry." He sighed. "So many lost."

I nodded, unsure how to respond to his statement.

He blinked and then fiddled with his bow tie. "But don't let me keep you from the party. I'm off. Have you seen Edward? I want to thank him for tonight's festivities."

"I think he's in the kitchen. How's Lady Margery?"

"About the same. The doctors say she'll have to travel to the Riviera again this winter."

"I'm sure you'll miss her. It must be difficult."

"For both of us. She's already lining up her companion. I'll have to do my part. And there are ways, no matter what one feels about them."

"Tell her I'm thinking of her." And what ways her

husband found to finance her expensive trip.

He nodded. "Good night. And good luck, Mrs. Denis."

The party was a success, particularly since Carol tended to stint on the appetizers and the guests had brought plenty to drink. And because of their location, we all wandered off in small groups into the late evening chill toward the train station, hoping to get taxis or the final train into town.

As luck would have it, we ended up with David Peters, who lived in the same direction as my flat. David tripped over a couple of cracks in the pavement on the way to the station and burst into song while we waited for a cab to show up. When we piled into the back seat, I was squished between Redmond's broad shoulders and David's boozy breath.

"Nice party," Redmond said.

"You thought sho?" David said, slurring his words. "What did you think about that argument between Hawthorn and Martingale?"

"Which one's Martingale?" Redmond asked.

"The short, square man with the thin wife who kept worrying that the baby was all right. He kept saying to her that his sister was bright enough to take care of a baby for a few hours," I told him. "So why did Paul Chambers separate them?"

"Did Paul tell you how happy he was that Reggie got himself killed? He jumped right into Reggie's spot. Started working on Rankin as soon as he got the word. Don't trust him," David said in a confiding manner, although he didn't bother lowering his voice.

If he was right, not everyone in the department had been as sorry about Reggie's passing as they acted. I added Paul's ambition to his debts as a motive to kill Reggie. But David moved up a spot, too, and he could also be striving to get ahead.

"Rankin?" Redmond asked, watching out the window.

"Sir George Rankin, department head. He was there tonight," I said.

David leaned closer, nearly choking me with his breath. "And he was in talks with the higher-ups as soon as they heard Reggie was shot. They were in a panic that morning. I got in early, but they were there earlier. Running around like fools."

"Why? You don't have access to anything that amazing, do you?" Redmond asked.

Instead of tapping the side of his nose, David stuck his finger in his eye and jerked back. Just as I thought he'd forgotten Redmond's question, he said, "Not the whole department. But a few lucky souls see the secret minutes on foreign affairs from the cabinet."

"Reggie was one," I said.

"Peters is another," Redmond replied.

"I'm not saying a thing. My lips are sealed."

"We're not going to ask you for any secrets, David. We know that would be wrong," I assured him. "But why were Edward and Martingale arguing?"

"Response to an alliance with Germany that von Ribbentrop's pushing. Not supposed to be discussing it." David gave me a superior smile.

"Is there such an agreement?" I asked, still staring at David. I was vaguely aware of a powerful engine passing us on Redmond's side of the car.

"Maybe." David shrugged. "It has its backers in Parliament. Those who are more concerned with the empire than Europe. So—"

"Get down," Redmond shouted and leaped on top of me. I

was shoved forward with my head between my knees.

I couldn't move. Redmond's weight pressed on me as thunder rolled through the cab. I heard breaking glass and brakes squealing. The cab swerved, Redmond's body shoving me against David's with the next blast. All three of us were in a tangle with our knees in each other's faces. A car engine roared as it sped past.

The cab jerked to a halt. "I didn't sign up for this," a man's voice shouted from the front seat. I peeked out in time to see the driver run off, leaving the door open.

Leaving us stranded at the mercy of an assassin.

CHAPTER TWENTY

REDMOND ROSE off me and climbed out of the cab. By the time I had shaken the broken window glass out of my hat, he was in the driver's seat and we were moving again. "Are you all right?" he called back.

"I'm fine. David?"

He sat up, groaning. I didn't see any blood, but he'd taken on a greenish tinge. I scooted away from him in case he became sick.

"No one's hurt. Those were gunshots, weren't they?" I couldn't imagine anything else so loud.

"Yes."

"Why would someone shoot at us?"

"Peters knows government secrets, your husband was murdered for some reason, and I've made a few enemies in my job. I wondered why someone was staying even with us on empty roads. Then I saw the gun barrel." Redmond was racing down the empty streets now, chasing the taillights of the car some distance ahead of us. Air blew through the jagged remains of the windows on the front passenger side and the back where I sat behind him.

Redmond continued to speed down the streets, swerving here and there, as the sedan pulled away from us. I sat forward, holding on to the back of the driver's seat and wishing he'd hurry. David leaned back in the far corner, moaning.

"He's making for the city," I said, excitement filling my voice.

"Yes."

"You'll have to hurry if you want to catch him."

"I know." Redmond sounded as if he were speaking through clenched teeth. "What does he have under the bonnet?"

"It's a Mercedes-Benz 540K with a 5401cc straight eight-cylinder engine," David said without opening his eyes.

"How do you know?"

"I saw it while we were waiting for a taxi. Beautiful machine." David had a smile on his face.

"I'll never catch it in this tug," Redmond said.

"He can't drive this fast once he reaches the bridge. Too much traffic," I told him.

We raced across Putney Bridge. Then Redmond gave a crow of delight. "He's gone down Kings Road. Got you now, you bugger."

We had other cars to contend with, but so did our speedier attackers. Traffic lights forced both cars to stop time and again. Through savvy lane choice and aggressive maneuvers, Redmond soon had us only a few car lengths behind the Mercedes.

I'd never known anyone who could drive so expertly.

He stayed a few car lengths behind, even letting another car get between us. "What are you doing? Aren't you going to catch up to him?"

"And do what? Let's see where he leads us. Try to get his number plate, will you? I have my hands full."

I leaned farther forward, my head next to Redmond's. We stopped at a light, this time in sight of the Mercedes.

"Got it?"

"Got it."

"Then scoot back. You're in my line of sight."

With an outraged huff, I sat back and scrawled the number on my handkerchief with my lipstick. When I looked up again, we were turning left onto Grosvenor Place. Moments later we were on Piccadilly.

"I knew it," Redmond growled.

"Carlton House Terrace?"

"I think that's where they'll lead us. Sloppy of them if they do."

The Mercedes turned in from Pall Mall and we went around the block in time to see them disappear behind the German embassy.

Redmond drove away, whistling.

David Peters sat up, groaning. "Pull over."

Redmond jerked the taxi to the curb. David opened the door and leaned out over the gutter.

When he was finished and had shut the door again, Redmond looked in the rearview mirror and said, "Thanks for not doing that before."

David grinned at me. "It was a close thing. But I knew Livvy would kill me."

I turned away from David, shaking my head. Still breathless from our wild drive, I asked Redmond, "What do we do now?"

"The cab's probably been reported stolen or for speeding. We get out and walk as soon as I can find a less public place to abandon it."

Redmond found a parking spot for the glass-strewn taxi off Charing Cross Road. We brushed glass fragments off our clothes and walked away as if arriving in a windowless cab was an everyday occurrence.

David had sobered up considerably after our mad race through the early morning streets. "I'm getting too old for this drinking and partying. It's time I settled down."

"You just have to find the right girl," Redmond said.

"I thought I had. What a fool I was."

It was the perfect time for me to ask. "David, what happened in Italy?"

"What do you mean?" He sounded guarded and far more sober. I could see him redden in the light from the street lamps.

"The woman and the visa and having to come back to London."

He glanced from me to Redmond and back. "Her name was Sofia. She was beautiful. She was passionate in that Italian way. I loved her." He made a noise deep in his throat. "She was a double-crossing whore."

He kicked at a broken piece of paving. "She told me her brother was being harassed by a German officer in Rome. She wanted a visa for him to get him away to safety, saying she had a cousin here who would give him a job. I gave her the visa. I loved her, but I didn't trust her story. I filled out all the paperwork so they were able to trace him when he reached England. It turned out the German officer was her lover and they worked it out between them to send a spy over here.

"When her so-called brother was picked up after he landed, the German officer came looking for me. Put me in hospital. The officer was Liestran."

"So the whole thing was a plot?"

"Yes. The embassy learned about the beating and my involvement with the lovely Sofia, and that led to my return to England in disgrace. Fortunately, I'd done all the paperwork properly and that saved me. Liestran and Sofia wanted to get a German spy in place as soon as possible. They weren't as careful as they should have been with the information they gave me. Set off red flags in Whitehall."

He glanced directly at me for the first time since I'd asked about Italy. "You think I'm a fool, don't you?"

I laid a hand on his arm. "I think you must have cared for her very much."

David huffed and shook his head. He left us with a wave as he wearily headed on to Baker Street, and Redmond and I continued walking to my building.

Sutton was nowhere to be seen and the front door was unlocked when we arrived. Redmond gestured for me to stay in a corner of the lobby while he looked around. Was the shooter working with someone who'd arrived ahead of us? I watched the empty street and wondered when Redmond would reappear.

A minute later, I heard men's voices and then Sutton clearly saying, "I understand. Women can be such fearful creatures, and her a new widow and all."

As Redmond came out of the back hallway, I glared at him. Fearful? Then I gave the doorman a smile as he appeared with a cup of tea in his hand and said, "Good night, Sutton."

"Good night, ma'am."

"I'll walk you upstairs, Olivia."

Actually, we took the lift. I wondered during the slow progression up if Redmond would kiss me. The elevator was barely big enough for the two of us. We stood facing each other, nearly nose to nose. Despite the tight squeeze, he didn't try to kiss me. I was surprised to find I was disappointed.

I decided my desire to feel Redmond's strong arms around me, to taste his lips, must have been due to the shock from the bullets ripping apart our cab. I knew I couldn't be falling for Captain Redmond. It was too soon after Reggie's death and Redmond wasn't my type.

Was he?

"Thank you, Captain, for rescuing us tonight."

A quick smile crossed his lips. "I'd hardly call it that."

"Don't be so modest. Neither David nor I had any idea what to do until you did it." I was impressed.

"Glad to be of service."

I knew when I was being teased.

Once inside my flat, I took my handkerchief out of my purse. "Can you read my handwriting?"

"Clever. Yes, I can read it. I'll find out tomorrow who the Mercedes belongs to, but I think we can guess."

"And once we find out, then what do we do?"

"Nothing."

"Nothing?" That wasn't what I wanted to hear.

"We can't act against a member of an embassy staff, if we even knew which one. No, it will just be confirmation." He ran the tip of one finger down my nose as he leaned forward. "Don't worry. We've got them under surveillance, and they know it. I suspect Monday there will be a protest lodged over a traffic incident involving one of their cars, and they will promise to look into it. They'll know that we know."

"What good will that do?"

"None that we'll know about, but someone will be warned not to get carried away again and fire shots for intimidation."

I crossed my arms over my chest. "I don't feel intimidated. I feel angry."

"Good. Dinner tomorrow night?"

The offer brightened my mood considerably. "All right."

"I'll pick you up at seven."

The phone rang as Redmond picked up his hat and gloves. He lingered by the door as I answered.

"Olivia, it's Derek. I'm sorry it's so late, but I've been trying to reach you all evening."

"It's fine, Derek," I said, glancing at Redmond. "What can I do for you?"

"I had to let you know. I asked everyone about the book."

"Good. I did, too. Did you learn anything?"

"Yes, but I'm afraid I've done something foolish. I guess it'll be all right. He told me it wasn't what—oh, hold on a moment, someone's at the door."

His words reached my brain an instant too late. "Derek, no. Wait." Panic squeezed my throat. I squeaked as the receiver thudded against something solid. After a moment, I heard something that sounded like a shriek and a moan. Then there was a click and the line went dead.

I hung up, pulled on my gloves, and grabbed my coat. "Come on. Someone's broken into Derek's."

"Again? Every time I bring you home..." Redmond muttered, opening my front door and letting himself be hauled into the lift.

"It sounded like him. And then something that sounded like an attack." The lift crawled down at its usual slow pace. I stomped on the floor in a futile attempt to speed it along.

We finally reached the ground floor, but Redmond stopped me with one hand. "This could be a trap, set up to get you to leave your flat tonight."

"No. It was Derek. He's in trouble. Let's go."

He nodded and led me outside while Sutton flagged

down a cab, but I could tell by the way he watched the pavement and the few passing vehicles that he was being super-vigilant. Once we were in the cab and on our way, I heard him release his breath.

"Did he give you any hint as to who was breaking in?"

"No. He mentioned the book, and saying something about being foolish." Why couldn't the cab go faster? The streets were practically deserted.

We pulled up in front of Derek's building and clambered out. While Redmond paid the cabbie, I rushed to the front door. It was locked. I hammered on it and roused the doorman by the time Redmond arrived at my side.

"Hold your horses. What's the emergency?" the doorman said, shouting through the door.

"We need to see Derek Langston immediately. Has anyone been to see him?" I asked, shoving against the door.

He unlocked it and opened it partway. "Yes. A gentleman was here not ten minutes ago. Why—?"

I pushed past him and ran to the lift, Redmond behind me. We finally reached Derek's floor and turned toward his front door. It was shut, but when Redmond turned the handle, the door opened.

He blocked my view with his shoulder. "Livvy, stay outside." Then he walked in and I peered around his side from the doorway.

Derek was on the floor on his back, blood covering his shirt and leaking onto the floor.

I leaned over the railing by the lift and shouted, "Call the police and an ambulance."

"What?" came back at me from the lobby.

"Call the police and an ambulance." I could hear a few doors opening around me, but no one stepped into my view.

"There's no need for an ambulance," Redmond said directly behind me. I jumped, and he put a hand on my shoulder. "Can you wait here in the hall and make sure no one enters? I need to find out about the man who visited Langston before the police arrive."

I nodded, unable to speak.

Redmond ran down the stairs and I walked over to the doorway. This time Derek's flat hadn't been turned upside down. Nothing was disturbed, not even Derek. He'd been laid out neatly except for all the blood.

Even his phone had been hung up. I'd heard that at the end of the call. No doubt by his killer.

Derek, who'd been murdered for helping me hunt for Reggie's killer. It wasn't fair. I hoped the murderer left a calling card behind this time that would lead to his arrest, because I hadn't a clue to his identity.

No, I had one clue. Derek had spoken to a man he and Reggie had gone to school with about the borrowed book. And Derek felt he'd been foolish as a result.

And whoever the man was, I wanted him to pay.

CHAPTER TWENTY-ONE

I LOOKED AT Derek's phone table, which held only a phone on a doily. Surely he hadn't memorized my phone number. Where did he keep his appointment book with important telephone numbers?

Striding into his parlor, I went straight for his desk. A glance through all the drawers told me there was no appointment book here. Was it taken by his killer?

The sound of voices told me I'd waited too long to get out. I met Redmond and a constable in the doorway to the parlor.

"You shouldn't be in here, miss."

"I know. I made sure no one came in, but as I was feeling faint, I thought I'd better sit down. I didn't want to collapse on the body."

"Go and sit down again, Olivia," Redmond said before the bobby could throw me out.

They remained talking in the hall while I went back to the center of the parlor. If I were a phone book or a diary, where would I be? I saw the constable look in at me from the hall, so I sat down on the sofa.

There was something hard under the cushion, and I absently moved it while I studied the room. My hand felt something like a square, thin book. I pulled it out and glanced through it. Address book and diary in one.

Why had Derek hidden it under a sofa cushion when he'd telephoned me or when he heard someone knocking? Did he think the person outside his door was in his book? And how would I smuggle it out of there?

It wouldn't fit in my tiny purse. My dress coat didn't have pockets, and the dress I'd worn to Carol's party wouldn't let me conceal a handkerchief.

As more voices sounded in the hall, I knew I couldn't spend my time studying it now. I slipped it under the cushion next to me.

I was left alone in the parlor listening to the officers going about their duties. Finally, a detective questioned me and then said I was free to leave.

"Could you ask Captain Redmond to come in here for a moment?"

"Can't do any harm now, I suppose. Redmond."

They passed each other as Redmond stepped in front of me. I slipped out the address book and flashed it at the captain. He frowned for a moment before giving me a hand up in a way that left me holding the book. Then he took it as he slipped it under his evening suit jacket and around to the small of his back.

In that way we got it out of Derek's flat and into a cab. Once in the cab, Redmond said, "What was that about?"

"Why would Derek hide his personal phone book and diary under the sofa cushions when he called me unless his murderer was there?"

"Mmm."

That didn't tell me what Redmond was thinking. I pressed on. "The doorman's description of the man?"

"Muffled up over evening clothes. Didn't look closely. Obviously a gentleman."

"He wasn't curious about why the man was calling so late?"

"When I tipped him well before the police arrived, he told me the man caught him indisposed, which I suspect means napping, and tipped him well for his trouble. He didn't see him leave, just heard him, a minute or two later. Probably gone back to his bunk."

"It was definitely a man?"

"According to him."

"I hope Derek's appointment book will help us." It had to. I was desperate.

"I'll take it back with me and study it."

"No. Hand it over. Derek was my friend, and Reggie's, and I want to go through it first."

"You wouldn't know what to look for."

His scoffing tone grated on my ears. "Don't be too sure of that." Still, he had possession of it, and I didn't see a way to remove it from beneath his jacket without a tussle. Since we were in a taxi in our evening finery, it would have been scandalous behavior. "Perhaps we should work on it together. Say, tomorrow afternoon?"

He grinned. "I'll be over at three."

* * *

I came back from the grocers and the chemist the next morning, ready to attack the housecleaning. I was still finding the odd thing left over from my break-in under the furniture. I needed mindless scrubbing to work off my nervous energy from the horrors of the night before.

As soon as I walked in, the phone began to trill. I set down my purchases in the hall as I shut the door with my rear, catching the phone on the third ring. "Hello?"

"Olivia, it's Carol Hawthorn. I just heard the terrible

news."

She didn't know Derek. "What—what's happened?"

"Why, you were shot at last night after you left our party, weren't you? I had no idea we had gangsters in Wimbledon."

How had she heard? "I don't think they were gangsters, Carol."

"Well then, who were they?"

I was about to answer when some of Carol's statements from the previous night sounded in my head. Words I'd not thought to pass on to Redmond because of all the excitement. I decided to be noncommittal. "Well, not gangsters. That's beyond belief."

"There are too many Americans in this country, bringing their music and their wild ways and their gangsters with them."

"Rather like that Wallis Simpson woman?"

I could picture Carol gnashing her teeth. She had been a big supporter of King Edward and his pro-German sentiments, but she'd made unfavorable comments about his wife and her brash American ways. "I think we all believe she's been a disaster for our country."

I smiled at the telephone. "I won't argue with that."

"Anyway, I'm coming up to town and I wondered if you wanted to go to lunch. I've been remiss in not checking on you more since you lost Reginald."

I bit my lip, knowing how much Reggie hated being called by his given name. And how little I wanted her "checking" on me. What was she up to? She'd certainly had little time for me before he died. "Lunch would be lovely."

"Say, noon at the Aerated Bread Company on Oxford Street."

"That sounds nice, Carol. Thank you."

I rang off, knowing one good thing would come of this. I had an excuse not to clean today.

I walked to the restaurant, enjoying our autumn weather with my umbrella opened, my coat collar turned up, and cursing every splash on my stockings. I arrived, shaking water off me, to find Mary had joined Carol.

Mary leaped up from the table and gave me a hug with warmth I felt down to my bones. Carol's handshake was stiff, but she made the effort and had invited Mary. I shouldn't be so critical of her.

The tea was already on the table and I fixed myself a cup, savoring the heat as it slid down my throat. Mary and I chose the meat pie, while Carol shuddered at the idea and ordered a chop.

After we ran out of remarks on the menu, the weather, and Carol's party, lunch arrived and we all dug in as if we were starving. As time drew on, the silence became uncomfortable.

Mary broke it by saying, "I'm glad you had to come up here this afternoon, Carol. We never seem to have time to do this."

"And after I got that terrible news this morning about Olivia, I just had to call."

"What horrible news?" Mary looked from one of us to the other, worry etched in lines around her forehead and mouth.

"Why, Olivia was shot at last night. She and David Peters and Reginald's cousin. What was his name again?"

"Adam Redmond. How did you hear about it?"

"Edward said the police came to our house this morning, wanting to know what time you left and if we'd seen or heard anything."

The cabbie who'd run after his windows were blown out

must have gone to the nearest police station. He'd picked us up at the Underground station and the police somehow traced us back to the Hawthorns.

"Livvy, what happened?" Mary grabbed my hand.

"Some crazy person fired into the cab we were in. He blew out two of the windows and frightened us all. The cabbie ran away. Redmond drove us back to town. He appears to be more accustomed to being shot at. I guess it comes of being in the army." Now that I thought about it, he was rather brave.

"How could you stay in that taxi? I'd have been terrified." Mary's eyes widened and she gripped my hand harder.

"Whoever shot at us was long gone, and we still had to get home. The taxi seemed like the best way." I took a bite with my free hand as I glanced at Carol. She was listening politely, not appearing affected at all by my story.

And it was a story. I made no mention of the Germans, the Mercedes, or the car chase.

"Why did they shoot at you?" Mary asked.

"That's a good question. Carol thinks it was gangsters."

"Definitely. This goes on in America all the time."

Mary looked at Carol in amazement. "But why shoot at Livvy? She doesn't look like Jimmy Cagney."

"Thanks for that, Mary." She'd almost made me laugh, and nothing had been humorous since we left the party the night before.

She let go of my hand, apparently comforted by my smile.

"Maybe they were looking for someone in a cab, and you were the first one they saw," Carol said.

As a suggestion, it was terrible. "Even Americans know how many taxis are on the London streets. And why look for this person in Wimbledon, unless you're living in a nest of crime, Carol, and haven't told us."

Temper flared behind her eyes for a moment, but then she settled in her chair and smiled. "I'll have to look at my neighbors more closely. One of them must have been the target."

"Good luck finding out which one," I told her.

"That's the job for the police," she admonished me. "Otherwise, they might shoot at one of us next time."

"It sounds like fun. Sneaking around Wimbledon, trying to find out who the target is that Livvy was mistaken for," Mary said. Her fear over, I guessed she was now considering taking on an ill-conceived investigation.

Carol and I both cried, "No."

"It might have been David Peters or Adam Redmond they were shooting at, not Olivia," Carol suggested.

"Oh. That does make it more difficult." Mary looked deflated.

"Why would someone shoot at Peters or Redmond?" I asked, looking at Carol.

"Said that way, it sounds political," Mary said.

"Unless one of them is having an affair with a married woman," Carol said, her thin eyebrows arched.

I shook my head, but I had to admit to myself that I didn't know either one well enough to be certain.

"David Peters had that unfortunate affair with the Italian girl before he came back to London. The girl was also having a tryst with a German officer. He and Peters came to blows. That's how the Foreign Office found out he'd been doing favors for the girl."

"Really?" I tried to sound surprised. I wasn't about to tell Carol what I'd learned.

"If you don't believe me, ask Sir George. He's the one who told me about the scandal." Carol gave a delicate sniff.

"That's worse than the story Lester told me about Blake Fielding," Mary said. "At least he married the girl."

Carol's eyebrows rose. "But why did he go to the trouble of marrying her? It's so permanent."

Leave it to Carol to be uncharitable. "What happened?" I asked.

"It seems Fielding fell in love with this German girl while he was living in Prague. He wanted to marry her, but the Foreign Office wouldn't approve because her father is a high-ranking Nazi. Fielding married her anyway, but she can't get a visa to come over here. He slips over to the continent every few weeks to meet her," Mary said.

"That's sad, except now the Foreign Office can't trust him," Carol said. "Unlike Chambers, who's just pathetic."

She certainly had information. "Why are you so hard on Paul?"

Carol lowered her voice slightly. "He's gambled away a small fortune. Annabelle would have been furious if she'd known. She inherited the money from her parents, who were not impressed that their daughter chose Paul for her husband. Thank goodness she and Paul never had children."

But were any of these a reason for treason?

The table fell silent.

"But back to last night. We certainly weren't followed and shot at," Mary said, leaning forward as if ready to hatch a conspiracy. "Were any of the other guests?"

"Of course not. We live in a respectable neighborhood." Carol sounded perturbed.

And I couldn't resist needling her further. "I thought so too, until last night."

"You and Captain Redmond must have led them to our door."

Mary and I exchanged glances and then stared at Carol.

Under our scrutiny, Carol looked around and then blurted out, "You were the only people who hadn't been to our home before."

"I've been to your house before."

"But not with Captain Redmond. I've heard he's been involved in a scandal or two. Did Reggie trust him?"

I didn't want to lie. The two men had never met. But if they had, Reggie would have trusted him. And I was determined not to pay attention to Carol's gossip about Redmond's behavior.

Better to change this conversation now. "Of course, if this is political, then both Lester and Edward should know what's going on."

"Lester's not that well placed," Mary said, "since he's dealing with colonial credentials. And he's not the man in charge. Politicians never have questions for him. But Edward has the middle European belt. Austria, Czechoslovakia, Poland, Hungary. He must be kept busy, being in charge of the group that has to deal with invasion threats."

Carol studied herself in her compact. "Yes, he's important, and yes, politicians come to him for answers, but he works with visas and credentials and diplomats. He doesn't have to create British policy toward those countries, thank goodness." She rose from her chair. "I'm going to put on more lipstick. Are you coming?"

I smiled. "No. You go ahead. I want to finish my tea." And think about the mischief Edward could get into with the knowledge he had about Britain's policies toward the countries Hitler wanted for his own. Was that why Carol said,

Hitler has no interest in fighting with Britain. He promised. And *don't believe the English warmongers.* Had her husband assured her with knowledge from his job?

* * *

Redmond knocked on my door precisely at three o'clock. When I opened the door, he grinned and walked in, his belted coat and dark fedora damp from the rain that beat down on the town. "At least we didn't have wet weather to deal with last night."

"Then you probably would have been skidding all over the road and killed us on a roundabout."

"Give me a little credit." He gave me a quick smile.

Oh, I did that. More than a little. He seemed ready to handle any emergency, and we needed to work together to solve these murders. "I've made tea. Come into the dining room with that book and let's get started."

By the time I returned to the dining room with the tea tray, Redmond had draped his coat and hat over the radiator and was sitting at the table with Derek's address book, a pad of paper, and a pencil. "He noted some of his appointments recently by initials and marks after them. I wish I knew his code," he said without looking up.

I pulled up a chair next to him. "Let me see."

He slid the book over to me and then leaned in my direction. Umm. He smelled clean and masculine and I had to drag my mind back to our task. I opened to the calendar section of Derek's book and began on yesterday's date. It read: *S?!*

"Good grief. We could do with a key."

He gave me a wry glance. "I looked. There isn't one."

"Was he shot like Reggie?"

"No, he was stabbed. A deep wound. Nicked the heart.

And whoever the killer is, he took the murder weapon with him."

"How gruesome. Oh, Derek, what were you trying to tell me?" I stared at the entry. "He said he'd done something foolish. And he said 'the book.'"

"Which book? This one or the missing *Far from the Madding Crowd*?"

"I don't know, but I'd guess this *S* has something to do with it. Since the marks are in this book, that would mean he meant the book by Hardy."

"I'd guess this *S* has something to do with his death. Whoever's behind this, and I'm still betting on the Germans, moves fast. *S*. Could that be Schreiber?"

"He doesn't know Schreiber. He'd have no reason to have ever met him. It must refer to someone Derek knew."

"You're sure he didn't know Schreiber?" Redmond stared at me.

The colors in his sweater vest matched the shades in his hazel eyes. I wondered who knitted it for him. "Quite sure. Derek worked in a bank as an accounts manager. He had nothing to do with foreign affairs aside from his friendship with Reggie." I flipped open the address book to S. No Schreiber.

Redmond raised his eyebrows at the word "friendship."

"I believe this *S* is much closer to home. He was so familiar to Derek that he opened his door to his killer after midnight."

"The Germans went after Manfred as soon as they knew a document was missing. The same night, someone shot your husband. Hans Manfred threatens Schreiber and he's killed. Derek says he did something foolish and those are his last words before he's murdered."

"Well, let's look backward and see if we find a pattern." I flipped through week after week. In the past week, there were several letters with punctuation marks after them as well as a note that read "Library 4:30" on Thursday. Before that, the entries were dull things like "Dentist 10:00" and "Cleaners." Occasionally, there would be individual capital letters, a *V* or a *P* or a *Q*, or even more rarely, a pair or a few letters, like *QPW*. Sometimes they followed a time, while on other days there was just the letter, but until the last week, those mysterious letters weren't followed by punctuation.

It was a riddle, but I doubted it was one involving Germans.

"Learn anything?"

I gave him a dry look. "I think we can rule out the usual appointments that everyone has."

Redmond made a huffing noise and moved the book along the table in front of him. "Come on, Livvy. You knew Langston better than anyone else I can think of. What do these letters mean?"

I glanced over my shoulder at him. "When I mention people by initials, and it's not often, I use two or three. People have first and last names. Why is he just using one?"

Redmond stared at me, waiting for me to continue.

"They're appointments with specific people. People he doesn't want to name in case someone gets hold of this book. People of his persuasion, maybe?"

"That would be smart. What they're up to is illegal. This way no one is incriminated." He nodded. "How long has it been since your husband died?"

I had to count back to know how long it had been since I'd lost my best friend. I couldn't forget that day, but I'd lost track of time since then.

Redmond flipped back to that wretched day. Then he looked back several weeks and then ahead to the present. "The Thursday your husband died is the last time Q appears on these pages. I'd guess that was your husband. Why?"

"I don't know."

He shut the book. "If you can't do better than that, Mrs. Denis, there's no sense in continuing."

I scrunched up my face in thought. "Why would Derek associate the letter Q with Reggie?"

When I didn't continue, Redmond said, "That's the question. Well?"

I tried to remember a scene from early in our marriage. I'd found a book Reggie had kept from school days, *The Complete Plays of William Shakespeare.*

"Just a moment." I went into the parlor and scanned the shelves.

Redmond called in, "S doesn't appear in here until two days ago. Not at all. Obviously not a close friend of Derek's. So why did he trust him?"

"Maybe he didn't. Not really." I found the volume I wanted, looking scarred and wilted and faded. I carried it back to the dining room and set it on the table.

"I found this when Reggie and I first married." I opened to the flyleaf. There, in a boyish hand, was written *Quigby.* "It was his nickname in public school. No one called him that now."

"Then all these letters may refer to school friends of Langston," Redmond said, looking at the pages of Derek's phone number and appointment book.

"And Reggie. They went to school together."

"Who did they go to school with?"

"I never paid any attention. I only know what Derek said

about Hawthorn, Fielding, Chambers, and Babcock."

Redmond's expression was dark.

"Don't look at me like that. Reggie rarely talked about his school days. I don't think he was very happy. And I never could keep his school friends straight from his university friends. Most of them went on to Oxford with Reggie and Derek, where they met up with more boys and their circle grew larger."

"And all of them must have had nicknames. Like 'Quigby.' Who would know them now?"

I felt as dejected as Redmond looked. "And who of that possible group do we trust to tell us who had which nickname?"

He nodded. "Because any of them could be the mysterious *S*." He put on his still-damp coat and hat and slipped Derek's book into his inside pocket.

"And what do these punctuation marks mean? He only used them in the last week. When he was asking old school friends about the missing book."

I shuddered as if someone walked across my grave. Those marks had to mean who knew about the missing book. I wished again that Derek had stayed on the phone with me instead of answering his door.

* * *

Redmond returned at seven to take me out to eat. My mind had left the problem of boyhood nicknames and gone on to other worries as I'd readied for dinner. When he helped me into my coat, I asked, "Did you find out who owns the Mercedes? And please don't tell me American gangsters."

He was immediately serious. "No. Not gangsters." When I turned to face him, he said, "The German embassy."

"Did Edward Hawthorn say anything odd to you?"

"No. Why?"

"Because last night Carol Hawthorn said Hitler promised to leave Britain alone if we don't interfere with what he does in Europe. And not to trust British warmongers."

"He *promised*?" From his expression, I guessed I'd finally shocked Redmond.

"And then this morning after the police went to her house about the shooting, she called me and invited me out to lunch. She never would have had lunch with me before."

Redmond hadn't seemed to have heard me. "Hitler promised? Who? Mrs. Hawthorn?"

"The way she said it, his words almost sounded like they were addressed to her. Of course, in learning to write society page copy, I've been taught ways to make things sound like some person was talking directly to me when they weren't."

"Does she have any ties to Germany?"

"I wouldn't think so. She can trace her family back to the Conqueror." I read his thoughts on his face and groaned as I realized I'd be spending more time with Carol. "I hope you'll take a look at Edward Hawthorn. He's the one who has reason to be talking to diplomats."

We were about to leave my flat when Redmond suddenly came to a stop. "Why did the police go to her house?"

"To find out if they saw or heard anything about the shooting."

"We were far from their house when the shooting took place. And the police don't know who was in the taxi. What did you tell her, Olivia?"

What had I said to her? "That it was you and me and David in the cab. I said after the driver ran away, you drove us to town. Nothing about the Mercedes or the German embassy or anything. Carol kept insisting it was either

American gangsters, or you or David were having an affair with a married woman."

"What did you say?"

I raised my eyebrows. "I didn't think so."

Redmond didn't reply. As he escorted me downstairs, I wondered if her guess was a good one.

"How would the police have learned where we'd been before we picked up the cab at the Underground station?"

"They wouldn't have." Redmond kept going, but I stopped on the stairs.

"Then how did Carol find out?"

"From Peters or whoever shot at us." When my jaw dropped, Redmond said, "Either answer is at least as likely as the police going door to door to find out who had guests last night."

It wasn't until we reached the front door that I discovered he had a taxi waiting. "We only have to walk around the corner."

"I thought tonight deserved a nicer meal. How does the Ritz sound?"

"It sounds like I need to go back upstairs and put on my best evening frock." I started to turn around.

A grin flashed across his face. "That's not where we're going. There's a new restaurant in Soho, a place called Viennese Nights, where your dress will fit in perfectly."

"The owner is from Vienna?"

"And so is the cook. Expect to be fattened up."

"Oh, I hope not." I couldn't afford to put on weight and need a new wardrobe. And with all this running away from my tails, I had to stay slim and quick.

CHAPTER TWENTY-TWO

WHEN WE arrived at the restaurant, we checked our coats and waited while the maitre d' disappeared in back. A moment later, another man came out wearing a smile that looked painful enough to have been stuck to his face with hatpins. "Captain Redmond, I see you decided to come back to our restaurant. And brought a lovely lady this time."

"Your invitation was too tempting to pass up," came out of Redmond's mouth sounding like a challenge. "Herr Ostmann is the owner, Olivia."

We nodded to each other. Then the owner glared at Redmond. When he looked toward me, he put a weak smile on his face and picked up the menus. He led us over to a table by a window where we'd be visible to anyone outside in the night. After last night's shooting followed by Derek's death, I felt vulnerable. My feet refused to take me the last few steps.

Redmond put a hand on my back, and when I didn't budge, said, "Somewhere a little less obvious from the street. The lady doesn't want to draw admirers."

The owner pursed his lips together. "Of course" came out as a grumble. He took us to a table near the back, giving me a chance to look over the other diners. Long dresses with plenty of jewels and furs for the women, and evening suits with bow ties for the men. Except for my lack of jewels and furs, we fit right in.

Redmond, with his erect carriage and martial steps, looked born to wear evening suits with braid down the side of the trousers. I watched him brush past me while I hoped I disguised my interest.

This early in the evening, several of the tables were empty, but some diners sat close enough to hear our conversation. I knew a lot of Austrians were fans of Hitler. This couldn't be a working dinner. I sat a little taller and smiled at Redmond.

He ordered for us in German. Once the waiter left, I murmured, "I didn't know you spoke German."

"Enough to get by. Do you speak the language?"

"Yes. Plus French and Italian. All of them rusty by now."

"I'm surprised your father doesn't use a foreign language to speak to you, to keep you in practice."

I couldn't resist answering, "Oh, he speaks in a foreign language, but the words he uses are all in English."

Redmond's face fell. I began to suspect he admired my father. After a brief pause, he spoke quickly. "I enjoyed the party last night. Thank you for inviting me."

"Did you really enjoy it?"

"Yes. It was nice seeing men I work with in a more relaxed setting."

"I didn't realize you worked with them."

"I do. Because of my current assignment."

I assumed he meant as camouflage for his counterintelligence work. Not wanting to think about it, I looked at the oil paintings covering the back wall. Chubby cherubs cavorted around chubby, underdressed women under voluptuous skies. A style of painting I'd disliked since my student days.

Redmond's prickly relationship with Herr Ostmann

made me suspect this was a restaurant full of Nazis. My back was to the front of the building. I hoped Redmond would at least warn me if we were about to be attacked.

The food was good, but our courses were arriving faster than at the other tables. We barely had time to taste our soup before it was whisked away and our salads arrived. "I get the feeling they want us out of here."

"I'm not Herr Ostmann's favorite person. Which is a shame, since the food is delicious." He shrugged.

"What did you do to him?"

He gave me a quick smile. "Nothing much."

I had a sudden thought that made me grin. "You want me to improve our service?"

"Can you do that?"

"Watch me." As soon as the waiter came by to refill our glasses and reached out to remove the salad I was enjoying, I said, "Could you please have Herr Ostmann come to our table? I think it would be unfair not to let him know my review of his restaurant will appear in the *Daily Premier*."

The waiter jerked his hand away from my salad plate and said, "Of course, madame."

Herr Ostmann bustled out a moment later. "You are from the *Daily Premier*?"

"Yes, I am, Herr Ostmann, and I want you to know my salad has been excellent. Too bad I barely had time to taste my soup. I only hope the rest of the dinner is as good and that we can enjoy our food with impeccable service. I know you don't want my experience with hurried service to color a review." I spoke softly so he had to lean forward a little to hear me.

Ostmann was silent for a split second before he gushed concern. "The waiter is new. If he's been rushing your enjoyment of the meal, I will certainly speak to him. I wish only to please our patrons."

"I know you do, and so I thought I'd give you a warning before anything negative would have to appear." I gave him what I hoped was a charming smile.

"Let me get you another bottle of wine on the house as a token of my embarrassment that a waiter in my establishment has not been serving you properly."

"You don't need to do that. Just have your waiter take a deep breath and slow down a little. I'm sure he's just been overeager in his efforts to please."

After that, our dinner and our service were perfect. We talked about the upcoming Remembrance Sunday ceremony. Redmond didn't mention security for the event, which I guessed was his role. We spoke of Guy Fawkes nights of years past, of stuffing effigies of Guy and blazing bonfires. He told me about a golf match he'd been in that ended with the other pair insisting they finish despite standing in a downpour with lightning flashing around them. His descriptions made both of us laugh.

As we drank our coffee, I told him about a feud between two of my neighbors over a dust bin. Their pranks against each other had escalated, as neither would yield what they saw as their prerogative.

We were both laughing when Redmond froze as he looked past me.

I had the presence of mind not to turn around. "What is it?"

"Your friend Carol Hawthorn was in town for more than having lunch with you. She and her husband are here with the Austrian cultural attaché and his wife. Both staunch Nazis."

"Edward Hawthorn handles ceremonies and credentials for Austrian officials. There's nothing unusual about them having dinner together at an Austrian restaurant."

"They're now being joined by Major Liestran, in evening dress tonight, and Claire deLong."

"You're in evening clothes, too."

"I thought he slept in his uniform."

I grinned, not accustomed to hear Redmond sounding catty. "Now why would they be joining their party? He's head of security for the German embassy. Edward doesn't handle Germany. And I can't imagine Carol approving of Claire deLong." I gazed at Redmond, wondering what would happen next.

A grin flashed across his face as he looked past my left ear. "If looks could kill, Mrs. deLong would be on the floor. She missed it, but Mrs. Hawthorn's husband saw the look his wife gave her and he said something. Mrs. Hawthorn's reply was to glare at him."

"Good for Carol." I couldn't stand Claire deLong, even though Reggie's unsigned will must have been fake.

"It's a good thing you found a way to lengthen our dinner. Now, are you sure you can't have a Viennese pastry with another cup of coffee?" He gave me the briefest of smiles as he took my hand.

Warmth tingled up my arm from his touch. It had been too long since any man had looked at me the way Redmond was at that moment. I'd have agreed to anything he suggested. Fortunately, this was a good plan. "An excellent idea. The newspaper can't recommend an Austrian restaurant if we don't sample the Viennese pastries."

When the waiter returned, we added pastries and more coffee to our order. After he left, I said, "What are they doing now?"

"Ordering."

This was going to turn into a long night.

The food had been heavy and rich. We'd both eaten carefully, not finishing any dish, so I had room for a few nibbles on my pastry. Redmond ate almost half of his. Before we finished our coffee, I excused myself and headed for the powder room. Fortunately, it was down a flight of stairs in the back, so I didn't have to walk past the Hawthorns' table.

I was washing my hands when I looked in the mirror and found Carol Hawthorn staring at my back. "What are you doing here?" she asked. She sounded as if she were interrogating me.

I decided not to crassly remind her we were in the ladies' loo and said, "Having dinner. And you?"

"I can believe it of you, but not Captain Redmond."

"Believe it. The man knows how to tuck into his dinner."

"Humpf." She stood in front of the other mirror and opened her purse. Fishing around, she came up with her compact and powdered her nose.

She'd barely started dinner. Needing an extra coat of war paint this early in the evening wasn't a good excuse for being in the powder room.

Eyeing me in the mirror, she said, "Major Liestran told us Reggie's supposed cousin works for counterintelligence."

"Reggie's *cousin*," I said, emphasizing the words, "told me Major Liestran is head of security of the German embassy. Odd he isn't dining with Paul Chambers. Does Paul know about this dinner?"

"It's certainly none of your business."

"No, but it is interesting." I decided to use my restaurant review ploy again. "You know I work for the *Daily Premier*."

"I heard. How can you stand working for that odious Sir Henry Benton?"

I shrugged. "Tonight I'm writing a review of this restaurant. Have you eaten here before?"

Her lipstick held forgotten in one hand, she said, "Once. We were here opening night."

"How do you find the service?"

"Excellent."

"And the food?"

"Excellent."

"Not what Londoners are used to. I found it overly rich, but that could be my taste. I don't want to misjudge them." I watched her over my shoulder as she applied lipstick.

"If you'd spent any time in Vienna, you'd know Ostmann is one of the best restaurateurs in the city. I think his food is divine."

"I've never been. I guess with Edward working that desk, you get to travel there and try out the restaurants." I tried to sound a little envious.

I must have struck the right note, because Carol said, "Yes. We try to go over at least once a quarter. The food and the opera are first rate. The last time we were there, Herr Ostmann told us about his plans for this place."

"Reggie used to take me to the opera in Berlin when he had to go over there. I don't remember the restaurants being anything special, but the operas were superb." Another happy memory of Reggie and me from the past.

"I didn't know you were an opera fan." Her tone indicated that maybe I wasn't the tart she thought.

"Yes." I gave her a smile I didn't feel. "Do you find this restaurant the equal of his place in Vienna?"

"Yes, except perhaps for the ambiance. He attracts a

higher class of clientele in Vienna."

Ouch. As a snub it was pretty good. I decided to ignore it. "It's still early days. I'm sure his restaurant in Vienna didn't start out catering to the upper crust."

"Perhaps not. It's been open for at least a decade." She dropped her lipstick into her purse. "Well, I mustn't keep my host waiting."

"Your host?" I said, following her out.

"Herr Mann. The Austrian cultural attaché."

"What do you think of Claire deLong? I would have thought you'd find her a little scandalous."

She turned at the bottom of the stairs and looked at me. "Just because she's American and more flamboyant than the rest of us, people find it necessary to gossip about her." With a huff, she faced the stairs and nearly raced up them.

Full of dinner, I found myself going slower. Carol might not like Claire deLong, but she wouldn't criticize her to me. I wondered why. They weren't friends. And Carol certainly didn't mind spreading dirt about anyone at any time.

Redmond had already settled our bill when I reached our table, but that still left walking out past the Hawthorns, Claire deLong, and the frightening Major Liestran. Custom decreed I lead the way. I hoped Redmond would find a way to let me know how he planned to handle this.

He did, by following me closely and keeping a hand on my elbow. When we reached their table, he pulled me to a stop and said, "Major."

"Captain. Good evening." He rose, along with the other men. Introductions were brief. "Mrs. Hawthorn was just telling us Mrs. Denis is a restaurant reviewer." His gaze bore into me as if he didn't believe the story. "I hope you found tonight's meal adequate."

I forced a smile and said, "More than adequate. Have you eaten here before?"

"Yes."

"Then you know what to expect."

"Indeed I do. I hope you know what to expect, dining with Captain Redmond." It sounded a bit like a threat. But then, everything Liestran said gave that impression.

I decided to try something brazen. "I'm afraid Mrs. deLong would know better than I would."

I could hear Carol Hawthorn suck in her breath, but Claire deLong just smiled and said, "I hope you find the captain as amusing as I do."

I returned a cold smile. "Every bit as amusing as the major?"

Frau Mann, the Austrian attaché's wife, knew the makings of a catfight when she heard one. "It's been very nice meeting you, Mrs. Denis, but I'm afraid our soup has arrived."

"Of course. Enjoy your meal."

The men sat down. Redmond and I picked up our outerwear from the coat check as the waiter set down their bowls. We were a block away before Redmond said, "Well, that was interesting. You and Mrs. Hawthorn have a nice chat in the ladies' loo?"

"Ostmann has a restaurant in Vienna patronized by the wealthy."

"I know. He's also a big Nazi sympathizer."

"Where the Hawthorns eat when they visit Vienna at least every three months."

"How did that get past us?" he muttered. Then he looked at me and said, "Would you like to walk or would you rather take a taxi?"

"I need to walk off that meal. Ooh, that was heavy. Worse

than those stuffy formal dinners I had to attend with my father and later with Reggie."

The Soho streets were busy at that time of night, but once we left Oxford Street heading north toward my flat, the roads were practically deserted. Add to that a wispy fog settling down from the rooftops, and I was becoming nervous.

"I'm not going to let anything happen to you," Redmond said in my ear.

When I glanced at Redmond's face, I saw he was watching a man walking toward us. The brim of the man's hat was pulled down. He made me suspicious, too. I huddled a little closer to Redmond, but the man walked past without glancing our way.

Cars, most of them taxis, drove past without slowing.

"Surely we won't get a repeat of last night." I hoped.

"We won't." Redmond sounded grim. "That was a warning. The next attack will be more accurate."

I stumbled in my panic.

Redmond gave me a quick smile. "Don't worry. They won't strike while you're with me. They want the Nazi restaurant to get a good review."

"I'd better speak to Colinswood Monday morning about getting a review in the paper."

"Will he do it, do you think?"

"I don't know exactly what Colinswood and Sir Henry Benton have in mind, but they're willing to put in articles with the details I give them. Not news articles, just general interest, and without a byline."

The screech of tires snagged my attention. I looked toward the street as a black car stopped and three men jumped out.

Redmond pushed me forward behind a parked car and slipped his knife out of his sleeve. "Run!"

CHAPTER TWENTY-THREE

I RAN.

I'd only taken a few steps when a man grabbed me from behind and swung me around. Angry, I cried out and stomped on his instep with my high heel.

He groaned and then wrapped his arms around me, pinning my back against his chest. Behind us, I heard grunts and shouts.

"Help!" I screamed to the empty street. Where were the police? I lashed out with my heel again, meeting empty air and knocking myself off balance. The man pulled me toward the idling car.

Out of the corner of my eye, I saw Redmond fight with a man carrying a club while another was writhing on the ground, clutching his bloody stomach.

Was this what had happened to Reggie? I wasn't going to let this thug drag me into the car. I wriggled and struggled, but he kept pulling me closer to the open back door of the auto.

I stopped resisting and drew my legs up under me. Since I no longer supplied any support, I made myself a weighty object. In that second, the man lost his grip on me, but not on my coat.

My arms slid out of my coat sleeves as my rear smashed into the pavement. I shrieked from the pain. Redmond, having wrestled the second man's club away and knocked him down with it, came after my attacker.

I heard the car engine rumble louder. The man who'd grabbed me threw my coat over Redmond and dashed for their car. Behind Redmond I saw one of his attackers drag the injured man toward their car as well.

Squealing tires followed by silence signaled that it was safe for me to stop screaming. I climbed stiffly off the ground.

Redmond fought his way out from under my coat and tossed it on the pavement. He took a step or two toward the speeding car.

"They won't strike while I'm with you?" I said, my trembling voice rising with hysteria. I picked up my coat, shook it off, and put the torn garment over my arm.

"Everything all right?" a man's voice called out from the street where he'd stopped his coupe.

"Yes," Redmond replied in a calm tone. "Robbers, but you frightened them off. Thanks. We'll be fine from here."

"You're certain?" He hid behind his open driver's door, wide-eyed at the violence he'd witnessed.

"Yes. Thanks."

"Good night, then." The man slid back inside his auto and drove off.

"Where's a bobby when you need one?" I snapped.

"We don't want a bobby," Redmond muttered, hurrying me down the street.

"We don't?" I tried digging in my heels, but I found I couldn't slow Redmond any more than I had the villain.

"That's the last thing we need. I'm trying to get you home and safe as quickly as possible. We don't want to attract attention from the police. Too much explanation required." He put an arm around me and hustled me forward.

Safe sounded good to me. And an explanation to the police would mean one to my father. And Abby and John. Not wanting to face that, I sped up.

We reached my building without further incident and he took me up in the lift, still holding on to me. Once we were inside my flat, I took stock of the dirt on the skirt of my evening frock and the damage to my coat and grumbled, "I'm having a brandy. Would you like one?"

"Yes. Thank you." Once we settled in the parlor with our drinks, he said, "You took care of yourself very well out there."

"I was afraid he'd take me away in their car. I couldn't fight him, so I made myself a dead weight. He didn't expect that." My rear still hurt, but the pain was worth it since we'd escaped capture.

"Fortunately, they weren't armed with anything but clubs. And one man didn't know how to use it properly."

"You stabbed him?" The thought was nauseating.

"I wasn't going to let them kidnap you."

"They would have kidnapped you, too."

"No. The men I fought with were keeping me away from you. They made no attempt to grab me. But apparently you're valuable enough to kidnap." He raised his eyebrows at me.

What a ridiculous notion. "I don't have any money, and neither does my father."

"Then they want something other than money."

"What?"

He gave me an appraising glance. "What did they search your flat for?"

"And Derek's flat. Don't forget that." He'd said something or learned something that made him dangerous enough to kill. The same with Hans Manfred. I'd spoken to them both, and now someone was after me. I trembled, making the brandy slosh in my glass.

Redmond studied me over the rim of his snifter.

I rose and paced the room in my stocking feet. "We still don't know what they want, except possibly a letter. Something so tiny it could be anywhere. Not like the heavy book Reggie borrowed the night he died."

"*Far from the Madding Crowd*. Think there's a clue there?"

"They'd kidnap me to learn where a book is? That's insane."

"We need to find that document. And until this is over, you need to keep your door bolted when you're home and don't open it unless you know the person."

"That didn't help Derek." The thought made me depressed.

"But it might save you."

We finished our brandies, but I was still cold down to my bones. "I'm tired and I'm frightened and I can't wake up from this nightmare. Hold me, Adam."

He stood and led me to the sofa. We sat next to each other and stared into each other's eyes for what felt like minutes. The greens and browns in his irises darkened as I drew nearer.

Then his lips went to my eyes, my ears, my mouth. We quickly tangled in each other's arms, kissing, touching, with tears on my part, until he pulled back. "If you don't want me to stay the night, you'd better tell me now."

I couldn't spend the night alone. "Stay."

* * *

Adam left after a cup of coffee in the morning. The combination of evening clothes and his need for a shave made him look roguish and even more desirable, but I resisted asking him to remain. Just barely.

I sat at the table, sorting through my jumbled emotions. I'd been married to Reggie for three years, but we seldom had any physical contact beyond a kiss on the cheek. Especially in the last year or two. Now I'd discovered Reggie had been going through the motions. Redmond had shown great enthusiasm and I'd happily joined in.

I'd been frightened. Two more murders in the last few days. Multiple attacks on me. I'd needed to be held by another human being. Well, I'd gotten what I needed, but it came with a busload of guilt.

I felt disloyal to Reggie. Ridiculous, I knew. My husband was dead. But I shouldn't be having an affair while his killer was still at large. It was as if Reggie and I had unfinished business and my new life couldn't begin until the mystery of his death was solved.

Odd. It might not make any difference to Reggie, but it did to me.

And what did Adam think? He said he was very fond of me, but did he consider me a woman of loose morals? Was I another in a long line of easy conquests?

I was still trying to sort out this new experience when my father showed up to take me to lunch. He knew I would never turn down a free meal. I suspected he had some sort of fatherly wisdom to impart or he wouldn't be offering.

I hoped he hadn't somehow heard about last night's attack on the street.

After I dressed, we set out by taxi to a very posh hotel's restaurant.

We'd started on our soup when he spoke very quietly. "The body of an East End thug was found along the banks of the Thames this morning. The body hadn't quite reached the river, the water level being at low tide, so it was easy to identify the man and see he'd been stabbed."

This was not the sort of conversation I expected of my father in a restaurant with pristine white linen and a countess with her school-aged granddaughter at the next table. "You're not trying to ruin my appetite, are you?"

"Captain Redmond had already reported he'd stabbed a man last night while in your company."

Oh, here it comes. "He prevented me from being kidnapped."

"General Alford believes, and I concur, that Redmond was the target. You were merely in their way."

"Is that what Redmond believes?"

My father gave me a sharp look. "He argued quite strenuously against it. Tell me, Olivia, what is going on between you two?"

I considered telling him, and then decided he'd never forgive me for imparting such news in an elegant restaurant. "Who's this General Alford? I thought Captain Redmond reported to General Lord Walters."

"Officially, he reports to Walters."

"And unofficially?"

"It's a complicated arrangement."

"It usually is when spies are involved." And now I was certain my father also had performed clandestine duties under General Alford.

"That doesn't answer my question."

It didn't answer any of mine, either. "He's been helping me figure out why Reggie was murdered and our flat searched."

"He didn't tell me that." My father seemed annoyed

someone wouldn't tell him something he wanted to know. "Was your flat searched before or after you met Redmond?"

"Before."

"He had probably already shown an interest in you. And he's put you in danger more than once."

I cared about and admired Adam. "He's rescued me from danger more than once. There is a difference, Father." At this point we were both sounding huffy.

"Not where Redmond is concerned. He brings trouble with him. You do know he'd caused trouble yesterday for the owner of the restaurant where you ate last night."

"I'm not surprised." I had suspected as much. It explained why our service had been so hurried. They wanted to get rid of him. "What exactly did he do to Herr Ostmann?"

That earned me a glare. "You don't need to worry about that. I believe it's high time you gave up the flat and moved home."

"You don't want me home."

"I'm your father. It's my duty to look after you as well as I possibly can."

"I don't want to live with someone who's inviting me because of duty. And I can afford my flat with what I earn at the *Daily Premier*."

"That scandal rag." My father was no longer keeping his voice down, and the countess at the next table glanced our way in horror. He nodded and gave her an apologetic smile before turning to me and saying in a quieter voice, "I'd rather you gave up that job. It's embarrassing me."

"Well, it's not embarrassing me." I gave him an innocent look and turned my attention back to my food. "This is good soup. I'm glad you suggested coming here."

Once our main courses arrived, I decided to use my

father as a source of information on Derek's address book. And I had to be very careful how I asked my questions, or he'd never answer because he'd be sure it would lead me to embarrass him further. "I was talking to Mary Babcock, and she told me Lester had a schoolboy nickname. He wouldn't tell her what it was. I know he went to Oxford, and you did, too. Did you have a nickname at Oxford?"

"No. Like most schoolboys, I got mine in boarding school. I suspect Lester Babcock did, too. Probably why he won't admit to it now."

"They were in questionable taste?"

"Rarely. Mostly silly. Reggie's was Quincy, or something like that. A cartoon character he used to doodle on scrap paper."

"So by the time he was at Oxford, no one would call him that anymore?"

"Not necessarily. Young men entering Oxford are still boys at heart. His public school friends would still tease him with it, and so his new friends at Oxford would probably hear it. By the time they left Oxford, they were all too grown up and serious to call each other by nicknames, unless they were very close. There was a war on, you know." My father took a bite. After he swallowed he added, "Hard to tell what your generation has done. It seems like you never grew up."

Leave it to my father to turn a simple question into a statement of displeasure with young people. And he was about to become angrier with me. "How well do you know Sir George Rankin?" I asked.

"I've known him for years. Trust him with my life."

"How does he afford to send Lady Margery to the Riviera every winter with a companion?"

"It's for her health."

"I know that. How can he afford it? He sees everything that comes into the office. He's in charge. How do you know he's not the leak?"

When my father finished spluttering, he said, "That's absurd. How can you even think that?"

"Because I don't know where he gets the money to pay for her travels. There's a leak in that office, and the Nazis must be paying very well for such important information." And the traitor probably also killed Reggie.

My father toyed with his food. He seemed to be on the brink of saying something twice, but kept silent. Finally he said, "If it will make you happy, I'll find out."

Actually, I thought it would make him happier now that I'd made him consider that possibility.

It wasn't until after our coffee had arrived that my father leaped into dangerous territory again. "I've had General Alford tell Redmond to stay away from you."

I narrowed my eyes. "You didn't have the nerve to tell him yourself."

"I can't make it stick. The general, um, has a hand in assigning his work. He can."

My temper flared, but I tamped it down. Arguing with my father required cool nerves. "Why are you interfering with my life?"

"It's for your own good."

"And when do *I* get to decide what's for my own good?"

"After I'm dead."

That was probably the truth of our relationship. "Must I wait that long?" I gave a dramatic sigh.

"Don't be smart with me, young lady. I could cut you out of my will."

"Don't threaten me, Father. We both know you have little

else but your salary and the house. On your death, your salary would stop and I doubt I could keep up the house on what I make." Actually, I liked the house. I'd love to live there if it didn't come furnished with my father.

My father had the grace to look chagrined. "Look, Olivia, why can't you go along with this? Redmond deals with some very unsavory characters. They see him squiring you about, well—they might get all sorts of ideas."

"Like kidnapping me?"

"Exactly."

"I'll take my chances." I lowered my voice to a murmur. "Reggie had something when he died that the people who killed him are still looking for. And I think those people are German. I need Adam's help." Actually, I could use him for a great deal more, but I didn't need to tell my father that. Especially since I didn't yet know how I fit into Adam's plans.

"Olivia. Leave Reggie's death to the authorities."

"I would have, if people hadn't searched my flat and followed me. And the man who questioned me lied about his identity. I didn't go looking for trouble. It found me."

He was scowling now. "Lied? How?"

"He said he was a British army officer. I've now found out he's German. An SS officer."

"They're interested in you because of your friendship with Redmond." I could tell my father was keeping his voice down only with effort.

"No. They want something tangible. And I believe Reggie didn't have this thing until the evening he died."

My father frowned into his coffee. He wore the same face every time he was trying to decide whether to tell me something.

"What is it?"

"It's only a rumor." He looked as if his tie were suddenly too tight.

"What?" I whispered.

"There's a rumor that a German who was killed the same night as Reggie stole something from the embassy. Something they are still looking for."

"What did he steal?"

"Something small. A document, presumably. The man was a clerk."

"You do realize I know all this."

For once, my father looked astonished. His eyebrows almost reached his receding hair line. "How could you possibly—?"

"By speaking to people you've warned me against."

"As I am part of His Majesty's government, perhaps you'd better tell me what you've discovered."

We went back to the house, where I told him a sanitized version of what I'd learned and what I'd guessed.

When I finished, he said, "I think we need to get Sir George Rankin involved. It's his office that is under suspicion. While he went to Oxford several years before the men working for him, he may know their schoolboy nicknames."

"Even though he may be the source of the leak?"

"I'll check his finances for you, but I think he's the best person to ask about the nicknames."

I nodded. "Call him and see if we can meet this evening."

"No. I'll ask him and let you know."

I couldn't trust him to ask the right questions, much less find out what I most needed to know. Who was *S*? "Then I'll talk to him on my own."

My father and I stared at each other across his study. Neither of us was ready to give an inch. There was only one way out of this impasse and I didn't have time to wait while he thought of it.

"We're both going to ask for this information. We might as well do it together and only waste Sir George's time once." I suspected Sir George wouldn't tell me without my father's presence, but I'd never admit it.

"Very well." He picked up the phone and called. Sir George had a dinner engagement, but if we could get over there quickly, we could discuss this "urgent" matter.

Sir George himself answered the door. "Margery has warned me not to be late in getting ready. What can I do for you that couldn't wait until we get into the office tomorrow?"

"This is something we shouldn't discuss in the office," I told him. "We've uncovered some evidence that leads to a member of your staff being involved in Reggie's death. But this person is only known by his schoolboy nickname."

"You're joking." Sir George looked from me to my father. Seeing our serious expressions, he nodded and said, "Come into the library."

After we were seated, he said, "A member of my staff killed Reggie Denis? Preposterous."

"I'm afraid Army Intelligence thinks so too."

Sir George looked at my father, who nodded. "Very well. What is this nickname?"

"I don't want to say. If this evidence proves untrue, I don't want to cast aspersion on this man's name," I told him. "Could you just run through all the schoolboy nicknames you've heard and who has them?"

He seemed about to argue, but then he glanced at the clock and then at the ceiling. We could hear someone walking around the old house's upstairs. "I know Denis's was Quigby."

"I thought it was Quincy," my father said.

"No. It was Quigby after that caricature he scribbled. Peters's was Poltergeist after some stunt he pulled sneaking in after curfew. Hawthorn's was, I'm afraid to say, Snitch. There's some bad feeling behind whatever happened to earn him that name. And Babcock's was Squeaky. He has a lovely singing voice now, but his voice changed late. I'm afraid those are all I can remember."

"What about Chambers and Fielding?"

"If I ever knew them, I've forgotten."

Two of them started with an *S*. How many more did? "How would I find out the rest of them?"

"I'd check with the schools they attended. Someone there must remember."

I shot a quick glance at my father and decided this was as good a time as any to ask. "Why was Reggie at St. Asaph's Hotel the night he died?"

"Why do you think I'd—"

"Because you and General Alford were there and it wasn't for a drink. Unless the two of you and the hotel manager were going to share a room upstairs."

"Olivia," my father snapped, clearly shocked.

"I was afraid you'd start putting things together," Sir George said. "Did you know your father once served under General Alford? I guess you didn't."

I looked at my father, but he was studying the red patterned rug.

Finally, he said, "One of the biggest hurdles for espionage work is finding office space that isn't known to belong to the government, or at least the intelligence services. Things in Europe are heading downhill. We're going to need more people breaking codes and processing intelligence, and we're going to need more places for them to work. The St. Asaph's is one possibility."

Now Sir George wouldn't look me in the eye, either. "We'd heard the bar was being used for some meetings that wouldn't fit well with our use, if you see what I mean. Reggie was tasked with finding out if this were true."

"Was it true?" I asked.

"We don't know. Reggie was killed before he reported back." He stood and patted my father on the shoulder. "I'll speak to you tomorrow." Then he showed us out.

My father was very quiet as he went on his own way. As soon as I returned to my flat, I called Adam and left a message. He called back within five minutes and I told him what little I'd learned about the schoolboy nicknames.

"That's not surprising. Rankin went to public school years ahead of the men we're interested in. I'll begin working on the others. Just our luck we already have two starting with the letter *S*."

"What was yours, Adam?"

I could hear his smile over the line. "I don't think you're ready to hear that. And thank you for finally calling me Adam."

How could I not call him by his given name after the night before?

"I'm going to be out of town for a few days. I hope to be back by the weekend." His tone was oddly tentative.

"Why?" Hurt slipped out in my voice.

"It's not by choice. It's the job."

"Adam…"

"Don't ask me. I can't tell you anything."

I hurried to assure him. "I understand. Anything to do with our government these days is secret." I'd learned that from Reggie.

His tone changed, telling me he believed me. "You're going to have to trust that I care about you, Livvy."

CHAPTER TWENTY-FOUR

I'D NO MORE than hung up the phone when it rang again. "This is Sir Henry Benton. Do you have a passport, Olivia?"

"Yes. Where do you want me to go?"

"Berlin."

I felt a rock hit the bottom of my stomach. I'd found Berlin intimidating even with Reggie and his diplomatic passport protecting me. This time I'd be alone.

Not waiting for a response, Sir Henry said, "I want you to pick up a package for me and bring it here. And I don't want anyone noticing that you'll be dressed differently on the return trip than on the way over."

How odd. "Maybe you'd better explain more."

"Not over the phone. Can you come over? You'll remember the house from when you and Esther were girls."

I recited the address and said, "I'll be right over." I put on a trench coat and a wide-brimmed hat in an attempt to hide my identity from anyone watching my building. Sutton called me a taxi and I was at Sir Henry's door in the suburbs in fifteen minutes.

After we settled in his study, Esther came in. "Livvy, we need you to do something you'll think is outrageous."

"In that case you know I'll do it." I smiled. We'd enjoyed our girlhood pranks.

She sat in the chair next to me. "We need you to travel to Berlin and smuggle out jewelry from my aunt. My cousin escaped Germany on a tourist visa and wants to stay here. Wants to go to university. He needs money, and his mother's jewelry will provide him with enough funds to get a visa and continue his education."

"She agreed to this?"

Esther nodded. "Of course. All you'll need is a small suitcase for an overnight stay. And don't wear a coat over. You'll be wearing a fur one back. You need to leave in the morning. There's a ticket waiting for you at Croydon Aerodrome. You'll land in Brussels and then Hamburg on your way to Berlin. You should get there by early afternoon. Go straight to the address we give you and pick up the package."

"No." Sir Henry shook his head. "First, you're going to Berlin City Hall. You're going to ask the mayor to describe his favorite meal. We'll do a series in the women's section on favorite meals of famous men. Then you'll have a reason for a short visit."

"Won't the airport staff recognize me as being better dressed on the return flight? There can't be that many people flying between London and Berlin on the same day." The last thing I wanted was to be noticed by the Gestapo.

Esther chewed on her lower lip, a sign she was worried. I hadn't seen that since her last mathematics exam. "That is a problem."

I looked from Esther to her father sitting behind his desk. "What if I travel back by ferry? I can take the train to Amsterdam and catch the ferry there. I shouldn't run into the same officials."

He grinned. "That sounds like a good solution. You'll

need German currency."

"Get some from my aunt. She won't mind. They can't take money out of the country." Esther sounded eager now instead of worried.

"Is anyone watching their home? If I go in dressed one way and come out another, someone might notice."

"No one is watching. They're in a block of flats on a well-traveled street. Maybe change your hat along with putting on the fur coat and no one will realize you're the same person."

"And your aunt knows I'm coming? There won't be any trouble there? Or at the paper if I don't show up?"

"She knows, and I'll square it with Colinswood and Miss Westcott. Tell my sister-in-law Sir Henry sends his love. That's your password."

After receiving an assignment like that, I couldn't sleep a wink. But I was ready and at the airport early the next morning wearing a wool suit and carrying a small suitcase. I'd flown that route before with Reggie, and the trip held no surprises.

I went through customs quickly with much smiling and speaking German on my part. I got a second look from several men in trench coats, but the expression in their eyes said "relative" or "girlfriend." Sir Henry had changed the return portion of the ticket to be open ended, which gave more evidence to their guesses.

I was glad to find a taxi and get away from there.

Berlin was full of uniforms, all smart and black-booted. The city had been spiffed up for the Olympics the year before and still looked well scrubbed. But most of the leaves were off the trees and the flowers had all died. Civilian pedestrians hurried along, not looking to the right or left. I had the impression of a city boasting that all was well while plague lurked in every alley.

I was terrified.

My German was strong enough to tell various officials several times each that I needed to interview the mayor for a maximum of five minutes. Finally, I got in. He was bemused, but told me his favorite meal was sausages and beer. He even gave me a potato salad recipe given him by his mother.

I wrote it down in my notebook, thanked him, and caught a taxi to my true destination.

I wished Reggie was here with me. I felt cold and unsure without him. I paid the cab driver with the marks I'd gotten in exchange at the airport, climbed out of his cab, and shivered. Traveling without a coat at this time of year was folly.

I knocked on the door of flat 3B and the door was opened a crack. "Hello. Sir Henry sends his love," I said in German.

The chain came off and the door was opened long enough for me to slip through. I was led down the hall and into a large, high-ceilinged parlor that was comfortable in an old-fashioned way, with heavy, stuffed furniture and layers of curtains at the windows.

The woman who led me was perhaps fifty. Or maybe the strain of being Jewish in Berlin was showing on her face. "I'm Ruth Weisz, one of Sir Henry's sisters-in-law. It is my son you are helping."

"And perhaps you as well?" I asked.

"Perhaps." Then she glanced behind her at an older couple standing nearby. "These are my parents, Simon and Sarah Neugard."

I stepped forward and we shook hands. "Esther sends her love. She wants you to visit her in England."

"I know what my granddaughter wants. Things are not so bad I need to move to England," Mr. Neugard said. "I was born here. This is my city. I will remain here."

I nodded. Esther had warned me he'd say that. "We need to get moving. I'm taking the evening train to Amsterdam."

Ruth produced two long, jeweled necklaces, some gold bracelets, rings, and a fur coat. Then Simon produced a small strip of cloth in which some metal discs could be felt. "Put this under your clothes," he directed.

I was shown into a bedroom where I took off my suit. Ruth helped me put the sash around my waist so it wouldn't show when I donned my tea gown of black silk. I slipped the necklaces under my dress and put on thick gloves to hide the rings and bracelets. I changed my tan cloche for my chic black slant-brim and my low heels for slightly higher ones. Then I switched my traveling purse for a black bag.

When I came out, Sarah Neugard gasped. "It is not the same girl."

"I am, and now I must catch my train. Wish me luck."

Ruth helped me on with the fur coat. "Tell Sir Henry thank you. And I appreciate your help."

"You're welcome. Esther's my best friend. I'm doing this for her."

"You'll need marks for the taxi and the train. Here." She gave me a stack of bills that I slipped into my wallet and then I was on my way.

I felt as if I was being watched as I flagged down a cab and told him to take me to the bahnhof, the train station. The muscles in my arms began to shake from tension. How would I explain all I was carrying if I was stopped and searched? What if I missed my train?

I gripped my hands together and willed them to relax. I

was doing nothing illegal. *Then why the secrecy?* I asked myself.

When we reached the train station, the feeling that I was being watched returned. Once I purchased my ticket to Amsterdam, all I had to do was look bored while waiting. I found that was difficult when rabbits were hopping in my stomach.

I purchased a German magazine aimed at housewives. I sneaked a glance around me as I took a seat. No one appeared to be watching me. In just a few minutes I'd be leaving Berlin.

I kept telling myself nothing could go wrong as I tried and failed to absorb an article on how to make a bomb shelter comfortable.

When a man sat down next to me, I ignored him and prayed he'd go away.

"Ah, yes, one of their more popular articles," the man said to me in English.

I glanced up in terror into the dark eyes of the man from the German embassy party.

"As I recall, some of your sketches were better than this," he added, pointing to an illustration.

"Thank you." *Please, please go away.*

"What are you doing here, Mrs. Denis?"

"I was sent over to do an interview. What are you doing here?"

"I live here."

That fell like a boulder between us.

I finally forced out through my dry mouth, "What is your name?"

"I am Oberst Wilhelm Bernhard, German army liaison to some embassies. I suspect we're traveling in the same direction."

"I suspect we are." That could be either a good or a bad thing, depending on how much he suspected. As an oberst, a colonel in the German army, he carried the same rank as Sir John.

He tapped the magazine again. "I didn't know you read German. Or is that just camouflage?"

"Yes, I read it. And speak it, although not like a native," I said, switching to German.

He nodded. "Your accent is not good."

I smiled. "About what yours is in English."

He chuckled. The Nazi actually chuckled. "Mathematics. Machinery. Science. These things always made sense to me. But languages? Eh. I could never get them right."

"I enjoy languages because I enjoy literature." I could feel myself unbending to this personable man even as warning bells went off in my head.

"How are you getting back to London? Through Amsterdam on the ferry?"

"Yes."

"That's the route I'm taking also. We can travel together."

I didn't manage to hide the shocked look that crossed my face.

"I understand. British women do not like to talk to men they have not been introduced to."

I shook my head. Better to sound truthful. "This is my first trip to Berlin since my husband died. Traveling alone makes me wary."

"Our countries are not enemies. You have no reason to fear."

Even his tone put me on edge. "I'm sorry, but I don't know you. And we haven't been properly introduced."

He gave me a teeth-baring smile. "That is true. But the trip will take all night and I can't sleep while traveling. Talking is much preferable to staring out darkened windows. And between us, we should be able to cross borders without difficulty."

Oh, how I wanted to cross the German border without trouble. I smiled shakily. "I'm sure we can find topics to discuss that don't involve bomb shelters."

They announced our train and we crossed the ticket barrier without problems. I breathed a sigh of relief when we found an empty compartment in a first-class carriage. We sat across from each other by the window in silence, while from outside, I could hear shouts and clanks. I couldn't wait to leave.

Oberst Bernhard seemed on the verge of speaking when two heavy-set, middle-aged women came into our compartment. With many apologies, they took over three quarters of the space with their coats and bags and the smell of sauerkraut.

The train had no more than begun moving when the ladies began to unwrap and eat their dinner. Sausages were accompanied by sauerkraut, black bread, and beer in copious quantities as they chatted loudly. I glanced at the oberst and then nodded to the window. He rose and opened it from the top, letting in cold, smoky air.

The women glowered at him. I smiled, glad I had on a fur coat.

Once their meal was finished and the containers put away, the woman next to the oberst looked me over from head to foot. She turned to her friend, nodded toward me, and smirked.

The other woman studied me, moved a little away from

me, turned to her friend, and they both started giggling.

"Oberst," I asked in my best German, "how much longer until we reach our destination?"

He replied in English. "Several hours. We have two stops in Germany and one in the Netherlands before we reach Amsterdam. Don't worry. This train always makes it in time for the ferry."

"You'd rather speak English?" I asked. The women were staring at us now.

"I need the practice after speaking German for a few days. And I doubt these women can understand us."

"They'll probably report us at the next stop."

"Probably. But we have no danger there." Then he looked straight into my eyes. "Do we?"

"I'm a foreigner and I no longer travel under a diplomatic passport." And I was smuggling jewels.

"No reason to worry." He gave me a brief smile.

The women got off in Hanover and took all their bags and boxes with them, leaving behind a faint odor of sauerkraut. I stretched slightly and smiled.

"What a relief," Bernhard said in German.

"*Ja.*"

The train started again without anyone joining us. Now I knew I'd be in for a grilling.

Instead, he asked in English, "Do you have children?"

"No. And now that I have to go out to work every day, I see that as a good thing. And you?"

"I am a widower. I have two children, a boy and a girl. They are young, and I travel a great deal. My sister and her family are raising them."

"Then I hope for their sakes there won't be a war."

He gave me the saddest smile I'd seen in a long time.

"Thank you. Too bad your wish won't come true. I doubt it can be avoided much longer."

"Then I wish for you a quick defeat, but I hope you and your family remain safe."

"I wish you the same. But if you're not a fan of the Nazis, why did you come over here?"

I smiled. Sir Henry's idea sounded so silly it had to be true. "We're running a series on the favorite meals of famous men. I interviewed the mayor of Berlin."

"What was his answer?"

"Sausages and beer. He even gave me a recipe for potato salad."

"You could ask Ambassador von Ribbentrop as well." His words warned me to stay on my guard.

"We plan to. I imagine he'll get a promotion after his current assignment."

The oberst shrugged. "He does seem ambitious. May I close the window now? I think the compartment is aired out sufficiently."

"Please. And despite your accent, your command of English is excellent."

After he closed the window, he sat again and stared at me. "Why did they send you to interview the mayor?"

"I speak German. I'm the only one on the society pages who can."

We circled each other warily until we stopped at the border. I stared at the corridor. Just the sight of the black-uniformed soldiers with their rifles and pistols following the armed border guards made me shiver.

When they finally stopped at our compartment, the oberst handed them his diplomatic passport and some papers that were probably his orders. The guards saluted and returned his documents.

Then I handed them my passport, hoping they couldn't tell that sweat was leaking from my underarms and back.

The guard studied my papers, then handed them to a soldier who also studied them before handing off to a man in a trench coat. A man who had "Gestapo" written all over him.

"Why such a short trip, Frau Denis?" trench-coat man said in English. He had a pointed nose that could probably smell my fear.

"I had an interview with the mayor of Berlin. Now I need to return and write up my story to make the deadline for my paper."

The man seemed impressed with my German. "And the subject of your interview?"

"His favorite meal."

The soldiers around us broke out in smiles, but trench-coat man said, "I think you should come with me." He raised a hand and two soldiers moved into the compartment. I shrank back in my seat. They each grabbed one of my arms and lifted me upright. I struggled against my desire to wail or thrash around to fight them off. That would be fruitless.

"Why? What is wrong?"

"No one travels this far for a few hours if the reason for their trip is innocent." He made innocence sound like a crime.

My heart stopped and I couldn't get any air in. This could only mean a search uncovering the jewels I was smuggling. A search followed by torture. Imprisonment. And death.

CHAPTER TWENTY-FIVE

I STOOD THERE trembling. Panic made everything around me move in slow motion. My limbs under the soldiers' grips felt weak and my stomach hurt. How could I keep from going with them? I would die.

The moment they discovered all the jewels I wore, they would take them from me and throw me in jail. They would torture me. They would demand to know who owned the jewels and that would endanger Sir Henry's relatives. I had to stop them from searching me.

And I had to stop myself from crying out in terror.

Oberst Bernhard looked relaxed but his voice took on a tone of command. He gestured to the soldiers to let me go. "Not so fast. Mrs. Denis is the widow of a British Foreign Service official and is now a well-known newspaper reporter. We don't want her to get the wrong opinion of us."

The soldiers paused, waiting for orders from whoever was in charge. I stood between them, praying.

Herr Trench Coat considered this challenge while I held my breath. Finally, he held out his hand for Bernhard's passport. The oberst handed it to him after displaying the diplomatic cover.

"You are traveling with this woman?"

"And she's acquainted with Ambassador von Ribbentrop. I'm sure he will hear if we are discourteous."

Trench-coat man handed Bernhard's passport back and saluted. "Heil Hitler."

Bernhard returned the salute. "Heil Hitler."

The Gestapo man in the trench coat signaled to the soldiers to let me go and I was handed back my passport.

Border guards, soldiers, and Herr Trench Coat went on to the next compartment while I collapsed onto my seat.

I clung to my passport and released a deep breath. "I thought somehow I'd gotten in trouble," I told Bernhard in English.

He nodded. Once again I worried. Would he denounce me? Did he have any reason to?

After a few minutes that dragged along like hours, the train began to move. We slowly passed the guard shack and then came to a stop a few hundred yards beyond. Dutch guards came on, looked at our passports with disinterest, and kept moving.

This time the train picked up steam.

I was out of Germany. Nothing could go wrong now. I felt my whole body relax.

After a few minutes of watching me, Oberst Bernhard said, "You have nothing to fear now. But next time, I would spend a few days vacationing in Germany before returning to London. It doesn't look as suspicious as a visit of a few hours."

Instantly, all of my tension returned. "How do you know how long I was in Berlin?"

"The same way the Gestapo knew. Your name showed up on the arrivals manifest. Since I was planning to return to London, I thought I'd travel with you. Imagine my surprise to find out you were leaving by train the same day." He smiled. Snakes must smile like that.

I took another deep breath. "I need to get back to file my copy."

He shook his head, still smiling. "You made this trip for your employer, Herr Benton?"

"Yes."

He lowered his voice. "But not for a spur of the moment interview."

"Why do you say that?"

"Because I followed you from city hall to an apartment block where you changed clothes."

The fear that left me at the German border returned. "I thought I was being followed. Was that you? Who else was watching me?"

"No one else. No one else is concerned that Herr Benton has Jewish relatives in Germany, or that you work for Herr Benton."

My stomach churned. I was glad I hadn't eaten. "Will you tell anyone?"

"Why should I? I am a soldier and I care about my country. I have no interest in the politics of destroying small groups."

"Thank you."

"Tell Benton things will not get better in Germany for his relatives. They will get worse. They need to get out very soon." His voice was little more than a whisper. "And if you say I told you, I will make your subsequent trips to Germany far more dangerous."

"I understand. Thank you for not letting the soldiers drag me away."

"They are much more suspicious than I am." Now he was definitely laughing at me, at least on the inside. What game was he playing?

"Were they SS soldiers? Like Herr Schreiber and Herr Rickard?"

"No. Schreiber and Rickard are SS officers."

There was a chill in his tone that frightened me. "What is it you want?"

"Merely your company, Frau."

"If I may ask one more question, why were you speaking to David Peters in his office the day before the diplomatic reception when I saw you the first time?"

"I needed to present my credentials. I had only arrived in your country the night before."

Such a simple solution. This man hadn't been there when Reggie was killed or my flat searched. And I had no reason to suspect David any longer. He simply hadn't paid any attention to a man with an ordinary request.

We finally reached Amsterdam in the small hours, stiff and tired. The oberst flagged down a taxi and we rode together to the ferry terminal. After we bought our passages, Bernhard said, "May I buy you breakfast, Frau Denis?"

"Yes. That would be very kind."

The cafe in the terminal was just opening up. The coffee was hot and strong, the eggs greasy, and the toast crispy. Bernhard added sausages to his breakfast order.

We ate in silence until Bernhard said, "Where is the document Manfred gave your husband?"

"I don't know where it is. If he even received it." I set down my fork as my mistake sank in and stared at him in wide-eyed terror.

"He received it."

"Then you know more than me."

He studied me over the rim of his coffee cup. "Let me tell you a little story. A fable, if you will. A man takes a letter from the king and sneaks it out of the castle. He is spotted and followed. Watched at a distance until it is decided to search him and his lodgings. The letter is gone. But a member of the British Foreign Office is seen visiting him. The British official is located and followed. He doesn't have it either. It's not in his flat. It's not in his friend's flat. He couldn't take it to a bank because they were already closed. He didn't pass it to his friends. It has disappeared. Poof."

"Your story doesn't explain why his brother Hans was murdered."

"He knew too much. He might know where the document is and might tell an English person. Someone like yourself."

By now my breakfast smelled rancid. "You ordered him killed when I went to see him."

"No. And I didn't find out in time to stop the killing. I would much rather Manfred were alive so he could tell us what he knew."

"Maybe someone feared the document and destroyed it."

"No. No one believes that. What would you do, Mrs. Denis?"

"I don't know. I have trouble believing Reggie would take anything stolen. It wasn't in his character." I needed to puzzle this out, because his story wasn't a fairy tale. "Was my husband killed in the search for this missing letter?"

"No. Someone killed him before we could learn where the document is. Your husband's death has complicated our work." He stared at me with such intensity in his dark eyes that I believed him.

"Is that why you stopped the soldiers from taking me off the train?"

"I need the letter. And your death would be such a

waste."

There was no way I could finish my breakfast now.

He ate his with relish.

We boarded the ferry and found comfortable chairs indoors on the upper deck. We discussed the odds of a smooth crossing while passengers filed on and scattered over the lounge. After the ferry had left the harbor, I spotted Blake Fielding.

"Excuse me a minute, Oberst. I see someone I need to talk to."

Suspicion clouded his expression. "On this ferry? Really?"

"One of the suspects in the murder of my husband. They went to the theater together and shortly after, Reggie was killed. I want to know what he's doing here."

"I'll save your seat."

When I rose, he draped his overcoat on the chair. I gave him a smile and went in search of Fielding. I found him staring through a window into the first streaks of dawn.

"Blake, what are you doing here?"

He froze and then looked around, clearly wondering who else might have spotted us. "I could ask the same thing."

"I was sent to Berlin on assignment for my newspaper. Have you been meeting your wife for the weekend?" I decided to be daring. "Or your Nazi friends?"

He glared at me, anger rising into the air like heat from an oven. He swiveled his head around to face the window again. "They're no friends of mine. Of course I was meeting my wife. I do every chance I can get away."

"Surely she'll get a visa soon. As soon as they find the leak in your office."

"If Gretchen's father wasn't such a swine—say, how

much do you know about this?"

"I know you're under the same suspicion Reggie was because of the leaks."

He held up his hand and looked around. No one was nearby. Then he murmured, "How do you know about that?"

"Reggie was murdered, maybe by the person giving away Foreign Office secrets. Since the police won't do anything—" I decided to take a chance, whispering, "It's true, isn't it? You're under the same suspicion and that's why your wife can't get a visa."

He nodded, his mouth set in a grim line. "Her father's the reason she can't get a visa and join me here. We could start a family. Have a normal life instead of sneaking away weekends in the Netherlands or France like we're having some cheap affair." The sorrow and bitterness in his tone just about convinced me.

"Can't you pull some strings? Talk to some people in the office?"

"I've tried. I'm still trying. But this leak—" He closed both his mouth and his eyes.

"You're not the leak?" I was pressing him now, but I felt safe enough in this public place.

"No." His voice snapped with fury. "If I were, I'd have moved to Europe and be living full time with my wife. No, we both hate the Nazis. And her rotten father."

I nodded and walked away, eliminating Blake Fielding from my list of possible traitors. And possible killers.

I returned to my seat and gave Bernhard a smile as he retrieved his coat. "Another possibility eliminated."

He left his coat on his chair as he strolled around the deck. In my mind, I tried to trace Reggie's movements, guessing where I couldn't be sure, but I kept coming back to the book. The novel by Thomas Hardy was not a theater playbill you could slip behind a chair cushion.

Where was it?

I dozed off, waking to a recollection of Reggie getting onto a double-decker bus. I thought I'd glimpsed Reggie from my taxi on my way to my grandmother's. What if I'd only thought I'd lost sight of him because the bus was blocking my view? What if he'd climbed aboard? What if he was already being followed according to the oberst's tale and left the book on the bus?

When I realized Bernhard was watching me closely, I wiped the smile of triumph from my face.

We landed at the docks at mid-morning. After crossing through customs, I said good-bye to Oberst Bernhard and took a cab to Esther's home.

She welcomed me inside and then whispered, "How did it go?"

"Successfully. Let me change clothes and get out of all these jewels." When we entered a bedroom, I stripped down to my slip and took off the length of fabric with discs sewn in to discover it had been gold coins digging into my waist the entire trip.

Esther was elated. "This will be enough to get two or three visas, not just my cousin's."

"Good, because I don't think there's much time left."

"What do you mean?" She gripped my hands.

"The Gestapo and soldiers are everywhere. And from what I saw, it isn't safe to be Jewish in Berlin. Your aunt Ruth would like to leave, but your grandparents want to stay."

"Oh, Livvy, I fear they won't leave." Her shoulders heaved.

I hugged her. "I'm sorry. I told them you wanted them to

visit England, but your grandfather seems determined to stay. If you can change his mind, I'll help where I can."

"I know you will. Aunt Ruth sees it as her duty to take care of them. My mother's other sister and her family are in Vienna. I have some cousins in France, but they should be all right." She pulled away and dried her eyes.

"We can hope they are. I have an errand to run before I go in to the paper. Let me call your father."

"He'll want to hear how you did."

After I dressed back in my wool suit and tan cloche and called Sir Henry with promises of more information, I took a taxi home for a bath and what I needed for the day. Then I walked to the Baker Street Underground station and the Lost Property Office next door. I explained to the clerk what I was looking for, and he went back into the shelves and bins where all lost property items were stored.

But the box he finally brought out was all small books, paperbacks, and pamphlets. "Don't you have any heavy books? *Far from the Madding Crowd* is a long piece of literary fiction. Hard bound."

He nodded and took away the box. In a minute, he returned with another box filled with hard-bound volumes. I grabbed the book I wanted from the mix, clutching it to my chest and smiling as if I'd just won a prize. "Thank you so much."

"You should be more careful with your things, miss. Now, you'll need to fill out a found property report."

While he found the paperwork, I opened the book and found a single piece of thick paper, folded, between two pages. I slipped the letter into my purse and the book into my string bag and filled out his report. "I know the day, but I don't remember which bus I was on. What do I put there?" I asked.

He thumbed through a large ledger. "It was found on the 37."

I put that number down, signed the form and left the office. I'd nearly entered the Underground station when a strong arm linked elbows with me.

I was jerked to a stop and looked at the man next to me. Oberst Bernhard.

CHAPTER TWENTY-SIX

"YOU ARE NOT a gifted liar, Frau Denis. That is refreshing. I could see on your face when you realized what your husband did with the letter."

"With what letter?" I squeaked. I knew immediately it was a foolish response.

"Please, Frau Denis. You are much too intelligent to play those games with me."

"Unhand me or I'll scream," I said with as much conviction as I could muster on shaking legs.

"And have us following you, searching your flat again, threatening you and your friends? No, I don't think you will. Not when it would be so easy to give us what we want and have us go away."

I glared at Oberst Bernhard. "My husband was killed for the letter. Why should I give it to you?" I didn't trust him. But I certainly didn't want him killing me.

"No, he wasn't. I have no idea why an Englishman wanted to kill him."

"A Nazi sympathizer?"

He shrugged. "He didn't act on orders from the Reich."

I put a hand on Bernhard's free arm. "Do you know who killed my husband?"

"I only know that he was killed."

That was a weird response. "Did you see my husband

shot?"

"Not personally. I wasn't in the country at the time."

Drat. I knew that. And his dry tone told me he knew I knew. "One of your friends, then."

He cleared his throat. "A contact we have in this country works in the St. Asaph's. He had gone out through the kitchen to have a cigarette when he heard a loud noise. He saw one man fall and another drop the pistol and run in the opposite direction."

"He must have seen something of this second man."

"There wasn't much light, and he wasn't very curious."

"He didn't stay to search Reggie for your letter?" I could hardly believe that.

He shook his head. "He knew nothing of the letter. Later, we expected to hear from your government that they had found the letter on his body. We were surprised as time went by without word."

"So then you ransacked my flat."

"I'm afraid it was considered necessary." He sounded apologetic. "At least they made sure you weren't home."

I was thankful I hadn't been, or I could have suffered a beating like Derek had. "So you claim your people followed my husband, saw him murdered, tore my home apart as well as Mr. Langston's, and followed me for weeks, but you didn't kill my husband."

"We weren't following your husband when he was killed."

"You said you were following him."

"Earlier in the evening, but not after he left the theater."

This made no sense. "Why did you stop?"

"A mistake in assignments. We do make mistakes, Frau Denis." Then he murmured to himself, "More than anyone knows."

I was on a busy public street. I decided I was safe enough to ask, "Four men have been killed, including my husband. Why?"

Bernhard shook his head. "You'll have to look elsewhere for the answer to your questions. Like your husband's death. Why would we bother? What good would any of this do us?"

"What good has it done anyone?" If I could answer that question, I'd know who killed Reggie.

"Your questions seem very complicated. Our need is simple. We want our document back. Now, please. Hand me the book."

"Very well. Here." I pulled the heavy book out of my string bag and handed it to him with a scowl.

He let go of me and ruffled through the pages. His satisfied expression turned to fury. "It's not here. Where is it?"

"It's not?" I kept my eyes on the book.

"German lives depend on getting that letter back. Where is it?" For the first time, he showed signs of panic.

"I thought it would be there. If it's not, I have no idea." I widened my eyes, trying to look as surprised as he did. "Maybe Reggie refused to take it. He had very high standards. He would never take something stolen."

"The loss will have a huge bearing on the war. People will die if the contents of this letter get out."

"That wouldn't have mattered to Reggie. A principle was a principle. He told me that many times." All of that was true. I wondered why he'd changed his mind this once.

"You realize we'll have to continue to follow you. We must have the letter back."

"What is so important about a letter that lives depend on

it?"

"Oh, no, Frau Denis. I will not answer that." He smiled at me. "May I keep this book?"

I sighed and nodded.

"If it's not in here, I'm sure I will see you again."

"That's not the worst thing that could happen." I reluctantly smiled back at him. He was a German officer, but he seemed honest and he hadn't hurt me. He'd saved me from the Gestapo at the border. In another world, I could probably like him.

"Thank you." He nodded to me and walked off.

I went straight down into the Underground and headed toward the *Daily Premier* building. If I was followed, I couldn't spot my tail. The crowds heading to work were gone, but the trains were still busy and the street as I headed to the building was bustling. I kept my purse tucked against my side and prayed no one had seen me remove the letter.

At least no one approached me. As soon as I entered the *Daily Premier* lobby, I breathed a sigh of relief and headed upstairs to Mr. Colinswood's office.

He was in conference when I arrived, and I paced the area outside his door until the other man left. I then burst in without knocking and sat down opposite his desk.

"Come in," he said belatedly.

"Don't let anyone come up behind me," I said as I fished the letter out of my handbag.

"What's going on?"

I shook my head as I scanned the single-paged letter written on good-quality paper in German. My eyes widened when I read the signature beneath the words *Der Führer*. Adolf Hitler.

Glancing up, I said, "It's a letter signed by Hitler himself to von Ribbentrop requesting those details of southeast England they discussed previously for the invasion. He calls it 'Operation Seelowe.' I think that translates as 'sea lion.'"

"Good Lord." Colinswood slumped back in his chair.

"I wonder if the answers have been sent to Berlin already."

"Probably. How did you get this?"

"Reggie borrowed a book from a friend, put it inside, and left it on a bus the night he died. I think he knew he was being followed."

Colinswood picked up his phone and called up to Sir Henry's office. When he hung up, he said, "He's not in the building right now. We'll have to wait."

Waiting was the last thing I wanted to do. It didn't seem safe. "Do you have a contact at 10 Downing Street?"

"Yes."

"You need to get this there. Have your contact give it to the prime minister. Then it becomes the government's problem. And hopefully no one else dies over it."

"Not until Sir Henry sees this and decides if we're going to print this or not."

My heart leaped to my mouth. "You can't print that. Not without the permission of our government. People have died because of that letter and more will unless the whole cabinet sees it and decides what to do. Then it will be too late for retaliation." Otherwise, I'd be the first one under fire.

"It's the scoop of the century."

"Call Esther's house. Sir Henry might be there."

"Do you know the number?"

I walked around the desk and dialed. When the maid answered and confirmed Sir Henry was there, he came on the line immediately. "We have a situation here, sir. I have something that Mr. Colinswood wants to print, but I believe it should go to the government instead. Please come back here as soon as possible." Panic leaked from my voice.

"What are you talking about, Olivia?" Sir Henry sounded puzzled.

Caution made me reply, "You'll see when you get here."

Colinswood got us both coffee while I waited at his desk with the letter in my hands, wondering if Nazi thugs would crash into the office at any moment. Maybe my lack of sleep had sharpened my fears, but I jumped a foot when Sir Henry bustled in.

He read the letter and turned pale. He listened as I told him how I recovered it. "I'll take this to Downing Street now. Not a word of this to anyone."

We both nodded.

Then Sir Henry said, "This letter confirms my worst fears. Shame we can't run it, but the government needs to see this."

Once he left, I said to Colinswood, "I was planning to come in yesterday morning to ask a favor. We need to run a review of Viennese Nights. It's a restaurant in Soho. Owned by a Nazi sympathizer, or so I'm told. I said I was a restaurant critic so I could keep an eye on someone. I'll write up my notes for you."

He grinned. "Along with your notes on your meeting with the mayor of Berlin. Sir Henry told me. You can use that desk right outside my door. I know you don't want to go far since Sir Henry will call me when he returns."

I received a lot of strange looks while I worked in the newsroom, but no one said a word to me. I had finished writing both pieces by the time Colinswood came out and said, "We're to go upstairs now."

When we arrived, Sir Henry was pacing a trench in his carpet. "The prime minister was shocked and dismayed by the letter. He'd hoped it was fake until I assured him people had already died getting this to him. He has called for an emergency cabinet meeting."

"Will we be able to publish the story?" Colinswood asked.

"No. We've been warned not to publish and never to hint at the letter's existence. The government fears a panic," Sir Henry said.

"But the government will use the information?"

"Yes. They've been warned that Germany plans to invade us. You did good work, Olivia."

I gave them a broad grin. Those weren't words I often heard around the *Daily Premier* building.

CHAPTER TWENTY-SEVEN

SIR HENRY TOLD me to go home and get some rest. I gave my stories to Colinswood and did exactly that. If anyone had broken into my flat that night, I would have slept right through.

I went into the office the next morning with a spring in my step. I'd given Esther's relatives help in obtaining visas by smuggling some of their wealth out of Nazi Germany, and I'd delivered the letter Reggie had hidden in hopes of getting it to our government someday.

I could feel him smiling down on me.

Miss Westcott came up to me as soon as I entered. "Are you feeling all right?"

"Yes. Thank you."

"Mr. Colinswood warned me these migraines come on very quickly, but don't happen too often. My sister suffers from them, too. They are a curse."

"Yes. Tell your sister I sympathize with her." And bless Colinswood for giving me a perfect excuse.

"Do you feel up to an assignment with Jane Seville?"

"Yes, ma'am. I'm back and ready to work," I said briskly.

"The Guy Fawkes Day tea in aid of the policemen's fund is being held this afternoon. We need the usual frock details and quotes from the high ranking among them. Here are tickets for you and Jane." She scowled at me. "You're sure you're all right?"

"Yes, ma'am."

"It's just you're dressed up today. As if you knew where you'd be assigned."

"What good luck" was the only reply I could manage. Actually, I hoped I'd see Adam once he heard about me finding the letter. I was hungry for his congratulations.

Buoyed by my successes, I tried hard to continue the streak and get the best descriptions and quotes I could for my article. Jane noticed my new-found confidence and congratulated me.

My confidence lasted through a quick trip to the shops after work until I walked into my flat. The light was on in my parlor.

I stopped dead in my tracks. Should I confront my burglar or back out? Or scream?

"Come in, Frau Denis," a familiar thick German accent said.

Taking a deep breath, I walked to the doorway. Penetrating dark eyes stared at me from the center of the room. Familiar eyes.

I stared back at Oberst Bernhard, blinking when I realized he'd walked into my flat as if it were his own. When I finally found my voice, I asked, "Do you think you can just break in anywhere you want?"

"It is better if we are not seen talking to each other."

"Better for whom?"

"The political situation being what it is, for both, I would say." He smiled, and I found myself wanting to be on his side.

Odd. He was German, and everyone from my father to Colinswood thought we'd soon be at war with his country. And yet, he'd made sure I returned from Berlin safely. For the sake of the letter. My voice was cold. "Why are you here, Oberst Bernhard?"

"I wanted to congratulate you. It is not easy to fool me, but you did. You had the letter all the time."

"No. You were right. It was in the book. I slipped it out while I was filling out paperwork in the Lost Property Office."

"I never suspected. And all Germany loses." He shook his head above his slumped shoulders.

"Perhaps it will help us avoid war between our countries. And then everyone wins."

"It's not that simple. Eventually, we will have war. Being a soldier and a father, I would prefer to minimize the lives lost."

I thought of Captain Redmond, who'd be sure to be on the front lines. "I wish you and your family well. I want you to lose, but I don't want you hurt."

He gave me a slight nod. "I also came with a warning. Your part in taking the letter to your government is now known in Berlin. No, no, I didn't tell them, but I would advise you most strongly not to return there to help your Jewish friends."

I thought of Ruth and her parents. "Are they in danger because I was there?"

"No. I'm the only one who knows about them so far. But if you return, at the very least you'll have the Gestapo tailing you and then your friends will suffer."

"You're frightening me." My shivers should have told him that.

"I hope so. It will make you more careful."

"I will be." I decided to take a chance. "As long as we're being honest, was Major Liestran the one who organized searching my flat, shooting into a moving taxi, having me followed, and attempting to kidnap me?"

He stared into my eyes for a moment before he nodded.

"All in search of one letter?"

"Yes. It was that important. As you saw."

"Does anyone at the embassy know who killed my husband?"

"Someone thought maybe someone else knew. Nothing but gossip. Rumor. I deal in facts, not rumor."

"I appreciate your honesty."

He smiled and headed for the door. "I admire your bravery and your quick thinking. Too bad you are not German."

We stood looking at each other, not enemies, but certainly not friends. Then he walked past me, opened my front door, and saluted military-style before he left.

I had the strangest feeling I'd see him again.

Bernhard hadn't been gone five minutes before my telephone rang. "Livvy, I heard what you did. Well done! Would you like a celebratory dinner? It'll have to be at your corner restaurant." Adam's voice boomed through the telephone wires.

"I'd love it." I was glad I had dressed up that day.

Adam arrived ten minutes later. He came in, tossed his hat on a table in the parlor, and gave me a long and satisfying kiss. "I'm sorry I wasn't around to congratulate you before now."

"Where were you?" I tried not to press.

"Scotland. I can't say more than that. It's the job. I don't want to keep secrets from you, but I have to. And as we get closer to war, it'll only get worse."

I had to trust someone, and I'd found that someone was Adam. I took a deep breath and said, "All right. I accept that.

I'll try to curb my natural curiosity."

When I gave him a big smile, he answered with a kiss. He broke it off to say, "You have to tell me. Where was that blasted letter?"

"In the book Reggie borrowed from Derek Langston. He knew he was being followed, so he left it on a bus. I thought I couldn't see the man I suspected was Reggie because a bus got in the way, but really, he'd boarded the bus. I went to the Lost Property Office by the Baker Street station yesterday morning when I returned from Berlin."

"Berlin?" He whistled. "You have been a busy girl."

Oh, blast. I didn't need to keep the trip secret, but I didn't want to invite more questions. I stared into his eyes and saw affection and encouragement. "But I still don't know who killed Reggie."

"It wasn't the Germans in their search for their missing letter?"

"They say it wasn't."

"What were you doing in Berlin? Asking them if they murdered your husband?" He still clung to me as if he were afraid I'd disappear into a Nazi prison.

"Of course not."

"Well?"

I stuck to the official story. "I was interviewing the mayor of Berlin on his favorite meal."

Adam seemed to find that more astonishing than my trip to Berlin. "Why?"

"Because Sir Henry wants to do a series on famous men's favorite meals."

He burst out laughing. "It sounds like he's ready for the House of Lords. Barmy."

I didn't want to get into too close a discussion about Sir

Henry's motives. "So tell me about the nicknames."

"No. Dinner first. I'm starving. I've been traveling all day."

We went downstairs and around the corner to the restaurant, hand in hand. After we ordered and our soup arrived, I said, "I'm dying to hear about the nicknames."

"And I'm dying to hear why you really went to Berlin." He gave my hand a quick squeeze. "It's not safe anymore."

"Thank you, but there are things I do for my job that you may not approve of."

Adam and I stared into each other's eyes for a long time. Anyone looking at us would have thought we were madly in love. Love on both our parts, possibly, but Adam was also visibly worried and I was feeling mulish. Finally, he broke the silence. "I guess I'll just have to accept that we both need to keep secrets for our jobs."

I nodded.

"I checked on public school nicknames for men in Reggie's office. Besides Lester Babcock and Edward Hawthorn, I only found one who had a nickname that began with an *S*."

"Who was it?"

"Paul Chambers was known as Snort." He wiggled his eyebrows at me. "I didn't ask why."

"And he's in debt from gambling. At least that's what I heard."

"It's more than a rumor. It's fact," Adam said.

"And he took over Reggie's job after his death." Another motive, but I didn't want to think it was Paul. "Did you learn the nicknames for all of them?"

"No, I missed a few. More than a few, probably. But I learned Fielding's was Blackie. I don't see how any of the others would have been involved in stealing the information that passed to the Germans, so I think we have only three to choose from."

I could eliminate Fielding and Peters by their nicknames and their lack of a motive. "And only two have a motive. Lester's transparent. He and Mary are frugal. He's not the law-breaking sort and he doesn't have any hidden vices, so Reggie wouldn't have been reporting him for anything."

"How do you know?"

I shook my head. "Mary couldn't keep a secret that big from me. She'd have come to me to ask for Reggie's help. And Lester has no aptitude for stealth. No. It's not them. It has to be the Hawthorns and their Nazi sympathies, or Chambers and his need for money."

"And both are in a position to see cabinet position papers and pass them on. So far we haven't seen how our unknown traitor does it. And without proof?" He shrugged.

"There's a Guy Fawkes party Friday night in Hampstead. Geoffrey Wallace of the Eastern Mediterranean desk has a house a good hike from the Underground station. His gardens are situated with a lovely view of the heath. Please come with me. And perhaps something can be passed on to Hawthorn and Chambers that would be too good not to hand off to their masters. Then we can tail them."

"I'll see what my office thinks of the idea. Understand we won't be the ones to tail them. Too obvious."

I had to ask. "If you catch the traitor, will you question him about Reggie's death?"

He reached across the table and squeezed my hand. "You can be sure we will."

CHAPTER TWENTY-EIGHT

MY TRAVELS made it a short week for me, made shorter by everyone sneaking away early on Friday for the Guy Fawkes Day parties. The women of the society pages at the *Daily Premier* wrote their copy in record time while discussing where they'd watch the bonfires.

Friday evening I dressed for the Wallaces' party, expecting from Adam's silence over the last two days to be attending on my own. I understood his assignments meant I couldn't count on him to always be available. I knew it, but I didn't have to like it. When the phone rang, I snatched up the receiver, hoping it was him.

It was my father. "You didn't go down to Summersby Lodge today?"

I tried to keep the disappointment from my voice. "No. I have something to do tonight."

"I hope it's not investigating Reggie's death. He committed suicide. I'm certain."

"I don't believe it, but no, that's not it. You didn't go to Summersby Lodge, either."

"I go in the morning for a golf match." He paused. "I spoke to Sir George this morning and told him of your concerns. He inherited a horse farm near Newmarket. It seems he's been selling off his horses to pay for Lady Margery's winter holidays. Poor man. He's distraught having to do it."

Another possible traitor eliminated along with his motive.

"See? You had no reason to suspect Sir George. I told you he could never betray his country," my father began to lecture.

Somebody had, and killed Reggie in the bargain. And I was left with Hawthorn and Chambers as my suspects.

Almost as soon as I hung up, the phone rang again. When I answered, I heard Adam say, "I'll be there in five minutes. Not too late, am I?"

"Not at all." I didn't try to hide the joy in my voice.

He was good to his word, leaving the taxi waiting when he came upstairs to get me. He wore his sharp black evening suit again and I looked him over as much as he did me. The gleam in his eyes made me glad I'd chosen my sleek green gown. It was simple, relying on the bias cut to draw the eye.

My outfit would have been spectacular with expensive jewels. Too bad I didn't have any like the ones I'd smuggled in from Berlin.

As we rode out to the Wallaces' house in Hampstead, I filled Adam in on our host. "It's his wife's house, really, but the location is terrific for parties. They're a private family, I don't think his wife is too well, but they throw a couple of marvelous open houses every year. There will be all sorts: school friends, people from the office, family members. And they're always lucky in the weather for their fetes."

"You won't be too disappointed if we don't learn anything tonight?"

I gave him a weary smile. "Then I won't be any farther away from finding Reggie's killer than I am now."

"Well, we can enjoy the bonfire and fireworks." He

grinned in anticipation.

"Geoffrey said the local bonfire's just a short stroll up the hill from his house." I allowed an eager grin to cross my face. I could use a respite. "Actually, I'm looking forward to the Guy Fawkes celebration. I always loved them as a child."

When we arrived at the Wallace mansion, Adam climbed out of the taxi and gave a low whistle. "You didn't tell me the place was this spectacular."

"I didn't want to ruin the surprise. Imagine. A lowly civil servant living in a colossal manor house like this. And you should see the grounds."

He paid the driver off and then said quietly, "You sure he doesn't have money worries?"

"Quite sure. The wife's family is loaded."

We went in to find the party in full swing. I wandered through three rooms before I found Geoffrey Wallace. "On your own tonight, Livvy?" he asked as his wife air-kissed my cheek.

"No. Reggie's cousin, Captain Redmond, came with me. He's putting a bottle of white wine in the kitchen. Hope I haven't lost him. This really is a crush." I raised my voice to be heard over the din of music and laughter.

"It's one of our larger ones," Marguerite Wallace said, her thin face drawn in pain.

"This isn't too much for you, is it?" I asked.

"If I should disappear for a while, please don't think I'm rude."

"Of course not. And if there's anything I can do for you, you only have to ask. I'm serious. Promise me, Marguerite." She'd sent me a lovely note when Reggie died. It was the least I could do.

She took my hand. "See if you can find Paul Chambers.

He's looking rather down in the mouth."

I nodded, and she smiled.

I wondered if I was helping with her hostess duties or if she was playing matchmaker.

I found Paul smoking on the terrace. He grinned when he saw me. "Livvy. So glad you joined us tonight. Lovely view in the twilight, isn't it?" He gestured down the hill toward the heath.

I could barely make out the trees beyond the reach of the house lights. "The last time I was here, you and Reggie got into a disagreement over the outcome of a cricket match when you were in school."

The memory stabbed for a moment, and then faded to a dull ache. How long until those memories brought joy instead of pain? I felt Reggie move further away from me into the twilight.

"Yes. I'd forgotten. You know, I think Reggie was right. Shame I can't tell him that. I can hear him now. 'Well, of course, Snort. I'm always right.'"

I laughed at his spot-on mimicry and remembered what Adam told me about the names. "Snort?"

"My schoolboy nickname. I used to be able to make this hideous snorting noise. The other fellows loved it. Our masters hated it. I'm afraid I can't do it anymore."

"That's quite all right." I took a glass of white wine out of Adam's hand as he came up behind me. "You'll never guess what Paul's schoolboy nickname was."

Adam raised his brows. He already knew.

"Snort," Paul said and chuckled, not noticing the look that passed between Adam and me. "Those were the days. Before the war and all that." He fell silent.

"Yes," Adam said quietly. "Mine was Wally."

"Wally? That's so dull," I said.

"Short for Walsingham."

"Sir Francis Walsingham? Queen Elizabeth's spymaster? That is most interesting. What did you get up to at school?" Paul asked with a laugh.

I decided Adam hadn't changed much from his school days.

"I'll never tell. Hopefully, no one else will, either." Adam glanced around the terrace. We were the only three outside in the cool evening. "Chambers, I would like to ask your advice on something. You're in charge of the Northern European credentials desk."

"Yes. Which means I know exactly squat about what Herr Hitler has planned."

"No. Nothing like that. I plan to travel to the continent soon—never mind, you wouldn't know the answer."

Paul focused his full attention on Adam. "I might. Try me."

"I have a friend. A German friend. She's a dancer in a cabaret."

"Oh, that's the way of it, eh?" Paul put on a smug smile.

"How much trouble will I get in if I visit her?"

"Possibly quite a bit with your commanding officer."

"I'm afraid of that. Any way I can get a message to her without everyone from the king to Herr Hitler reading it?"

"You mean by diplomatic pouch? It's watched as closely as everything else."

"Any other way? Through a friend traveling to Berlin? I'd be willing to pay for discretion."

Paul's eyes flashed at the word "pay." "Something might be arranged. I'll see what I can do, for the right price."

I kept a blank face, but inside, my mind was shrieking.

Here I thought Edward Hawthorn was behind the treason for ideological reasons, but all the time, it was Paul Chambers, committing treason for cash. Paul had access to the same cabinet papers as Reggie and Edward.

I wanted to ask him why he had to kill Reggie, but I didn't dare. I knew the government first had to stop the leak of secrets to the Nazis, and I still wasn't convinced he was the killer.

The sound of a door shutting made all three of us turn. Winter winds slid under my dress and down my spine.

"Did you see who that was?" Adam asked.

Paul and I both shook our heads.

"Give me a call Monday," Paul said, and walked back inside.

"What—?"

Adam put a finger up to my lips. "Not here."

The fear I'd felt traveling back from Berlin returned to sink into my stomach.

After that, Adam acted like this was any other party. He spoke to Geoffrey Wallace about his house and discussed our host's Postimpressionist paintings. He flirted outrageously with two of the wives, making me jealous.

Why should I be jealous of any woman Adam spoke to? I had no hold on him, nor he on me.

I took a deep breath, and then sipped on my glass of wine. I should know better than to lie to myself.

I shouldn't have slept with him. I'd been lonely and frightened, and he made me feel loved and cherished. But now I was fighting jealousy over flattering words spoken to other women.

I'd never had this problem with Reggie. He never flirted, and I suspected I wouldn't have minded if he did. I trusted

Reggie completely. I hadn't known the danger didn't come from women.

I had no hold on Adam and I was only beginning to trust him. So why did I have to care about him so much?

As I was helping myself to the nuts and sweets on the dining room table, Carol Hawthorn came up to me. "I saw the nice write-up you gave Viennese Nights."

"I found the food and the service to be excellent." That much was true. It was Carol's companions I found to be questionable.

"It's a shame you seldom got to go to the continent with Reggie on trips for the office."

"Reggie avoided travel as much as he could, but he always managed it when there was an especially good opera on." I smiled at the memory.

"Well." Carol leaned closer and whispered, "I guess he would have felt awkward. Especially in Nazi Germany."

"Why?"

"Well, his fondness for other men. It showed such a weakness in character."

Why did Carol continue to bring up Reggie's scandalous behavior, which should have had him thrown out of the Foreign Office? Why did she keep throwing it in my face?

A lifetime of training to be a lady kept me from slapping her. I glared at her instead. "Carol, let's not quarrel. Reggie and I had a very normal married life. Where this rumor started I don't know. But it's not true, and spreading it is cruel."

"Olivia, I didn't mean—" Her mouth rounded in surprise.

"Yes, you did, and I think it's hateful. Don't try to start a scandal where there isn't one." It was past time for me to set her straight. Or at least silence her.

I think Reggie would have been proud of me.

Carol Hawthorn's shocked expression looked as if I had slapped her. "I'm sorry. I was only trying to say I thought it was a shame you didn't get to travel more. Whatever the reason." The words came out sounding stuffy. "Please forgive me for saying aloud what everyone is thinking."

I took a deep breath and remembered my earlier suspicions of her husband. I needed to be diplomatic if I wanted to learn anything. "Forgiven. Neither of us can help the silly things that go through people's minds. When will you be traveling next?"

"Edward needs to travel to Vienna. The ambassador wants some assistance, so of course they called on Edward." She sounded insufferably proud of the fact. "We were supposed to go for the New Year, but apparently there's a problem now that only he can solve."

I wanted to gag over her superior tone, but I wanted to question her more. Something I'd never have wanted to attempt if Reggie hadn't been murdered. Running through possible responses, I chose, "This must be a lovely time of year there. And won't there be more credentials work during the holidays with all these foreigners coming into London? Maybe it's better you're going now."

"All the foreigners arriving will be from the colonies. Edward's section won't be busy. Although won't London be ghastly when it's even more crowded than usual?" She gave a shudder.

I would have been suspicious if I hadn't known Carol had always thought like that. "I hope you have a pleasant trip. At least you're here to see the bonfires for Guy Fawkes Night."

"Noisy, gaudy, dangerous. No thank you," she grumbled.

I smiled at her words. "To remind us of the dangers of

treason." I wondered if she knew I suspected her husband.

Carol gave a sniff. "I wish Edward had given me more time to pack for our trip."

That surprised me. "Why? When do you leave?"

Mary Babcock hurried up and grabbed my arm. "Livvy. I've been looking for you everywhere. I have the most amazing news. Lester and I are going to have a baby!"

For a moment my mind went blank. Then the shock poured over me like a landslide. "You're expecting?" I nearly burst into tears. I'd so wanted to make that announcement with Reggie.

"Oh, be happy for me, Livvy."

"I am." I gave her a crushing hug to make up for my initial sorrow.

"That's wonderful news, Mary," Carol said, giving her a sedate hug without touching anything but her shoulders.

"Thank you, Carol. This has taken forever," Mary said.

"Good luck to you." Carol smiled at her and walked off.

"I want you for a godmother," Mary told me.

"Oh, I accept. Happily. I want a chance to spoil this baby." *Oh, Reggie, why couldn't you have given me a child?* Then I realized, with a baby, I wouldn't be able to work and I'd have to move home with my father.

Thank you, Reggie, for your wisdom.

After Mary went off to get her coat to go outside and watch the bonfire, I saw Paul Chambers pull Adam aside. They spoke too quietly for me to hear their words.

Knowing neither would tell me what they were plotting, I went to get my coat. When I passed the front parlor, I saw Sir George on his own by the empty fireplace and walked over. "Are you coming outside?"

"Yes, of course. Although I'm afraid the celebration was

more exciting when I was younger. The war took away my love of fireworks and bonfires."

I walked out the front path with him, the crowd visible at a distance around the flames.

"What we talked about on Sunday, things like that make me miss Reggie's help. He was the best of the bunch. A gentleman and scrupulously honest. I hope they find out what happened. He deserves it." Sir George patted my shoulder and walked toward the fire.

I stopped and bit back tears, no longer in a party mood.

Reggie's killer was here. But was it Hawthorn or Chambers?

CHAPTER TWENTY-NINE

EDWARD HAWTHORN came up behind me as I again started up the path toward the bonfire. "How are you doing, Olivia?"

"Well, thank you, Edward."

"And your new job?"

"I'm enjoying it. It's not vital work like you do and Reggie did, but I like having a reason to get up in the morning and talk to people."

He put a hand on my arm to delay me. "I'd be very careful about the assignments Sir Henry Benton gives you. Especially when he sends you to Berlin."

"Why do you say that?"

"The Gestapo suspects you of smuggling for enemies of the state. For the underground."

I stared at him for a moment in bafflement. "How would you know what the Gestapo thinks? Germany isn't even part of your territory. Paul Chambers and Sir George haven't said a word and they're the ones who should know."

"I hear things. Things they apparently haven't. With Reggie gone, you're free to put him and his perversions behind you."

His face looked evil in the flickering light from the distant bonfire. His words about the Gestapo made me certain. "You're the leak. You're the leak in the office and you killed Reggie. Didn't you?" I tried to pull away from his grip.

As I turned toward the bonfire and opened my mouth to shout for help, I felt a searing pain. Then everything went black.

* * *

I awoke in the dark. I tried to stretch and found my limbs refused to move. Panic set in. Was I dead?

No, I couldn't be. My head ached too much. My mouth tasted bitter.

Where was I?

I began to become aware of things touching me. A cloth covered my eyes. A gag in my mouth. Rope dug into my wrists and ankles. Rough wool scratched my skin. My elbow was pressed against something solid. I couldn't straighten my legs.

I was a prisoner somewhere small. I understood that much. But where? And how long had I been unconscious?

I tried to move and my stomach wanted to revolt. A powerful stench, smoke maybe, filled my nose. I faded off...

* * *

The next thing I knew, I was stretched out full length on bitterly cold concrete. My wrists and ankles were still bound and I was still blindfolded.

My head spun and ached, but with the gag removed I could take great gulps of dank, untainted air. That made me feel better despite the smell of mildew.

I had to be a prisoner in a basement.

A man's voice said, "You can't just leave her here."

Another man said, "She knows. I'm not going to hang for murder. And I won't hang alone."

"What do you mean? I didn't..."

Their hurried footsteps died away, the sound of their

voices covered by creaking wood. I lay in silence for what seemed like forever, but they didn't return. The lack of sight and sound was disorienting. Probably what they wanted, so I'd be less likely to escape. I tested my wrist and ankle bindings. No escape was possible.

The cold damp quickly passed through my thin coat and flimsy party gown to seep into my bones. I pictured myself in a stone- walled prison inside a castle, water seeping in through the walls. Or was this an abandoned Underground line? The cellars under the Houses of Parliament where Guy Fawkes had taken his gunpowder? None of these were likely.

Time dragged on, and I began to think about all I was leaving behind. Had Reggie had similar thoughts in the moments before the bullet entered his brain?

I started thinking about all the people I'd miss. Adam, Jane and her cameras, Lester and Mary Babcock, Abby and John, Esther, Mr. Colinswood. Then I realized my father wasn't on the list and I nearly laughed.

I shifted on the floor and the covering over my eyes slipped. I kept wiggling and it came completely off. I could see a dimly lit brick-walled cellar with old crates stacked along the walls in places. Light came through cracks in the wooden floor above and I could see a staircase not far away.

But to get there, first I'd have to sit up.

That was a struggle. My head throbbed every time I moved, and the effort to jerk my body into a sitting position sent sparks into my vision and spears into my brain. Once I was upright, a coughing fit made my headache worse but cleared my lungs of foul diesel fumes.

Diesel. They must have moved me in a car trunk.

My hands were tied in front of me, and I found after a few tries that I could crawl toward the stairs by sliding my hands forward and then scoot my knees, destroying my outfit. My dress was ruined, making me even angrier at my captors. I liked that dress.

I ignored the ache behind my eyes and kept moving until I reached the steps. The boards had been worn smooth by thousands of shoes, so at least I wouldn't get too many splinters. If only I could find a way to climb them.

And then I heard voices and footsteps. Two men were arguing. As their footsteps headed toward the top of the stairs, I slid to the side.

The men came down, and as they came into my line of sight, I saw Paul Chambers and Edward Hawthorn. Before I could say a word or they noticed me, Hawthorn clubbed Chambers on the back of the head.

He began tying Chambers up, not glancing my way as he said, "Don't make me kill you, Olivia."

That was the last thing I'd want to do. "I'm still tied up. I'm no threat to you."

"And don't bother screaming. It's the weekend. There's no one around to hear you."

"I believe you." I didn't think my aching head could bear screaming.

"Good. If you keep quiet and stay down here, someone might come around to rescue you Monday."

"Why so long?"

"This building's never opened on the weekend."

"You can't get away with murder." I was speaking in clichés. I blamed it on the headache.

"Oh, but I already have twice. They were necessary. But now that I'm leaving, I won't need to up the score. If you behave."

"Where are you going?" I couldn't imagine anywhere

welcoming a murderer.

"My friends are sending transport to take me to Germany. I'd hoped to stay in the Foreign Office longer, but that's not possible, thanks to you and your husband. Why couldn't you believe he died at his own hand?"

"He couldn't shoot right-handed. If you'd shot him from the other side, you might have been able to convince everyone else that Reggie committed suicide."

"But not you."

"Never me. How are the Germans getting you out?"

"By U-boat. Wonderfully simple plan. It's been in place for some time." He finished with Chambers's wrists, and satisfied, began on his ankles.

"Tell me what happened. Please. I want to know why Reggie had to die. And since you'll be gone, it can't hurt to tell me."

I didn't think he would, but after a minute he started to talk. "A few days before the shooting, Denis saw me leave a newspaper behind in Hyde Park, and he figured out how secrets were being passed from our office to the German embassy. I told your husband some story and he was satisfied, but I knew he'd wait to see if anything else fell into the hands of the Germans."

"And then you passed more secrets to them?" Foolish man.

"Of course. That was my job. But then I knew I'd have to kill Denis. I had the fake divorce papers and will drawn up to keep you busy if you proved meddlesome."

I was pleased I'd proved meddlesome.

"That day in the office, before we went to the theater, he left me a note saying he'd found what I'd passed in the park. I used a piece of that message to provide a suicide note."

"A suicide note that didn't work."

"Humpf. After work, I broke into your flat and stole the gun. After the show, I left by taxi but only rode a block before getting out. When I left I saw the direction your husband had taken, and I followed."

"So you followed and killed him."

Was that a chuckle? "Almost immediately afterward, Chambers came up and saw Denis on the ground with the gun beside him. I told Chambers I'd discovered Denis was the leak, and he must have decided this was the only way out."

"He believed you?"

"I paid him well to keep silent about what he'd seen for the good of the department. He always needs money, so he was happy to believe me."

"And then you killed Derek Langston."

"Langston contacted me about a missing book. He told me he thought Denis was rotten and that the Reich had the right ideas. I confided in Langston. I told him now was the time for all Aryans to help the motherland and I was doing my bit. Then Langston turned on me, accusing me of killing your husband and threatening to tell. I had to kill him."

"And still he let you into his flat."

"I said I was Chambers and only let him see my trench coat and hat through the peep hole. Silly fag." He pulled on the ropes to make sure Chambers's ankles were tied tightly and then rose stiffly from the concrete. "Good-bye, Olivia."

"Will you send someone to free us?" I knew I sounded frightened. I didn't want to be left alone in this chilly hole and it was growing dark. Would I freeze first or die of thirst?

"Of course. Starting tomorrow, you're not a worry any longer." He gave me a cold smile and hurried up the stairs.

I didn't believe he'd have us freed.

I crawled over to Chambers's prone body and shook him to wake him. He groaned but his eyelids didn't flutter. I clumsily searched his pockets, hoping he carried a pocket knife. He did, but it was a small one.

At once I began to work on the ropes binding my wrists. It felt like I cut the rope one fiber at a time. A few times the knife slipped and I cut myself, letting out a curse into the cold to keep up my spirits.

The cellar was already growing darker when I finally freed my hands. My chilled, stiff fingers couldn't untie the knots, so I started cutting on the ropes around my ankles.

Chambers groaned.

"Wake up, Paul. Edward Hawthorn has left us here."

"Ow. What? Olivia?"

"I have my hands free. As soon as I get my ankles, I'll start on your hands. By the way, your pocket knife is rather dull."

"What? Edward tied me up? Oh, my head hurts."

I left him to figure out what happened while I tried to get my feet loose before it got too dark to see.

Work was slowed by the nicks in my skin bleeding and making the knife slippery. The ropes seemed tougher than the knife blade. Every cut ached and my fingers were numb with cold.

I had nearly cut through the ropes when Paul said, "Edward turned on me? He must have told you I killed your husband. It would be like him. But I didn't murder Reggie."

"No. He told me he killed Reggie after Reggie discovered he was a mole for the Nazis. He also told me you discovered him right after he shot Reggie."

"Reggie wanted to meet me at St. Asaph's Hotel that night, but not to tell anyone."

"Why?"

"I don't know. I've heard rumors the hotel is used for clandestine meetings, espionage meetings, but I can't imagine Reg wanted to see me for a spying mission."

"Especially since you kept your mouth shut about what you'd seen after Hawthorn paid you," I said with some heat as I viciously sliced at my bonds.

His voice was melancholy in the dark. "I'm a gambler. That requires quite a bit of wishful thinking. And more money than I have. Once I kept my mouth shut, it just seemed easier."

"Because of your gambling, you've been suspected of being the leak in the office. Of selling out your country."

"Good Lord. I'd never do that. I served in the trenches in the war. Do you think a man who would do that would sell out his country? And to those animals?" He moved and then groaned. "I've always enjoyed a flutter, but since Annabelle died, it's the only interest I've had. And it's cost me a packet. I'm in hock up to my eyeballs."

"You were thought to have sold out your country, and you sold out your friend. Reggie was your friend." I considered leaving Paul in this cold, damp hole when I left. Despite my anger, I knew I couldn't do that.

"Livvy, I'm sorry. Everyone in the office suspected Reggie's tastes, but no one said anything because he was a decent chap and we didn't want to see him get the sack. We were all shocked when he told us he was getting married."

I had to struggle to make any sound when I murmured, "Reggie and I were happy."

"Edward had always been angry about Reggie being a homosexual. Felt he had no right to be in the Foreign Office. He couldn't say anything while Reggie was alive because he'd once hinted about Reggie's proclivities and the whole office contradicted him immediately. In the last year or two, Edward had become more critical. Lately, he'd been making Reggie nervous." Paul shifted his body to look in my direction. "Livvy, I'm so sorry."

"Nervous?" Reggie hadn't seemed worried to me. If anything, he'd been placid.

"Edward and Reggie had words once or twice in the week before Reggie's death. It was like they were both trying to get the upper hand. I just assumed Edward had threatened to turn Reggie in about his—tastes."

I worked on in silence. It was full dark in the cellar by the time I finished freeing my ankles. "I have your pen knife. Talk to me so I can find you and I'll cut you loose."

"After what I've told you, I'd be surprised if you don't abandon me."

I found Paul's leg and followed his side to his wrists. Then I began to slice at the ropes, the knife slipping in my bleeding hands. I refused to consider why I was being nice to someone who hadn't spoken out about Reggie's murder, so I ignored his words. "This will take some time. Your knife is almost useless."

"Why are you being kind to me?"

"Because Reggie was a kind man. He'd never forgive me if I abandoned you. And I liked Annabelle. For her sake, you need to turn your life around." I snapped my words out.

Neither of us spoke as I chopped at bindings I couldn't see in the dark. Paul tried not to cry out too loudly when the knife slipped and I cut him instead of myself.

Suddenly, footsteps sounded overhead and I shouted, "Down here!" Then strong beams of light blinded me. Men's voices shouted above us and then more footsteps crossed the wooden floor.

I was still dazzled by the lights when strong arms lifted me off the floor. "Livvy, I've been so worried," Adam said as he wrapped his arms around me. Someone on the other side of a torch took the knife out of my hands.

I leaned on Adam in relief. "How did you find me?"

"After the bonfire, I realized you, Hawthorn, and Chambers were missing. No one else. I asked everyone, but no one had seen a thing. And Carol Hawthorn was furious at her husband for leaving her in what she called the middle of nowhere."

I didn't know if it was strain or relief, but I giggled. "That sounds like Carol."

"I got my people involved as well as the police. We searched everywhere, and then a bobby reported seeing Hawthorn's car parked outside of here earlier."

"Hawthorn's the leak. He's leaving by U-boat today."

"Did you get that, Sergeant?"

"Yes, sir. I'll put the coast on alert."

"And he killed Reggie and Derek."

"To hide his work at the Foreign Office? His real work?"

"Yes." I was shivering now and felt like I'd collapse if Adam didn't continue to hold me up.

"Think you can walk up the stairs? We need to have you looked over by a doctor. You have blood in your hair."

"He hit me with something. That's the last I remember until I woke up down here. Where are we?"

"A warehouse used for storing government records. Including old records from the Foreign Office. We'll probably find out Hawthorn helped organize the records here on occasion."

They were helping Paul Chambers up the stairs. "He

helped Hawthorn get me here and saw Hawthorn with Reggie's body."

Adam's breath was warm on my ear. "He's going with the police. You're coming with me."

CHAPTER THIRTY

THE DOCTOR HAD just left my flat when there was a knock on the door and Esther let my father in.

"You look like you'll live." Taking off his coat and gloves, my father set them down and took the chair next to me. "The police seem to think Reggie was murdered after all. The coroner's going to reopen the inquest. Who would have guessed?"

"I would have. I told you Reggie didn't kill himself."

"Well, you were just working on some feminine intuition. These are professional men who know what they're doing."

"And it took four murders before they did anything about it."

He looked startled at my reply before he said, "I'm glad to see you're looking well. A cup of tea for your father wouldn't go amiss."

He knew I'd do what he wanted because I wanted to hear why he was there. Before I could get up, Esther said, "I'll fix it, shall I? The doctor doesn't want Livvy moving around or using her hands any more than necessary for a few days."

"Thank you. That would be nice." I rewarded her with a smile. Then I turned somber-faced to my father. "When did you return from Summersby Lodge?"

"I didn't go. Not with you kidnapped. I've already called Abby and told her you're safe."

"You missed your golf match?" I was truly surprised and touched by his concern.

"Now that I know you're well, I can play in the morning without worry."

My jaw dropped for a moment. I finally managed, "I'm so glad."

"I'm glad you're safe, Olivia," my father said, his expression serious. Then he cleared his voice and said, "I came to tell you David Peters is now head of the Northern European desk since Chambers was demoted. Not reporting a death. And going into debt gambling. Humpf. Not very responsible."

"I'm sure David's pleased."

"And Blake Fielding has taken over the Middle European desk from Hawthorn. The less said there, the better."

"Will his wife get a visa now that it's known Fielding had nothing to do with the leak?"

"Yes. It'll be processed Monday."

"I'm glad for him. But the office will be busy, having lost two bosses in a day."

Esther returned with the tea. My father smiled as he took his time making sure his cup was fixed to his satisfaction. I sat curled up on the sofa under a blanket, waiting impatiently for my father to come to the point.

"Was Edward arrested? Were charges filed against Paul?"

When my father hesitated, stirring his tea needlessly, I knew Edward Hawthorn had gotten away with murder. Finally, my father cleared his voice and said, "Apparently, the German government smuggled Hawthorn out of the country."

"In a U-boat."

"Yes." My father sounded livid at his treachery.

There was another knock on the door and Esther went to answer it.

I remembered my conversation with Carol on Friday night. "And his wife? Carol told me they were scheduled to leave for Vienna, but she didn't tell me when. Is she being allowed to leave with a wad of cash or more secrets?"

"No," Adam answered as he walked in, sounding like Captain Redmond and not Adam. "She's staying. She and the boys have no desire to go to Germany. They might hold to the same prejudices, but they appreciate our freedoms. And Mrs. Hawthorn knows her sons would end up in the military a great deal faster in Germany than they will here."

"Her brother was killed in the war. She doesn't want to lose her sons." I sighed. "She told me that once."

My father gave Adam a hard stare. "If I were on the run, I'd call my wife and tell her to meet me and to bring all the secret material I'd gathered. That would give me leverage in Berlin and keep London guessing as to what I stole."

"We'll keep an eye on her, but I don't think she was too pleased with him. And now that he's embarrassed her in front of her friends and neighbors by being an enemy agent..." Adam winked at me.

"And I thought it couldn't be Hawthorn because he was being followed by Schreiber."

"What do you mean, Livvy?"

"I saw Hawthorn in St. James Park one day. Schreiber sat down on the bench where Hawthorn had been sitting and watched us talk. He even read his newspaper."

Adam shook his head. "It's called a dead drop. If one of us had seen that, we could have stopped Hawthorn's treason earlier."

My father picked up his teacup and set it down again.

"Olivia, I'm sorry about how things have turned out."

"What have you been trying to get up the courage to tell me?"

"Now that you know who killed Reggie, even if he can't be tried, why don't you move home?" His tone was conciliatory.

I wondered how long we could get along. "No. I've come to like my independence. I enjoy my work on the *Daily Premier*." I smiled at Esther and Adam. "And I'd like to see my friends without your interference."

A smile crossed Adam's face. "I'd appreciate that."

"You should be chaperoned," my father said in a no-nonsense tone.

Adam sat on the sofa next to me. "If war comes as soon as I think it will, you'll be safer living at your father's than here in a block of flats in the middle of London."

"You're worried about bombing?" The thought of my flat, lovingly organized by Reggie, being blown up was sickening.

Esther paled.

"Hitler has a massive air force, including bombers. He must plan to use them against somebody."

"I'll face that when the time comes. Meanwhile, my father will just have to guess about my comings and goings. And who my friends are." I gave Adam a wide smile.

"I can live with that." He grinned back.

"How will you manage for the next few days if you can't use your hands?" my father asked, glaring at Adam.

"I'll be looking after her," Esther said. "It's the least I can do."

"Really?" My father gave her an inquisitive look and she glanced away. "And if you're in danger from Nazi agents, Captain Redmond will no doubt be close by."

"My pleasure," Adam said quietly.

"I wish you'd move home, Olivia, but if you won't, please be more careful."

Amazing. My father would not give up. "I love you dearly, but you need to remember I'm an adult." I patted his cheek with my bandaged hand.

"Well, I need to be going. Good to see you again, Esther. Er, Mrs. Powell. Captain." My father and Adam both rose before my father left the parlor.

"I need to get an overnight bag and explain everything to James. I'll be back..." Esther looked inquiringly at Adam.

"In time for dinner, and bring your husband along. I'll pick up some fish and chips. I'm glad to have met you, Mrs. Powell."

"And you too, Captain." Esther left a minute after my father.

Adam sat down and gently took my hand. "I plan to keep hanging around until you get tired of me, Livvy."

"You'll get tired of me long before then." I tried to squeeze his hand, but the bandaging was too thick to move my fingers and they were still stiff from my time in the cold.

"No doubt Sir Henry will get you mixed up in something and I'll have to travel for my work. We'll be separated sometimes and we'll have to keep secrets from each other. But don't doubt I care about you."

I looked at the tender expression in his eyes and said, "I care about you too. But let's take it slowly."

He leaned in for a quick kiss. "Take all the time you need. I'll be here."

Also from Kate Parker
The Victorian Bookshop Mysteries

The Vanishing Thief

When a frantic woman approaches Georgia claiming that her neighbor, Nicholas Drake, has been abducted by the notorious Duke of Blackford, Georgia and The Archivist Society agree to take the case. But Drake is no innocent—he is a thief who has been blackmailing many of the leading members of London society. To find Drake and discover who is behind his abduction, Georgia and her beautiful assistant, Emma, will have to leave the cozy confines of their bookshop and infiltrate the inner circles of the upper crust—with the help of the dashing but dubious Duke of Blackford himself.

But the missing thief and his abductor are not the only ones to elude Georgia Fenchurch. When she spies the man who killed her parents years ago, she vows to bring him to justice once and for all...at any cost.

The Counterfeit Lady

A cousin of Georgia's dear friend Lady Phyllida Monthalf is brutally murdered in her home during the theft of blueprints of a new battleship designed by her husband—who now stand accused of her murder...and treason. The Duke of Blackford, in service to Whitehall, enlists Georgia and the Archivist Society to assist in the investigation. Playing the part of the duke's new paramour, Georgia gains entry into the upper echelons of London's elite, where amidst elegant dinners and elaborate parties a master spy schemes to lay hands on the stolen plans.

The duke is no stranger to the world of international espionage, but Georgia is out of her element in more ways than one. She must not allow her genuine attraction to the duke—or her obsession with finding her parents' killer—to distract her from her role. But when a mysterious stranger threatens to expose her, the counterfeit lady may be in real trouble...

The Royal Assassin

When the Duke of Blackford enters her bookstore, Georgia knows the Archivist Society is in need of her services. The tsar of Russia and his family are visiting Queen Victoria on the auspices of the engagement of the Russian princess Kira to the son of the queen's cousin. When Kira's bodyguard is found dead on a train returning from Scotland, the queen calls on Blackford to discreetly protect the princess and prevent an international incident.

The Russian royalty refuses help in finding the murderer, suspecting anarchists and demanding that every extremist in London be hanged. But that is far from the English way. To get the job done, Georgia must go undercover as Kira's English secretary. She soon discovers that anarchy isn't the only motive in the case—and that someone is determined to turn royal wedding bells into a funeral dirge.

The Conspiring Woman

When Georgia Fenchurch is called in to find Sir Edward Hale's missing son, she's soon embroiled in multiple mysteries. After discovering young Teddy's been taken by his mother, her worry lessens. But further investigation reveals other well-to-do women have disappeared. Have they been kidnapped? Killed? Or is there something even more sinister going on...

To muddle the mix further, the Duke of Blackford has asked to speak with Georgia when he returns to England. It's almost enough to distract any woman.

Once Lady Hale is found dead, Georgia knows the Archivist Society must focus their efforts on finding the truth behind her disappearance and rescuing her son. But then a villain from Georgia's own past resurfaces...

Acknowledgments

This book would never have seen the light of day without the help of a great number of people. As always my very patient husband has been unflaggingly supportive.

My daughter Jen has been helpful in researching Britain in the era before and during World War II. Her interest in counterintelligence during this period has helped shape this story. Her enthusiasm for research trips has been of even greater help.

The staff of the newspaper archives at the British Library were unfailingly helpful to this new user.

Technical and critical help has been freely and kindly shared by Hannah Meredith, Anna D. Allen, Nancy Bacon, the Ruby Slippered Sisterhood, and the members of HCRW.

I thank all of you for your help during this process. All mistakes are my own.

About the Author

Kate Parker grew up reading her mother's collection of mystery books by Christie, Sayers, and others. Now she can't write a story without someone being murdered, and everyday items are studied for their lethal potential. It's taken her years to convince her husband she hasn't poisoned dinner; that funny taste is because she can't cook. Her children have grown up to be surprisingly normal, but two of them are developing their own love of literary mayhem, so the term "normal" may have to be revised.

Living in a nineteenth century town has inspired Kate's love of history. Her Victorian Bookshop Mystery series features a single woman in late Victorian London who, besides running a bookshop, is part of an informal detective agency known as the Archivist Society. This society solves cases that have baffled Scotland Yard, allowing the victims and their families to find closure.

At the moment, Kate has brought her imagination forward forty years to the perilous times before World War II in the Deadly series. London society more closely resembles today's lifestyle, but Victorian influences still abound. Her sleuth is a young widow earning her living as a society reporter for a large daily newspaper while discovering new skills as she tries to solve her husband's murder.

As much as she loves stately architecture and vintage

clothing, Kate has also developed an appreciation of central heating and air conditioning. She's discovered life in coastal Carolina requires her to wear shorts and T-shirts while drinking hot tea and it takes a great deal of imagination to picture cool, misty weather when it's 90 degrees out and sunny.

Follow Kate and her deadly examination of history at www.KateParkerbooks.com

and www.Facebook.com/Author.Kate.Parker/

60968678R00185

Made in the USA
Columbia, SC
19 June 2019